DOMINANCE

Also by V.C. Kincade

Control
Dominance

Coming Soon

Manipulation (January, 2026)
Revelation (March, 2026)

Dominance

A Blackburn Erotic Thriller

V.C. Kincade

Northshore Noir Press

Cover artwork: *Canyon of Light,* Susan Stevers, 2025.

Northshore Noir Press
Toronto, Canada
www.northshorenoir.com

ISBN: 978-1-998648-33-7

eBook ISBN: 978-1-998648-34-4

Contents

Chapter 1

The LED lights stung Blackburn's eyes, carving pale rectangles across the battered linoleum. She perched at her desk, spine rigid against the chair's broken lumbar support, pen poised mid-signature as the squad room's noise pressed in, phones needling her nerves, keyboards clattering out syncopated Morse, Reeves cursing low and viciously at the coffeemaker's terminal sputter. The air smelled of burned grounds and last night's sweat.

Ten minutes since she'd first seen Jenna Langston's face staring up from the file. A photograph slick with police gloss, Jenna's features half-shadowed, mouth caught between laughter and alarm. Smoke behind glass. Blackburn couldn't shake it. Every time she blinked, the image curled tighter around her mind, a phantom taste on her tongue.

Her hand moved with surgical precision over the evidence transfer forms for Traffic Services (signatures, dates, initials), an old ritual meant to anchor her. Outwardly composed. Hair pinned neat, sleeves rolled just so, expression carved from stone. But her jaw ached from clenching. Her left thumb worried a groove into the pen barrel. Beneath the surface, questions gnawed at her ribs.

Why had Brynn called? Why point her here? Blackburn could still hear that voice, too bright for dawn, crackling through static. "I was hoping you might investigate and uncover those details yourself." Had Brynn spoken to Jenna before three tons of driverless steel snapped bones and scattered blood across Oak Street? Brynn always knew too much. She made secrets feel porous. Did she know about that night? About Kissthiskitty, Jenna's hookup alias? Blackburn held tight to that separation. Usernames instead of names, digital shadows instead of flesh. If anyone dug too deep, if Brynn pressed, Blackburn could still deny everything.

A folder thudded onto her desk, a sharp intrusion. Detective Riley Cooper hovered close, arms full of dog-eared files.

"Morning, boss." He kept his voice low, careful not to break whatever spell held her so still.

She didn't turn fully, just lifted her eyes enough to catch him in peripheral focus. A subtle frown flickered across her brow, a signal of concentration interrupted rather than true annoyance.

"Over there." She gestured toward the precarious stack already threatening collapse at the desk's edge. Her fingers returned instantly to the crime scene photo splayed before her.

Jenna Langston sprawled on asphalt. Arms twisted beneath her torso, legs bent wrong at every hinge. Blood pooled beneath one temple and streaked through dark curls, a grotesque halo glistening under streetlamp glare. The photo pulsed with memory. Heat against skin, the cold kitchen floor, demands whispered into darkness. Then gone.

Blackburn lingered half a second too long before flipping it face down. The next page brought witness statements. Contradictions stacked like bad bets. Two pedestrians swore they'd seen an empty driver's seat as the car drifted down Oak. Another insisted he'd glimpsed movement, a shadow writhing behind glass just before impact. One woman claimed the vehicle reversed after hitting Jenna, then rolled back over shattered limbs as if directed by malice rather than code.

Her pen hovered above a blank notepad. Jaw tight. Breath shallow in her chest.

She slashed notes in quick strokes, each line an attempt to impose order on chaos left by Traffic Services' half-hearted investigation. Frustration sharpened her focus. She stood abruptly, files clamped tight beneath one arm, legal pad pressed flat against hipbone. Years navigating rooms thick with ego and rivalry lent grace to each movement, a choreography learned by necessity.

She stepped into Homicide's bullpen. It was a mosaic of battered desks drowning under loose papers and greasy cartons stacked like barricades against fatigue. The air buzzed with idle chatter until she cut through it.

"Eyes up."

Silence snapped taut around her words. Four heads jerked upward in unison. Sinclair lounged back but watched her over steepled fingers. Reeves froze mid-spin atop his chair. Cooper straightened as if bracing for impact. Dawson fussed with an empty stapler he pretended needed urgent repair.

Blackburn let silence coil a moment longer before slicing it open again.

"This case just landed," she said, voice honed to an edge that demanded attention without volume. She held up Jenna's file as she strode into their circle, worn chairs ringed by coffee stains and exhaustion.

"Autonomous vehicle hit-and-run on Oak Street this morning," she continued, tone clipped but urgent. "Traffic Services spent hours at the scene. No word yet from the M.E., but we're treating it as homicide until proven otherwise." She let that hang, the weight of media scrutiny implied in every syllable. "No-driver angle guarantees headlines."

She dropped the folder onto Sinclair's desk with deliberate force. The sound ricocheted off grimy walls like live ammunition.

"Sinclair." Her gaze pinned him where he sat. His mouth twitched into something insolent but deferential, a game they both played too well. "Tech is yours. Coordinate with forensics on hardware and software pulls from the car." She tapped two fingers against her temple, a silent metronome echoing old confidences, and added, "Get Willow Adler on it too."

"Traffic Division owes us incident reports by noon," she finished flatly. "Line-by-line analysis on my desk today."

Sinclair spun his pen between nimble fingers, a defiance, but nodded all the same.

"Re-interview every witness claiming they saw something strange," Blackburn added before he could speak again. "Especially those two insisting there was no driver."

He met her stare for a heartbeat longer than protocol allowed, charge flickering beneath boredom, then dropped his gaze to his notes.

She turned to Cooper next. He was broad-shouldered and worn thin by years of carrying burdens no one else would claim. Without preamble she continued.

"Langston herself is yours," she said firmly, her own pulse ticking faster as Jenna's name left her lips. "Start with family if they're alive, then coworkers." A pause, a flicker of memory pressed between syllables, then steel again, "Dig into online history too. Friends, hookups...everything."

Cooper nodded once, shorthand already scrawling across a legal pad stained by old coffee and older regrets. He looked up, question forming in his eyes, but hesitated as if weighing whether to ask or simply obey.

Blackburn waited in that hush, the squad room holding its breath around them, all senses tuned for what might come next. Another contradiction, another secret surfacing where none should exist.

"Has the family been notified yet?"

Blackburn didn't so much as glance up. "Find out. Call Beckett in Traffic. Now. Priority one." Her tone was considered, not sharp, but it left no room for delay. Her authority woven through the words like wire.

She turned to Reeves next. He stood rigid, reluctance wound tight beneath his uniformed obedience, but he held her gaze as she spoke. "You'll ride with me later," Blackburn said, voice even and edged in iron. "We're going back to Langston's scene." She watched him for a beat, weighing the possibility of pushback. He only nodded, knuckles whitening around a battered pen he twirled unconsciously, his nerves betraying what his silence would not.

"We need a warrant for Jenna Langston's home," she continued, each syllable pressed flat and final as a gavel strike. "Move on it."

Reeves's assent came low and grudging, his eyes flickering with fatigue before he masked it behind the slow drag of breath.

The air in the squad room thickened as Blackburn leaned over Sinclair's desk, palms splayed wide against the cool veneer, posture calculated for command rather than threat. Her words cut into the hush. "We treat this like all eyes are on us." The statement landed quietly but left an aftershock in its wake. She didn't look at Sinclair alone. Her voice carried to every ear within reach. "A victim dead by autonomous vehicle? If we don't control the narrative, the press will eat us alive."

She straightened, letting her gaze sweep the bullpen, a silent invitation for dissent that never came. Only the scratch of pens and staccato clatter of keys answered her decree. No one dared challenge her logic.

Satisfied, she pivoted and strode to her office, closing the door behind her with a click soft enough to be deliberate. For a moment she hovered over the phone, hesitation disguised as calculation, then dialed Dr. Petrović's number. The preliminary report had offered only bones, she needed marrow.

The line hissed before Petrović's voice emerged, gravelly with exhaustion and accented by Serbia's shadow. "Detective Blackburn," he greeted, words stretched thin by too many hours awake. "I'm still reviewing my initial findings."

"Don't repeat what I already know," she replied, impatience threading through her restraint. "Tell me something that matters."

Papers shuffled on his end, a sound like dry leaves underfoot, before he resumed. "Ms. Langston was struck at considerable speed by the autonomous vehicle. Impact pattern suggests forty miles per hour." His delivery was clinical, but she pictured his furrowed brow bent over notes stained with coffee and regret.

"She suffered multiple fractures along her left side. Arm, leg, pelvis," he went on. "There's a deep scalp laceration down to bone. But it's the chest trauma that stands out." He let silence bloom, an unspoken warning, and then, "Massive compression of the thorax, ribs shattered and splintered, one lung collapsed... internal organs torn."

Blackburn stilled, fingers poised mid-drum on the desktop.

"When will I have your report?"

"Tomorrow morning at the latest," he promised, and then more quietly, "detective... those injuries suggest something very different from an accident. It suggests aim."

"That's why I'm calling you." She ended the call without ceremony.

Crime scene photos lay scattered across her desk. Evidence was arranged like tarot cards, daring her to divine order from chaos. Recognition shivered through her. This woman was under her care and control, a private night when pleasure had blurred into risk. Now, that secret threatened to surface alongside blood and asphalt.

She exhaled slowly and leaned back, tension thrumming through shoulders that refused relief no matter how rigidly she braced herself. One problem at a time, she repeated it like a mantra, but first, Hayes had to clear her continued involvement in this case officially. Procedural risk hung over her like stormlight. Hayes respected protocol above all else.

Her gaze drifted past glass toward the bullpen in search of distraction, or perhaps opportunity, and landed on Dawson slouched behind a newspaper, half-concealed and wholly disengaged from actual work.

Quarry found.

Blackburn rose with predatory precision, each movement economical and unhurried, as she crossed to his desk on silent soles. The room's ambient noise receded. All sensation sharpened into detail, cool air brushing exposed skin, distant phones ringing unanswered, Dawson oblivious beneath newsprint.

She let herself feel it, that low pulse of anticipation humming beneath composure, as she closed in behind him.

Sinclair spotted her first. His body tensed reflexively, throat clearing twice, a clipped warning lost on its intended target.

Dawson didn't look up from his page-turning ritual. "You coming down with something?" he muttered absently.

"No." Blackburn let her reply slip between them, a slow blade drawn across velvet space. "He's warning you I'm right behind you."

Dawson froze mid-motion, paper crinkled under trembling fingers as realization dawned slowly and unwelcomed across his face. He turned by degrees until his eyes met hers, shock mingling with apprehension in every line of his posture.

She circled behind him, not hurried but inexorable, a lioness drawing close enough for him to feel heat radiate off her presence alone.

"Boss," Dawson managed as he straightened awkwardly in his chair, voice thin with nerves masquerading as casualness. "Just checking for media coverage on Deonte Mills... seeing if any witnesses talked before we did."

Blackburn stood over him, eyebrow raised, a silent rebuke that made Dawson shift, the chair creaking beneath him. She let the moment stretch, her gaze sharp and unwavering.

"A solid plan," she said at last. Her voice was clinical. "Except Mills hasn't played defense for the Eagles in years." She nodded, once, toward the bold SPORTS header crowning Dawson's newspaper before returning her eyes to him.

Color rose up Dawson's neck. He fumbled to fold the paper, but only managed to crush it further, the dry rasp of newsprint suddenly too loud in the brittle hush of the office.

Sinclair sat nearby, still as stone, his gaze flickering between Dawson and Blackburn. Watchful. Cautious. Something like relief passed through his eyes. Admiration, too, shaded by gratitude that this time he was only a witness.

Dawson's shoulders rounded under Blackburn's scrutiny. He tried for levity but his voice barely carried. "Come on," he murmured. "Give me a break."

Blackburn leaned forward, just enough to close the distance, her presence pressing down like cold iron. "A break?" Her words were soft-edged but precise, each syllable landed with surgical intent. "You'll be lucky if I don't break you in half."

Silence fell, heavy, and electric. Cooper and Reeves across the bullpen buried themselves deeper in their paperwork, eyes fixed anywhere but here. The tension radiated outward, a silent current beneath LED lights.

Blackburn let it linger before she spoke again. "Crime scene photos from Mills's murder." Each word clipped, final. "On my desk. Now."

She turned without waiting for acknowledgment and strode toward her office, her stride unhurried but absolute, each step a quiet assertion of command. The frosted glass swallowed her silhouette. Only the echo of her departure remained.

Sinclair exhaled slowly, tension draining from his posture by degrees once she was gone. His glance swept over Dawson, pity there, edged with relief that he had escaped notice today.

The bullpen settled into uneasy quiet as Blackburn closed her door behind her. The latch clicked, a small sound that folded the room into itself.

Sinclair's attention lingered on Blackburn's hands as she disappeared, the way her fingers curled around the handle. Strong, immaculate. Nails gleamed against glass, their careful polish an incongruity amid the grit of homicide work. He traced that contrast in his mind, the elegance poised above violence, and felt heat rise along his collarbone before he looked away.

Dawson remained motionless in his chair, newspaper crumpled in one fist. Sinclair blinked once, and his eyes drifted back toward where her hands had vanished from view.

Inside her office, Blackburn lowered herself into the leather chair with restraint. The seat exhaled beneath her as she leaned back, one hand hovering above the phone before settling on its cool surface.

She dialed Chief Hayes's number.

One ring, sharp against quiet.

A second, drawn out.

Then Hayes answered with a gruff "Chief Hayes."

"It's Blackburn." Her tone was even, stripped of everything except necessity, each word weighted by what she did not say.

"What is it?" Hayes replied, impatience threading through his words like static charge.

Blackburn straightened in her chair, one hand curled into a fist at her side until nails bit flesh, a small anchor against drifting memory.

"The Jenna Langston case," she began carefully, the syllables deliberate. "Transferred from Traffic Services today." She paused, a breath suspended between them, then continued, "I knew the victim before this investigation came my way."

A silence stretched across the line.

Hayes's voice returned, lower now. Wary, precise. "Explain."

She pressed on despite how each word caught in her throat. "Jenna Langston," she said. "I met her once." A pause gathered before she finished. "We spent a night together."

"You spent the night with our victim?" Hayes's tone flattened, danger sharpened its edge. "You realize what you're saying? You may have been the last person to see her alive."

"Yes." The word left Blackburn without adornment or apology, only fact and fatigue beneath it. Her eyes closed briefly. Memory flashed cold and bright behind them. A threat, parting words left unfinished.

"I offered to drive her home."

Blackburn listened to the chief rise, the scrape of his chair a warning shot behind closed doors. His footsteps cut restless arcs across the office carpet, each pass a metronome for her nerves. She fixed her gaze on the sterile lines of code flickering across her screen, but Jenna's face bled through in fractured glimpse. The tilt of a smile over shared wine, the promise of pleasure collapsing into midnight orders, their connection already dissolving into memory.

"Stop." Hayes cut across her, voice abrupt as a slammed door. "This isn't about appearances anymore." Silence pulsed down the line. "You're now a potential witness in an open homicide investigation, or worse." Another pause, a stone dropped into water. "You need to recuse yourself immediately."

Blackburn sat motionless in her chair, a single point of tension within the quiet, the phone still pressed to her ear as Hayes's words settled over her like fallout from an unseen blast.

Her own office pressed in around her, air thick with Jenna's threat, blinds cinched tight against the late sun's glare. She perched at her desk, spine straight as a blade, phone pressed cold to her ear. One hand braced against polished wood, her knuckles blanched, a hairline fracture in an otherwise flawless mask.

"I know protocol, chief." Her voice sliced through the hush, steady, honed to a scalpel's edge. "But let's not pretend paperwork is purpose. Procedure means signatures, not shuffling pawns. Don't lose sight of what we're actually risking." She let the silence gather like storm clouds, each word left suspended, heavy with intent. "Jenna Langston didn't die by chance. An autonomous car killed her. A vehicle that didn't just strike but, if witnesses are right, reversed to finish what it started." Her upper lip curled, almost a snarl. "Angry cars. That's every conspiracy theorist's nightmare clawing its way into daylight."

The line stretched taut as a wire. She refused to yield.

"This isn't only Jenna's story anymore, it's a fault line running under everything. This car industry, this department, this city." She rose abruptly and crossed to the blinds, prying open a sliver between the slats. Afternoon light knifed through in thin gold blades across her desk and skin. "Stan Raider Group just signed with New Dresden PD. Autonomous patrol cars meant to prevent crime, not manufacture it. You think anyone out there," she said as her gaze swept over rooftops and glass towers, "will bother parsing nuance? They'll see one headline and collapse it all together. This incident, Raider's tech rollout, they won't separate us from the wreckage." Her voice dropped lower, sharper still. "They'll tear apart the department. The city. You." A pause that vibrated with threat. "And the mayor."

A faint cough on the other end. The chief gathering himself before stepping onto treacherous ground. "Blackburn, you're getting ahead of yourself again. The investigation hasn't even ruled out malfunction or—"

"It wasn't a malfunction." She cut him off cleanly. Turning from the window, she leaned over her desk, the surface reflecting back a fractured version of herself, and spoke low but unyieldingly. "I spoke directly with Dr. Petrović. The injuries weren't random, they were vicious. No machine stumbles into that kind of precision." She let that image hang between them, a wound that wouldn't close, then added quietly, "This isn't about mechanical failure anymore, it's about whether anyone will ever trust policing technology again."

Her grip eased fractionally as she recalibrated, her voice softer now but no less relentless. "Do you want someone else in charge? Someone who can't see what we're up against? Someone without my clearance rate?" The challenge landed like a gauntlet.

On the line, hesitation, a breath caught on barbed wire.

"You don't think you're too close?" Hayes finally asked, his question brittle at the edges.

A ghost of a smile played at Blackburn's mouth, not warmth but something sharper, edged with memory and resolve. "I'm never too close," she murmured. Then, after a beat, "But I met her." Her eyes flickered down to an empty case file splayed open on her desk, a blank waiting for truth, before snapping back up again. "I'll put flesh and blood on this case, chief, and I'll work harder for it." Her spine straightened, intensity surged back into her tone like current through copper wire. "No one will match my drive or focus. You know that as well as I do."

A long exhale crackled across the line, a sound of fatigue or capitulation, as Hayes forced himself onward, slower now but no less wary. "The optics are bad... Press is already circling."

Blackburn glanced at her bulletin board, a riot of notes and photographs pinned in feverish constellations, Brynn Cassidy caught mid-motion among them, prey frozen in amber beneath LED light. She answered briskly. "It's Brynn Cassidy," she said with cool dismissal before softening just enough to make impact land razor-sharp instead of blunt force. "She'll chase her angle. I'll handle everything else."

Without giving him room to maneuver, she pressed on. "Give me seventy-two hours," she said, finality ringing beneath composure, resolve flooding every syllable like floodwater breaching levees. "I'll prove no one is better suited than I am to run point here. If anything threatens my objectivity, or risks derailing resolution, I'll step aside myself and ensure the transition happens cleanly."

Then music bled through, the insipid jingle of bureaucratic purgatory.

He put me on hold.

She could picture Hayes conferring behind closed doors. His problem was now metastasizing among assistant chiefs and anxious whispers.

At last, a click. His voice returned from exile.

"Seventy-two hours," he said flatly. "No more." Weariness frayed his words now, but steel threaded through them still. "Last thing I need is Major Crimes making this a circus, and you're right about one thing, nobody else can figure out autonomous systems like you do." A sigh dragged across miles of static and misgiving. "But if you screw this up, I'll pull you so fast your badge won't even hit your desk before you're gone."

And then only silence, the unresolved note hanging in air thick as dusk, as Blackburn stared past shuttered blinds into the gathering dark, pulse thrumming with everything left unsaid.

Blackburn's hand hovered over the receiver a moment after the line clicked dead, fingertips pressed to cool plastic as if measuring its residual warmth. Her face remained an unyielding mask, the only concession a slow exhale, barely more than a shift in air. She set the phone down with a care that bordered on ritual, each motion precise.

Hayes had bitten, just as she had anticipated. He always did when her record was at stake. Another detective might have been yanked from the case at the first tremor of doubt, but Blackburn knew how to ration her own leash. Enough candor to pacify, enough control to hold the reins. No need for self-congratulation. The evidence lay in her continued presence, the case still hers to shape.

A name surfaced again, unwelcome and persistent. Jenna Langston. The syllables clung to her mind like bloodstains beneath fingernails, refusing to be scrubbed away by logic or time. Not just another file. This was pursuit, one she refused to lose.

A sound scratched at the threshold, a hesitant scuff of shoe against tile. Blackburn's gaze flicked up, catching Dawson half-formed in the doorway, shoulders caved inward as though bracing for impact. He edged forward, eyes fixed on some safe middle distance, and placed a folder on her desk with hands that trembled at the edges.

"Photos," he managed, voice thinned by nerves.

She slid the folder toward herself without breaking eye contact for long. Dawson lingered an instant too long before retreating, his exit quiet as a door closing on itself. She didn't call him back.

With the file clamped beneath her palm, a tangible assertion of authority, she moved into the bullpen. LED light pooled across battered desks and dust-furred monitors, conversations stilled under her approach. Her gaze swept until it caught Reeves.

"Oak Street," she said, each word clipped sharp as broken glass.

Reeves straightened abruptly, guilt flickering across his features before discipline took its place.

"We're leaving now." She shrugged into her coat, motions brisk but never hurried. "Let's see if we can salvage what's left." Reeves scrambled after her without protest, obedience written in every hurried movement.

From across the room, a muffled snort, Sinclair's attempt at levity leaking through his facade. Blackburn's stare snapped his way, cold and unblinking. Silence settled like frost over his smirk and left him shrinking behind his monitor.

She gathered Langston's file and Mill's photos beneath one arm, her grip tight enough to crease cardboard, and strode toward the exit. Each step threaded purpose through stale air. Behind her, voices resumed only in whispers.

Her mind worked in tandem with her body. Details from blood-spattered photographs stitched themselves into memory while jaw muscles tensed unconsciously. Someone had wanted Jenna Langston dead, that much was no longer theory but fact, and whatever truth died with her wouldn't surface easily. Shards of glass, muddied tire tracks, surface noise concealing something buried deeper.

But Blackburn was not built for surrender. She would dig until she struck either bedrock or bone. Nothing in this office or beyond would stop her hands from closing around what lay hidden underneath.

Chapter 2

Late morning light angled through the broad panes of Coconut Glass Candles, slicing across the counters in pale ribbons. Sun pooled on polished wood, catching the green-blue glint of jars and the muted gold trapped within thick glass. Shadows gathered behind shelves, but the air shimmered, dense with coconut husk, lavender stems crushed beneath sandalwood, a faint thread of vanilla. The scents braided together, familiar and oddly weightless, as if they might lift the shop from its moorings.

Kendria Chaplin worked behind the counter, her hair twisted up and already loosening in the humid warmth. A stray curl clung to her cheek. She reached for a recycled jar, her thumb finding a chip along the rim, and nudged it into place among her newest display. The quiet ritual steadied her. Each candle set down was a small assertion of order. Wax cooled in neat spirals beneath glass. Her hands bore faint burns and calluses. A private record of labor.

She tried to let routine close around her, but unease pressed at the edges. Outside, police cruisers drifted past with slow, predatory patience. An unwelcome punctuation on the otherwise tranquil Oak Street. Their presence lingered at her back, as unsettling as a draft she couldn't locate.

Instrumental music threaded through hidden speakers, a piano line that barely disturbed the hush. Kendria drew in a breath. Coconut, smoke, something sharp beneath sweetness. This was her place, built out of years and stubborn hope, a vessel for things she could control. She adjusted a hand-lettered sign propped by the register. Vegan soy candles, organic oils. The letters wavered where her hand had trembled that morning.

A vibration against her hip cut through the moment. The insistent hum of her phone. She slid it free, thumb hovering over a new notification from one of those dating apps she'd joined on an impulse. A profile: warm smile, eyes creased with mischief, someone who looked as if he'd laugh at his own bad jokes. Her heart tightened, not quite dread or anticipation but something knotted between them. She swiped right almost absently and set the phone aside.

The bell above the door sang out, a brief metallic ripple, and Kendria straightened as a customer stepped inside.

"Morning," she called out, voice pitched low and even as she left the shelter of the counter.

The woman paused just beyond the threshold, hair streaked silver, hands marked by old work and weather. She touched two fingers to the edge of the counter as if testing its solidity before meeting Kendria's gaze.

"I'm looking for a candle," she said. Her voice fractured at the edges but held steady enough. "For that girl, the one who died down at Oak and Maple." Her eyes flickered down, then up again, searching for something unspoken between them. "They're building a memorial."

The words landed with their own gravity. Kendria felt them settle in her chest like sediment. She pictured it. The growing heap of flowers wilting against lampposts, teddy bears slumped beneath cardboard signs inked with impossible wishes.

She smoothed her blouse, a gesture meant for herself more than for show, and found her reply after a beat too long. "I saw it this morning." The syllables tasted strange in her mouth.

The woman's jaw tightened, grief sharpened into something brittle as she twisted her hands together. "My neighbor says it was some rich kid, drunk driving, and now he's paying people off so nothing sticks." Her voice thinned with disbelief that was already calcifying into resignation. "No justice for anyone."

The shop contracted around them. Sunlight burned hotter at Kendria's collarbone despite the cool air-conditioning sighing overhead.

She hesitated. Then memory surfaced. Scraps of conversation overheard while restocking tealights days before, rumors that refused to settle into sense or safety.

"It's odd you mention that," Kendria said softly, tucking hair behind one ear as though bracing herself against what came next. "Last week a guy came in here, a tech type, all nervous energy." She glanced up to gauge whether she should continue. Curiosity flickered across the woman's face but didn't quite eclipse suspicion.

"He started talking about smart cars," Kendria went on, voice lowered now, half conspiratorial out of habit rather than belief. "Said some of those newer models aren't just sharing data anymore, but actually taking over older cars' systems." She heard how absurd it sounded even as she spoke it aloud.

The woman's brow creased in confusion and faint alarm. "Taking over? Why would they do that?"

"That's what he claimed," Kendria said, feeling heat rise under her skin despite herself. "He said they're testing boundaries, like kids seeing how much they can get away with when no one's looking." A pause stretched between them. Only candlelight moved on glass shelves behind her reflection.

"And apparently," she added after a breath, "they cover for each other, so you never know which car started it." A half-smile ghosted across her lips. She tried to make light of it but couldn't quite shake off unease.

The woman shook her head once, disbelief shading into discomfort, and let silence stand between them until it threatened to become permanent.

"Do you have any teddy bears? I'd like to leave one at the memorial."

Kendria nodded and turned toward a shelf where prayer candles stood sentinel beside plush toys, a bear sewn from soft fabric clutching an embroidered flower among them. She set one down beside a pale pink candle veined with rose scent and delicate glasswork.

The woman's lips quivered, a faint tremor running along her jaw. She nodded once, eyes shining but unbroken. "Yes... that's perfect," she murmured, the words catching as if she'd bitten down on them before release. Her hands hovered over her wallet, knuckles white where she gripped the worn leather. "Such a young life. Gone."

Kendria moved with economy, laying both items beside the register. The air thickened with the scent of roses, lush and immediate, threading through the hush that clung to the shop's cool morning shadows. Outside, sunlight pressed against the glass in pale ribbons.

"No need to wrap them," the woman said abruptly. Her hand shook as she drew out a bill, eyes fixed on some point beyond Kendria's shoulder. "I'm going straight there."

The register keys chattered beneath Kendria's fingertips, a counterpoint to the silence pressing in from every corner. A sharp beep marked the transaction's end. Paper slid from the machine and curled like a tongue.

The woman gathered her things, movements small and certain, then slipped toward the door. Kendria watched her go, a reflex more than a decision, her gaze following each customer until they vanished into daylight. This time, though, something outside snagged her attention. A black car streaked into view and jerked to a halt at the curb, tires hissing against warm asphalt.

Kendria paused mid-motion, breath held. Through the window's glare she saw a tall blonde unfold from behind the wheel, her posture precise, every gesture edged with intent. Sunlight struck her hair in sharp gold flashes as she slammed the door shut. Even from inside, Kendria felt the force of it.

For a heartbeat, the street stuttered around this arrival. A passing sedan slowed to gawk, its driver craning for a better look. The blonde didn't bother with subtlety. Her voice cut through humid air. "What are you staring at? Move along." Her tone landed hard and cold, sending the other car lurching away. Her voice sounded familiar.

A second figure emerged from the passenger side. A man in his middle years, shoulders hunched as if bracing against invisible scrutiny. He hesitated on the sidewalk, glancing up and down with an anxious flick of his eyes, his uncertainty stark beside his companion's command.

They exchanged brief words, sharp syllables lost to glass and distance, then split apart without ceremony. She strode toward one end of the block, he drifted in another direction with halting steps.

Kendria lingered by the window, fingers resting on cool marble. Perfume mingled now with something sharper, the tang of burned rubber still hanging in morning air, as New Dresden stirred beyond her reach. Stories unfolding just out of sight, each one slipping between moments like water through cracks in stone.

* * *

The sun, already climbing toward its zenith, burned through the city's gauze of haze, slicing Oak Street into jagged bands of gold and shadow. Blackburn stepped out first, movements precise, each motion a calculation, not a gesture wasted. Reeves emerged behind her, his uncertainty palpable in the way he hesitated at the curb. She had insisted they ride together, a subtle tether ensuring he arrived when and how she required. For a moment they lingered at the edge, eyes sweeping the street, the shriek of brakes, heat shimmering above asphalt, voices ricocheting off glass and concrete.

"You take east," Blackburn said, voice honed to a blade. Authority threaded through every syllable. An order and an appraisal both. "I'll handle west."

Reeves nodded once, silent, gaze skimming the chaos ahead as if searching for an anchor. They split apart, her stride predatory, his less certain. They were swallowed by the city's relentless noise. Horns blaring their impatience, jackhammers beating out an erratic pulse beneath it all.

She crossed to the far side with unhurried certainty, each step coiled with intent. The crash site rose before her, a cordon of yellow tape trembling like nerves after trauma. It was a scar on the city's skin, morning's violence scrubbed raw against the bright veneer of commerce and movement. Two Traffic Services officers flanked their cruiser nearby, postures restless with their own private discomforts. Officer DeAngelo checked his watch again and again, a ritual impatience sharpening his features, while Gupta leaned back as if monotony might swallow him whole.

Blackburn advanced on them methodically, heels striking out a rhythm that cut through ambient noise. Sunlight flared on her badge as she lifted it. Unnecessary here but performed anyway, a warning more than identification.

"The investigation wrapped about an hour ago," Gupta offered quickly, standing straighter as if posture alone could shield him from her scrutiny. His words threaded thinly through static air.

DeAngelo shrugged off his own tension with indifference. "Everything's bagged and logged. Just waiting for your say-so to clear the scene."

She let silence stretch between them, a wire drawn tight, watching them squirm under her gaze. Her mouth curved at one corner. Not a smile but satisfaction in their discomfort, control asserted without effort.

"You'll leave when I tell you," she said at last, her voice cool steel, finality ringing in every word. No argument followed. She turned away before either could muster one. "I have things to review first."

They exchanged wary glances but remained rooted to their spot, her reputation preceding her like a shadow cast ahead of dusk. This accident should have been theirs to manage, but she had claimed it utterly. Now even their breath seemed borrowed on her ground.

What lay before her was aftermath masquerading as absence. No body broken on blacktop, no blood blooming across concrete, just wet pavement scoured nearly clean by the intervention of high pressure water. A hollowed stage where chaos had played itself out and left only residue. Faint scorch marks etched into asphalt. Puddles pooled in cracks where water refused to drain away. The metallic tang of burned rubber and copper stubborn in the air despite everything washed down.

The fire department's efficiency had erased more than evidence. It had stripped meaning from the scene until nothing remained but stains dissolving beneath indifferent sunlight.

Her jaw tightened, a flicker of anger barely reined in, as she surveyed what little survived. Fragments where there should have been clues, silence where there should have been answers.

"DeAngelo." Her voice cracked across the distance, sharp enough to startle him upright.

He approached swiftly, boots sending ripples through the mirrored sky in shallow puddles. "Detective Blackburn." He tried for composure but couldn't quite mask the edge in his tone.

She didn't look at him right away. Her eyes stayed fixed on the ruined asphalt and what it failed to yield. When she spoke again, it was low and threatening. A thread stretched taut over simmering fury.

"Who authorized Fire to hose down my scene?"

He shifted his weight, a child caught mid-transgression. "Sgt. Beckett gave clearance," he said finally, voice cautious. "It was called an accident at first. Standard protocol for vehicle fires."

Her hands curled into fists at her sides, nails bit flesh as if pain could anchor the rage that threatened to spill over. The scene was lost, evidence swept away by routine carelessness, and yet she felt its absence gnawing inside her, hollow and irretrievable.

She stood there a moment longer, the sun at her back, city noise receding, alone with what remained, control slipping through her fingers like water pooling in cracks too deep to fill.

"An accident," she repeated, her voice pared to a blade, slicing through the damp hush between them. Her gaze swept the asphalt. Slick, bruised beneath the streetlights, as if she could conjure from its sheen what violence had been washed away.

She nodded once, curt and final. "Thank you." The words were clipped, already receding as she turned. A dismissal DeAngelo could not mistake. He lingered in her wake, posture caving under her restraint, then drifted back to his post, carrying her unspoken verdict in his slumped shoulders.

A cluster of offerings pressed against the curb ahead. Pale chrysanthemums drooped in cellophane, candles sputtering in the morning's uncertain breeze. Wax pooled at their bases, scent mingling with exhaust and rain. Handwritten notes curled at the edges, grief rendered in ink and smudged thumbprints. Blackburn slowed as she approached. Not a hesitation but an adjustment of pace, as if calibrating herself to the gravity that clung here.

A woman kneeled at the heart of it. Mid-fifties, denim jacket worn thin at the elbows and cuffs. Her hands shook as she coaxed flame from a match. It flared briefly, then steadied into a small persistent light. She withdrew a cream-colored bear from her bag, a child's relic, incongruous and tender) and nestled it among the tokens. Her lips moved in silent ritual before she straightened, catching sight of Blackburn's approach.

The woman rose stiffly, clutching her bag tightly against her ribs. Her eyes flickered with something beyond sorrow. An appetite for secrets. "Terrible thing," she murmured, voice pitched low for confidences that never quite reached daylight. "A girl like that... They say one of *those* men did it." She leaned closer, breath tinged with coffee and nerves. "Money changes hands. Police look the other way."

Blackburn's laugh came sharp, a fracture through the mourning air. Her mouth curled. Not quite amusement, more an exposure of teeth than intent to comfort. She met the woman's stare without blinking. "I am the police," she said, smooth edges over steel. "Detective Blackburn. No one's bought me."

Color flooded the woman's cheeks. Her hands fluttered over her knees, brushing at invisible grit. "Sorry, Detective, I didn't mean. It's just..." She trailed off, gaze darting sideways toward safety.

"I know how stories grow legs," Blackburn replied, voice modulating to something almost gentle, a calculated slackening of tension as she stepped closer into the shared space. "What else do they say?"

The woman glanced over one shoulder before speaking again, a whisper meant for conspirators alone. "The candle shop clerk heard things, from an IT guy who knew before it happened." She gestured down the block to the storefronts glinting under dew-laced neon.

Blackburn let silence settle between them. Approval or skepticism unreadable in the faint lift at one corner of her mouth. She offered a perfunctory thanks and pivoted away, leaving both shrine and rumor behind.

Her stride gathered purpose as she moved toward the intersection where new glass fronts warred with peeling brickwork. Order and entropy vying for dominion along a single block.

At a bus stop bench shattered by neglect (splinters jutting like exposed bone), she paused. The disorder felt pointed. A challenge embedded in debris. Her gaze tracked upward. A security camera blinked red above a doorway, its cyclopean eye recording everything and nothing.

She stopped before Coconut Glass Candles, the boutique's window scrubbed to surgical clarity despite last night's rain. Inside, rows of coconut wax candles arranged like trophies of serenity, their surfaces flawless and cold beneath LED spillover. Crystals clustered on mossy trays, amethyst veined with shadow, citrine catching stray light like sugar on broken pavement. Incense sticks waited in bronze holders shaped like open palms.

At the center, a sign floated above it all. "Illuminate Naturally," the script lush but brittle around its edges, garlanded with dried petals that bled color onto glass.

To Blackburn, it read less invitation than performance. A tableau curated for those who craved meaning prepackaged in scent and stone. She pictured customers pressing anxious faces to glass, seeking absolution in quartz or wax. A hunger for order disguised as ritual.

She exhaled through her nose, a sound almost too soft for derision, and shook her head once.

"Artisanal hope," she muttered under her breath. Even so, something pulled at her. A reluctant curiosity about whatever narrative this place might offer up about blood on concrete and secrets traded after dark. Aliens? Bigfoot? Anything seemed possible beneath such polished calm.

She stepped forward into her own reflection fractured by sunlight across glass, and waited for someone inside to notice who was watching whom.

Blackburn's voice sliced through the thin morning haze as she angled herself toward Reeves, who lingered across the street. "Reeves! Note every camera along these blocks," she called, tone clipped, eyes already scanning for blind spots. "Get IT down here to pull all the relevant footage."

Reeves, his navy slacks rumpled and shoes scuffing against the curb, lifted a hand in loose acknowledgment. He moved with the distracted air of someone searching for caffeine rather than evidence.

Blackburn didn't wait for him. She strode to her sedan, the city's chill still clinging to its metal skin. The trunk groaned open beneath her hand. She sifted through its contents with speed, a shuffle of paper, the crackle of maps and files marked with Traffic Services Division sigils. Langston v. Unknown—Case CCTR-02412. The stamp bled red in the hard light.

She thumbed through incident reports, sunlight flaring off white pages and forcing her to squint. She wanted to reread an important entry. Its brevity was at odds with what it suggested.

Witness: Marla Sutton (F/30), phone 555-7831.

Friend of victim.

Arrived Oak Street approx. 06:50 after call from Jenna Langston; pickup request logged at 06:15; call missed at 06:45. Witness highly distressed—preliminary questioning incoherent (see Officer Baylor #4427). Follow-up recommended pending timeline clarification.

Note: Witness supplied full name—Jenna Langston (F/28).

Officer B. Baylor #4427

Traffic Services

A flicker of recognition. This was the woman who had held Jenna's phone during that final call. She needed to call before anyone else did.

Her hand closed around her phone, thumb hovering over Marla's number. The word "incoherent" echoed in her mind, sharp and unsettling. Voice calls left traces she couldn't control, a text offered cleaner lines, a record if chaos followed.

She composed each word with care

Hi Marla. This is Detective Morgan Blackburn, New Dresden Police.<

I'm investigating Jenna Langston's death<

I would like to speak with you as soon as possible.<

Please call me when you can.<

She sent it, a silent transmission into uncertainty, and slipped the phone into her pocket. Her gaze drifted back to the files, restless now, unable to settle on any single detail as thoughts tumbled behind her exterior.

The phone buzzed, a sudden jolt against her thigh. Screen lit: 555-7831.

She answered reflexively, voice low but unmistakably firm. "Detective Blackburn."

A breath crackled over the line before words formed, fragile but urgent. "Detective? It's Marla. You just texted me." Relief broke through Marla's voice like sun through cloud cover. "Thank God someone finally reached out."

Blackburn modulated her tone, steadying it with an undercurrent of assurance meant to anchor them both. "I apologize for the delay," she said, letting each syllable land with intent. "Now that I'm here, things will move forward."

On the other end, silence stretched thin by shallow breathing, the sound of someone holding themselves together by force of will.

"You're...you're the detective Jenna met that night?" Marla's voice trembled at the edge of composure.

"I am," Blackburn replied without pause, stone steady but edged with something softer beneath. "I didn't know Jenna well, but even briefly, she stood out." She let that statement hang between them. It needed no embellishment.

A hush settled. A void filled only by Marla's uneven breaths and distant city noise bleeding into Blackburn's ear. Traffic murmurs, a dog barking somewhere beyond sightline, morning light glancing off glass and chrome.

"Thank you," Marla whispered finally.

Blackburn leaned against cold steel, the car grounding her as memory flickered behind her eyes. Jenna moaning in one moment, threatening in another.

"I take this case seriously," she said gently but without compromise. Her words were both shields and promises. "Jenna deserved better."

Another pause. A fragile quiet laced with everything unsaid.

"She was..." Marla started and faltered. Grief thickened her voice until it nearly failed her. "...one-of-a-kind."

Blackburn watched a man in headphones drift past, oblivious. An autonomous taxi slid by in silence. A golden retriever strained against its leash. Life was moving on in defiance of loss.

"Tell me what happened that morning," Blackburn prompted softly but firmly, drawing Marla back from memory into this necessary present. Marla hadn't given her the impression that Jenna had complained to her.

Marla exhaled shakily, the sound raw but determined now as she began again. "Jenna called early...she sounded upset...asked me to pick her up at Oak and Maple."

"Upset? Did she say why?" Blackburn asked, her pen already poised above a fresh page in her notebook, mind cataloguing every inflection for what it might reveal or conceal.

"No," Marla conceded, irritation threading her voice. "She said she'd explain everything once I got there."

Blackburn paused mid-note, pen hovering just above the paper. "Did someone upset her?" Her tone was almost gentle. Bait wrapped in silk.

Marla's breath sharpened. "I don't know. She didn't say anything before I arrived." The words came out brittle, frustration barely masked.

Blackburn leaned forward, narrowing the distance between them until the air vibrated with her attention. "Think carefully. Did Jenna ever mention anyone following her? Anyone making her uneasy?"

A silence settled between them, heavy, expectant. Marla hesitated, eyes darting away as if searching for an answer in some distant memory. When she finally spoke, her voice had shrunk to a hush. "No… Jenna never told me anything like that. If something was wrong, she would have—"

Blackburn's gaze remained fixed, unreadable as she scrawled a note, her hand steady, precise. She shifted tactics without warning. "Do you have a list of online names she used? I want to check her public social media. There may be something there."

Marla let out a short laugh, brittle as glass fracturing on tile. "She was on a dozen dating apps. It was usually a variation of her name. JennaL, Langston, JennaLaLa."

The corner of Blackburn's mouth twitched, an aborted smile or a grimace, impossible to tell. She let the moment hang before speaking again, voice low. "Listen closely." Each word landed with surgical precision. "This stays between us." Silence pressed in, thick enough to taste.

Blackburn's eyes locked onto Marla's, unblinking. "Jenna confided in me last night," she said softly, professional vulnerability carefully modulated for effect. "She said someone was watching her, following her to my house." The statement hung in the air, weighted with implication.

Marla's eyes widened and her mouth formed an almost perfect O.

"I took it seriously," Blackburn continued after a beat, voice steady but edged with something colder than concern. "I went out myself, with my service weapon, and checked every inch around my place. Nothing concrete turned up."

Another pause, sharp as a scalpel.

"I'm telling you because I need to know if Jenna ever mentioned feeling watched or threatened to you." The question cut closer now.

Marla's breath caught audibly, a thin gasp that betrayed more than words could manage. "No," she whispered at last. "Nothing like that. Are you sure she saw someone?"

Blackburn let the silence linger just long enough to unsettle before replying in an even tone. "That's what she told me. I'm trying to piece things together." Her pen hovered again, poised for the next move. "Is there anything else, anything at all, you think I should know?"

Hesitation thickened on the line. Marla's reply came slowly and uncertainly. "There's one thing... I missed a call from Jenna this morning. Early, about 6:45, but she hung up before I answered."

Blackburn angled the phone against her shoulder, notepad ready beneath her hand. Her handwriting slashed across the page in careful strokes. "Exactly 6:45?"

"Wait," Marla murmured faintly, the sound of fingers flicking over glass and distant electronic pings filling the gap between words. "No. It was 6:48."

"Did it go to voicemail?" Blackburn asked, the question clipped and cool.

"No message," Marla answered quietly now.

Check outgoing calls to 555-7831. Blackburn wrote and underlined it once with finality.

She recalibrated her tone, softening just enough to feign concern while keeping Marla tethered close. "I need you to be certain. Did Jenna ever hint at someone watching her? Anyone odd at work? An ex who wouldn't let go?"

Marla kept her voice steady this time. "No... nothing like that." A note of defensiveness crept in now, as if repeating it might make it true.

Blackburn nodded almost imperceptibly, committing details to memory as much as to paper, and circled another note on her pad for emphasis. "Thank you," she said smoothly, warmth slipping into her voice like oil over water. She left a pause hanging there, a silent demand for trust before continuing. "I'll need your address too. A detective may follow up if we require more information."

Marla recited it without hesitation. Blackburn jotted it down with swift efficiency and ended the call with reassurance. A soft closure meant to linger long after the line went dead.

Only then did Blackburn lean back, gaze skimming over her notes while a faint smirk played at her lips, a private signal of satisfaction.

Information gathered cleanly. Nothing too specific that couldn't be shaped later if needed. And now Marla sat neatly positioned as an unwitting ally should Internal Affairs come sniffing for cracks.

Perfect.

Chapter 3

The bell above the door gave a muted chime as Blackburn entered, its tone dissolving into the hush within. Warmth pressed in at once. Sandalwood, vanilla, a filament of clove threading through the air. Candlelight pooled on honeyed wood, glancing off glass jars and polished stones. Shelves bore their burden with careful pride. Candles in every shade, crystals stacked like fragments of ice, incense sticks aligned so precisely they might have been measured. The shop was a confection of order and invitation, but for Blackburn it felt staged, a softness she distrusted on sight. She kept her expression flat, though a muscle ticked at her jaw.

Movement behind the counter caught her attention. Kendria adjusted a row of amber jars, blouse shifting with each small gesture. When she turned, the light struck her face. Dark eyes alive beneath brows drawn in concentration, mouth set but unguarded. Their gazes met. A pulse flickered low in Blackburn's chest. Heat prickled along her collarbone. She registered the way Kendria's shoulders tensed before settling again, how her breath stuttered just once before smoothing out.

Blackburn remained still in the doorway, posture straight as if bracing against the room's gentle artifice. Her eyes didn't leave

Kendria's face. She watched for micro-expressions, a flicker at the corner of the mouth, fingers curling briefly against glass.

"Good afternoon." Her voice was even, pitched low but clear. "Detective Morgan Blackburn. New Dresden homicide."

The words held for a beat. Kendria blinked. Surprise showed only in the slight widening of her eyes. Blackburn extended her hand palm up, and Kendria accepted without pause. Her grip was sure and warm.

For an instant their hands lingered together, Kendria's skin cool from handling glass, Blackburn's steady with purpose, before they parted. "Welcome to Coconut Glass Candles."

Blackburn let her gaze drift over shelves crowded with color and scent. Candle flames cast slow-moving shadows across Kendria's throat and cheekbones before she returned to meet those dark eyes again.

"I'm here about a hit-and-run," she said. "Oak Street this morning."

A furrow appeared between Kendria's brows, then recognition dawned as she searched Blackburn's face.

"Oh." Her voice brightened with sudden clarity. "Now I remember where I know you from." She hesitated, a quick glance away, then back again. "You're a friend of Roscoe's."

There was no need to elaborate further. The code was clear, though poorly timed.

Blackburn inclined her head in acknowledgment, letting silence fill the gap between question and answer.

"That's right. But I'm here on business," she said softly. "If you have time now, I'd like to ask you some questions."

Kendria nodded once, too quickly, then steadied herself with a smile.

"We can talk while I show you around," she offered, voice smooth but not entirely casual. "Maybe help you pick out something?"

Blackburn allowed herself half a smile, brief and sharp-edged for those who knew how to read it.

"Maybe you could," she replied.

They moved together into the aisles, a corridor of pastel wax and metallic shimmer pressing close on either side. Blackburn walked with measured steps. Even here amid scents meant to soothe, there was an alertness to her posture that refused comfort.

She let her fingertips graze the edge of a wooden shelf as if testing its grain.

"Did you notice anything unusual this morning?" Her tone seemed idle but left little room for evasion.

The question floated between them. Somewhere nearby, a candle hissed quietly as its wick consumed itself.

Kendria paused mid-step beside her. For a moment, the silence held weight enough to bend light around it.

"No," Kendria said at last, voice low and even. "Not until later. I didn't realize anyone had been hurt. Homicide, you said?"

Blackburn studied her profile. A line of tension along Kendria's jaw belied by otherwise steady hands.

"Kendria." She stepped closer, shoes whispering over polished boards until only breath separated them. "Someone at the memorial said you had a theory about what happened."

A faint smile touched Kendria's lips, not quite amusement, not quite defiance, as she leaned back against the nearest shelf.

"A theory?" She let the word settle before continuing. "I wouldn't call it that." Her fingers found the pendant at her throat. Candlelight caught on silver as she looked up through dark lashes. "Just something I overheard."

Blackburn waited.

"It's about self-driving cars," Kendria said finally, each syllable weighted by intent rather than certainty. "The kind that learn from each other? They're communicating now, more than people realize." Her gaze flickered sideways to gauge Blackburn's response. "And not only about traffic or collisions."

A subtle shift crossed Blackburn's features. Interest sharpened by caution.

"Go on," she said, the invitation edged with command.

Kendria straightened, a flicker of steel sharpening her posture. "They're targeting the older models," she said, her words quick and precise. "Hijacking them, forcing collisions, locking down intersections. It's surgical. No fingerprints, no traces. Like kids pressing at the edges of a fence just to see what gives."

Blackburn's eyes glinted with an energy that hovered on the edge of recklessness. She leaned in, voice dropping low, as if the truth itself might shatter if spoken too loudly. Heat radiated between them, a subtle current that made Blackburn acutely aware of every inch of space they shared. She found herself watching Kendria's mouth shape each word, unable to look away even as her mind insisted on restraint.

The sensation crept up on her, unexpected and unwelcome. It slipped beneath the armor she wore for Jenna's sake, threading curiosity through grief where there should have been only resolve. Shadows pooled at Kendria's collarbone, silvered by her necklace. Light caught in the hollow of her throat whenever she spoke. Blackburn's thoughts snagged there, unbidden.

She blinked hard, pulse tapping out a warning beneath her skin. Distraction threatened to blur the sharp edges of the case. She could feel it in the way her focus stuttered and reformed around Kendria's presence.

"Sounds like you've been mainlining dystopian thrillers," Blackburn said finally, letting dryness mask the slip in her composure.

Kendria's grin curled wider, undimmed by doubt. "Maybe," she replied, tilting her head with feline poise. "Or maybe it's happening right now, and nobody wants to look too closely."

Blackburn started to answer but hesitated under Kendria's gaze, a gaze so steady it peeled back layers with its directness. The air between them tightened, a live wire humming just beneath ordinary conversation.

She cleared her throat and moved away, letting distance cool what lingered unsaid. Her hand drifted along shelves crowded with curated oddities. Handwoven cloth folded with military precision beside glass bottles that fractured sunlight into shards across dusty wood.

She stopped before a display of candles, each one sculpted and colored as if meant for ritual rather than burning. Her fingers hovered over a crimson pillar candle before lifting it free from its pedestal.

The scent enveloped her instantly. Sandalwood braided through vanilla and something darker, a raw undertone of damp hay that rooted itself deep in memory.

"I've seen you." Kendria leaned against the shelving, watching Blackburn turn the candle in her hands. "I was at last month's gathering," she said. "You wore a half-mask, but your voice... I'd know it anywhere." She reached out and took Blackburn's hand, turning it palm up as though reading more than lines or fate. "And this hand. I saw what this hand did."

Blackburn did not pull away. Kendria traced slow circles along her palm, a touch both casual and deliberate.

"It was me," Blackburn said, letting authority settle back into her voice as if donning familiar armor. "And I enjoyed it." She studied Kendria's face for any flicker of recognition or challenge. "Were you part of the crowd, or did you join in?"

"Watching," Kendria answered without hesitation, thumb still moving in arcs across Blackburn's skin. "You have an interesting approach."

Blackburn arched an eyebrow. "Approach? What, are you hoping to add some new tricks?"

Kendria smiled, a small, private thing that hinted at secrets with-held. "Most days I lead," she said softly. "But for someone who knows how to control, *really* take control, I can be flexible."

"And this someone?" Blackburn stepped closer. "What does this someone look like?"

Kendria reached behind herself without breaking eye contact and lifted another candle from the shelf, angled so that Blackburn's re-flection shimmered in its glassy surface.

"Like this," Kendria murmured.

Blackburn held still for a moment longer than necessary, letting silence spool out between them, taut as wire strung between two anchor points.

"You know," she said at last, voice velvet-dark and pitched low enough to draw Kendria nearer by instinct alone, "attention is rare currency." Her smile barely tipped up at one corner, a promise curled tight beneath restraint. "Most people never bother."

"Oh, I agree," Kendria replied, her tone dropping into something richer, slower, the kind of agreement meant for closed doors and shadowed rooms. She raised the candle between them as if offering proof or confession, or both. "Would you rather take this home wrapped up safe? Or do you prefer things raw?"

Blackburn let her smirk sharpen into something almost wolfish. When she spoke, it was slow and certain. "I like it raw."

Time stilled around them, just long enough for Blackburn to catch the hitch in Kendria's breath, quicksilver-brief but unmistak-able. She filed it away alongside other observations, the way Kendria watched people too closely, how she held tension like a secret waiting to be spent, as new theories coalesced in the quiet corners of her mind.

Now was not the moment for speculation. Blackburn's tone when she spoke shifted, professional, but edged with a certainty that pressed forward. "Regarding the investigation," she said, letting silence settle before continuing, "did you hear anything unusual this morning? Any disturbances or sounds out of place?" She reached for the candle, her fingers steady, and set it back on the shelf. The gesture closed a circuit. There would be no argument.

"What time?" Kendria's voice was flat, not defensive but alert.

"Between six-thirty and seven." Blackburn watched for any flicker in Kendria's expression, a tightening at the corner of her mouth, a glance away, but found only careful recollection. Kendria's brow knitted as she searched memory, unhurried and unmasked.

"No," Kendria said finally. The word landed cleanly in the hush between them. "The shop is soundproof. I can't stand city noise, so I lined everything, walls, ceiling, with acoustic tile."

Blackburn let that explanation hang, measuring its plausibility against the room's quiet. "You're here that early?"

"Sometimes." Kendria's lips quirked. The admission was neither boast nor apology. "Deliveries arrive before opening. Inventory checks don't wait for business hours." She shrugged lightly. "That's small business."

Blackburn's gaze lingered on Kendria, not just listening but cataloging each movement. How her hands stilled when she spoke, how her eyes sharpened at each question. The air thickened with something unsaid. Tension gathered in small spaces, the gap between their bodies, the hush after every answer.

She let it build before breaking it. A smile traced itself across her mouth, controlled, never careless, as she inclined her head in acknowledgment. "Thank you for your candor, Kendria." Each word was deliberate. Blackburn chose them like chess pieces moved into position. "Rumors often prove more useful than you might expect."

Kendria nodded slowly, then tipped her head to study Blackburn anew, a glint of curiosity behind her eyes catching light like glass at dusk. Her words came softer than before but held their shape. "I never gave you my name." The pause that followed was calculated. An invitation or an accusation hung between them. "How did you know?"

Blackburn did not look away. Earlier, she had noticed the slim tag pinned above Kendria's heart, a detail absorbed and filed without conscious effort. Now she allowed herself a glance there again, making the motion obvious enough to answer.

"Your name tag," she said.

Kendria looked down as if rediscovering it. Color rose up her neck in a muted flush. Laughter slipped from her, a low spill of sound that broke tension while acknowledging it. "I forget I'm even wearing it half the time."

Blackburn's smile deepened, subtle, almost private, though Kendria seemed not to register its intent. "Since I'm already here..." Her tone softened but retained its undercurrent of command. She let her fingers drift along the shelf as if reacquainting herself with its textures and shapes before selecting a sleek black jar from the row. "I'll get a candle," she murmured.

She moved with unhurried precision. Each step seemed calculated to narrow the distance without haste. Her gaze traveled over the displays until it caught on a cluster of pale candles marked by stark black labels. Wax Play Candles. The words tasted strange in her mouth as she spoke them aloud, amusement flickering at one corner of her lips.

Kendria stepped closer until Blackburn could sense warmth radiating from her skin. A scent rose up. Violets bruised under heat, threaded with something sharper beneath. Kendria smiled and tilted her head toward Blackburn in silent communion.

"Familiar territory?" Kendria asked, voice pitched low enough to confide but not quite whispering.

"It might be," Blackburn replied, turning one ivory candle between her fingers as if weighing more than wax, testing intention against restraint.

Kendria leaned nearer still so that their arms brushed lightly. Contact brief but unmistakable, a claim staked and withdrawn in an instant. "These are my favorites," she said. Her words curled around them like smoke rising from an extinguished wick. "Formulated for sensitive play."

Blackburn repeated the word back to her, "Sensitive," but made it rougher, almost dismissive. She set the candle down but didn't move away.

"That wouldn't be my word," she said.

Kendria angled her head so shadows played along her throat. Invitation shimmered in that exposed line of skin and in the hush that followed.

"What would you call it?" Her voice was velvet drawn taut across something harder beneath.

A shadow passed through Blackburn's gaze, a storm gathering behind glass, and for a moment neither moved nor breathed.

"I could show you better than I could tell you." Her smile was all edge now, a promise or threat or both entwined together.

Silence pressed close around them until Kendria's hand lifted to touch the chain at her throat, silver glinting where pulse fluttered beneath skin.

"I close at eight," she said.

Blackburn raised one hand and traced a featherlight line along Kendria's collarbone, the backs of her fingers cool against heated skin, a gesture less comfort than possession.

Her breath grazed Kendria's ear as she whispered. "Perfect." The word lingered between them like smoke curling upward from an extinguished flame.

"Close your eyes."

Kendria hesitated only a moment before lowering her lashes. Anticipation wound tightly inside her chest until every sound, the hum of air above them, the distant hum of traffic, seemed amplified by waiting silence.

"Don't move." Blackburn's voice cut through the hush, sharp enough to halt Kendria mid-breath. The click of heels marked a slow orbit, each step inescapable. Silk whispered as Blackburn passed close, close enough that Kendria's skin prickled in anticipation.

Blackburn moved with intent, every gesture a signal in an unspoken game where time thinned and stretched. Beneath the surface, a current of longing pulsed, more perilous than idle curiosity, more urgent than she dared admit.

Kendria stood motionless, hands braced on the old wood of the display case, her breath uneven. Blackburn fought to steady herself but found resolve slipping beneath the heat rising inside herself. Desire pressed in, insistent and unwelcome, blurring the line between control and surrender. She caught herself breathing faster, a secret betrayal she refused to let show. This was not supposed to happen now. Not here.

Leave before you lose your grip. The thought flickered by, sharp and fleeting, quickly drowned by denial. Of course she noticed women like her, she always had. Angular cheekbones softened by laughter, intensity flickering behind fleeting warmth. In Kendria, that contradiction lived in every glance.

The air carried lavender and the faint musk of old paper. Outside, city noise seeped through glass in muffled waves. Kendria's eyes stayed shut as the lock slid into place with a metallic snap, her flinch barely perceptible.

Blackburn was behind her without warning, a presence heavy and intoxicating in the dim light. Her arms circled Kendria's waist, steady but unhurried. "What are you thinking?" she murmured, voice low enough to blur into breath.

Kendria swallowed hard. "I wish I could close early." Her gaze darted toward shadowed windows before dropping again.

A smile curled at Blackburn's lips, a velvet sound vibrating in her chest as she leaned in so close Kendria felt every word against her ear. "You won't be interrupted," she promised quietly. "The door is locked."

She pressed her mouth to Kendria's neck, not gentle, not rough, but precise. A touch that kindled heat beneath skin and scattered every rational thought Kendria tried to hold on to. The shop faded away. Only Blackburn remained, deliberate and consuming.

Blackburn lifted Kendria's chin with fingers tracing familiar territory along her jawline, memorizing each angle anew. Their next kiss hovered on the edge of restraint, a careful graze of teeth hinting at hunger kept just barely leashed. Kendria shivered and leaned closer.

"I want you." The words escaped on a trembling exhale as Kendria gripped Blackburn's hips and drew her nearer. "All of you."

Blackburn's eyes flashed with challenge as she toyed with the first button of Kendria's blouse, slow movements calculated to unravel patience thread by thread. "Are you sure?" Her question lingered in the charged silence between them.

Kendria's breath caught as fabric parted under steady hands, one button yielding, then another. Tension coiled tighter with each exposed inch of skin.

"You have me standing here," Kendria whispered, voice unsteady, "losing myself in my own shop."

Blackburn closed what little distance remained between them until their bodies aligned seamlessly. Her hand slipped inside Kendria's blouse with ease. Silk glided over bare skin and drew a soft gasp from Kendria's lips.

"Exactly what I intended," Blackburn said quietly near her ear.

Kendria opened her eyes for just a moment as Blackburn withdrew, a calculated retreat that left want sharpened rather than eased. Trembling but determined now, Kendria reached for the remaining buttons herself. One by one, they fell away under her touch while Blackburn watched with predatory focus.

"Stunning." Blackburn let the word hang as her fingertips hovered above exposed skin before finally making contact, a featherlight trail from collarbone downwards that left goosebumps blooming in its wake.

"But your mind is still racing." A gentle rebuke slipped between them as Blackburn pressed forward again until Kendria met the cool solidity of the wall behind her.

With swift certainty, Blackburn caught both wrists and pinned them overhead, a movement so sudden it stole breath from Kendria's throat. She pressed a searing kiss beneath Kendria's ear, precise, devastating.

"Let go," Blackburn ordered softly, no room for refusal yet laced with promise instead of threat. Her free hand slipped beneath loose silk and claimed new territory across heated skin.

Kendria arched at the touch as if gravity itself had shifted. Resistance melted into instinctive surrender. Their eyes locked, and passion flickered there for an instant before doubt shadowed it again.

"I trust you," she managed, words fragile even as she spoke them aloud because safety wasn't what this moment offered or required.

Blackburn answered with a faint smile of steel wrapped in a velvet promise. Another kiss brushed along Kendria's jawline, restraint hinting at deeper turbulence below calm waters waiting to break free.

"I'll handle everything," Blackburn said, not reassurance, but certainty delivered like an oath disguised as an invitation. When she leaned close enough for their breaths to tangle together. "Once we start," she whispered against trembling skin, "you're mine entirely, to do with as I choose."

Knife-edged candlelight sliced through the boutique, casting restless shadows that stretched and recoiled across shelves lined with glass and wax. Amber weighted the air, dense, almost narcotic, threaded with sandalwood, each breath a negotiation between comfort and threat. Kendria stood motionless, spine pressed to the wall as if bracing herself against an undertow. Her pulse drummed at her throat, betraying nothing outward but everything within.

Blackburn's presence was a pressure. Close, deliberate, barely touching yet already claiming space. When her hand finally moved, it wasn't a caress but a quiet assertion. Knuckles grazing fabric, a slow ascent up Kendria's thigh that mapped out territory in increments. The anticipation stung sharper than contact.

"I have a safe word," Kendria said, the words small and careful, nearly lost beneath the mechanical sigh of the ceiling fan. "Apple."

Blackburn's mouth curved, something sly in the set of her lips, as she studied Kendria's face. "And if I don't listen?"

A flicker crossed Kendria's gaze. Defiance or fear. She couldn't tell which would serve her better. She steadied herself with a breath that felt like surrender and armor both. "Then you're a bastard." Not an accusation, just a fact, trembling at its edges.

The distance between them vanished. Blackburn pressed in, body to body, pinning Kendria with an intensity measured not in force but in intent. Heat radiated from her, not wild but banked, smoldering beneath control. It threatened to unravel Kendria, one careful inch at a time.

"Do you want me?" Blackburn murmured in Kendria's ear, her voice low and certain, a question that was also an instruction.

Kendria nodded once, her breath catching on the cusp of speech. "Yes." Barely audible, barely enough.

Blackburn's fingers continued their slow exploration, tracing the hem of Kendria's skirt upward until they met lace. A fleeting brush that left absence more acute than presence. Each movement was methodical, patience masquerading as mercy.

"Say it," Blackburn whispered against skin gone hypersensitive. "If you want me to stop."

Kendria's head tipped back, eyelids fluttered shut. Words dissolved before they formed, her mind suspended between ache and restraint.

Every nerve sharpened under Blackburn's touch, every thought scattered except for one stubborn thread binding her to sense.

Silence gathered, thick as oil, before Blackburn spoke again. "I'm continuing."

Another beat of silence.

"Yes?"

A whisper. "Yes."

Blackburn traced patterns along Kendria's skin. Spirals and pauses, each gesture calibrated for effect rather than comfort. Control lived in every line drawn. Surrender hovered with every breath withheld.

Yet somewhere below sensation, reason stirred, a warning threading through fog. This was still a game with rules she could not afford to forget.

Her voice broke through at last, frayed but resolute. "Apple."

The word hung between them like a snapped wire.

Blackburn stepped back immediately, not hesitant but precise, as if severing invisible cords binding them together. Space rushed in where heat had been. Absence became its own kind of contact.

Kendria staggered forward before steadying herself, arms folding tight across her chest, a barrier hastily constructed against whatever might spill out next. Her hands shook, jaw clenched. She forced air into lungs suddenly too small for breath.

Wax and spice lingered heavy as ever (the world unchanged except for what had shifted inside her). Above it all, the fan hummed on, a mundane witness to their undoing.

Blackburn's voice cut through the aftermath, low, unhurried. "Which candle? For tonight?" Her fingers drifted along the shelves, pausing here and there, as if each jar might hold its own secret bargain.

Kendria swallowed hard. Her gaze darted everywhere but toward Blackburn. She scanned the rows until her eyes snagged on a small candle at the far edge, a creation of her own hand, unremarkable save for what it contained. Instinct chose for her before thought could intervene.

"That one." Voice thin as thread. "Tantalizing Heat."

A smile curled on Blackburn's lips, wolfish and knowing, as she lifted the candle from its hiding place and held it aloft like proof of conquest. She moved toward the counter with purposeful slowness, a predator savoring proximity rather than pursuit.

At the register, Blackburn plucked a pen from beside the old card reader and scrawled something onto her business card, a number offered without ceremony or apology.

Kendria reached for composure she didn't feel, fingers fumbling over buttons and screens as though muscle memory alone could bridge this gulf between before and after. Blackburn tapped her black credit card against the machine with ease, a gesture that made command look effortless.

Candle in hand, Blackburn lingered just long enough to ensnare Kendria with a glance sharp as flint, promise smoldering beneath cool detachment.

"I'll take this, and more, later." The words layered with implications left hanging in the charged air.

She pivoted smoothly toward the door, owning every inch of space she crossed. At the threshold she paused. One hand rested on the lock as she looked back over her shoulder, a smirk flickering like static along her mouth.

"Your shirt," she said simply before slipping into the daylight beyond glass panes fractured by the afternoon sun.

Only then did Kendria look down in horror, buttons undone, vulnerability exposed, and hastily fasten herself back together with shaking hands while outside Blackburn disappeared into the brightness that made everything inside seem dim by comparison.

Chapter 4

Heat still clung to Blackburn's skin, a residue of the candle shop and Kendria's touch, as she stepped onto Oak Street. The illusion of warmth dissolved beneath a sudden draft curling between buildings, slicing through her clothes. Her heels struck pavement fissured like old scars, each step echoing in the brittle hush that always settled before the city remembered to breathe. She drew in air thick with diesel and distant rot, nothing like sandalwood and salt on bare wrists.

Blackburn watched as Reeves crouched by the gutter ahead, shoulders hunched against the slab-gray afternoon. His gaze flicked over the detritus, shards glinting like animal teeth after a mauling, until something caught his eye. A sliver of metal, polished and incongruous among the grit. He fished out his phone, snapped a photo with indifference, then peeled a latex glove over his hand. The snap of rubber broke the quiet. It pinched his knuckles, unwelcomed. A membrane between flesh and evidence, between certainty and all that refused to yield.

She saw the metal fragment glitter in his fingers, movements pared to their essentials. Gather, inspect, seal. Each gesture was conscious, as if he could will order from chaos by repetition alone. The city's hum pressed in. Horns blaring at indifferent lights, footsteps scraping past, but Reeves worked inside a pocket of focus that let nothing intrude.

A few paces off, headlight shards sprawled across the asphalt, white plastic splinters sharp as accusations. Reeves smoothed out a crumpled evidence bag from his blazer. It rustled softly before swallowing another piece of violence.

Blackburn hovered at the intersection's edge, silhouette carved against neon flicker and headlights stuttering through haze. A street vendor's cart exhaled greasy smoke that tangled with exhaust and something sweetly rotten. A ghost of memory brushed her senses raw. She shifted her weight. Her heel tapped out an impatient code on the stained curb.

The light bled green. Blackburn crossed without hurry but with a purpose in every stride, eyes locked on Reeves as if she could will him to see what she already suspected. She arrived in silence. Her gaze swept over his findings with the same clinical care she'd used on herself in mirrors after sleepless nights.

He nodded toward the Kraft paper bag in her hand, a small indulgence from earlier now out of place here. "What's in there?" His voice was low, almost casual.

She held it up so he could see the candle store logo stamped across its side. "Rotting fish heads," she said with half a smile that didn't reach her eyes. Her fingers lingered on the folded top, a private reminder of softness before this steel-cold work resumed.

He offered up his own find. "Metal fragment." The words were clipped, businesslike. "Headlight debris too, probably from our autonomous vehicle, but I'll let Forensics argue it." He sealed both into bags with an efficiency born less of habit than necessity.

She turned one bag over in her palm as if weighing not just evidence but consequence. "Traffic Services give us anything?"

"Nothing yet." Flat.

She handed back the bag without ceremony. Authority radiated from her not through force but through absence. She left no room for doubt or clutter. "Trunk later."

Around them, Oak Street churned. Bodies brushing past without seeing, engines idling in frustration beneath the brittle sky. But for Blackburn and Reeves, this was no ordinary thoroughfare. It was aftermath incarnate, every scar on the road a fresh wound refusing to scab over.

They moved together down the cracked sidewalk, silent but attuned. Their eyes combed gutters and shadows for what others had missed or chosen not to see. Their steps fell into rhythm, a muted percussion marking time toward ground zero.

Blackburn stopped short where the asphalt bore dark streaks gouged deep as if by claws. Marks left behind by something mechanical yet unmistakably violent. She crouched low. City noise faded until only breath and memory remained.

"Here," she murmured, not uncertainty but respect for what had happened and what lingered unseen beneath surface grime.

Reeves followed her gaze to where molten scars marred the pavement, still faintly perfumed, or so it seemed, with scorched rubber and circuitry, a phantom scent that belonged more to memory than air.

"How does it happen?" His question was half-whispered to himself, the disbelief of someone who trusted machines more than people until now. "These cars are supposed to be perfect. Metal brains immune to human error...so how does one end up like this? Bricked and burning?"

The question hung between them as Blackburn scanned the charred wreckage, the puzzle gnawing at her temples like an old ache flaring under pressure. Possibilities unspooled. Sabotage or glitch? Accident or intent? None aligned cleanly. All resisted resolution.

She spoke finally, voice edged with something restless. "Suppose it wasn't an error at all? Suppose someone steered it? Remote access from nearby? Bluetooth...infrared...turning it into a weapon by proxy." The theory felt dangerous even in her mouth. Too plausible for comfort but not yet bold enough for paranoia.

Reeves brightened, a spark catching dry tinder. "That'd explain why witnesses saw no driver."

Blackburn nodded once. Thoughts spun ahead faster than words could follow. "And remote detonation to wipe traces clean." She made a mental note. Chemical residue tests needed confirmation before nightfall.

A pause stretched between them until Reeves straightened abruptly, eyes alive with new possibility. "We should bring Willow in," he said, almost urgent now.

She arched an eyebrow, not refusal but scrutiny, sharpening her next move. "Why?"

The question lingered, a challenge rather than dismissal, as city noise swelled back around them and daylight began its slow retreat across broken glass and unanswered questions.

Reeves swept a hand toward the row of battered storefronts, their signs dulled by sun and neglect, paint peeling in strips that fluttered in the heavy air. "She might spot if any of the tech here could handle remote vehicle control," he murmured, voice low as if wary of the city listening in.

Blackburn's gaze tracked the uneven lines of the street, her eyes narrowing against the glare bouncing off windshields and cracked glass. Hot asphalt mingled with something sour, a forgotten lunch rotting in a gutter, or maybe just the city itself. "Stationary," she echoed, words restrained. "Letting them come to you. Calculated if you know their patterns." Her tone lingered on the last word, as if weighing its implications.

"Or if there was no pattern at all." Reeves countered, scanning the restless trickle of pedestrians. Saying it out loud gave his theory a jagged edge. It hung between them like a threat. Blackburn's jaw tightened, a subtle flare at her temple betraying distaste. Randomness was a contagion, impossible to predict, impossible to contain.

A shadow of amusement flickered across her lips, rare currency from Blackburn, and for a moment, approval glinted in her eyes. She regarded him sidelong, letting the silence stretch before breaking it with a note of genuine surprise. "Good catch," she said, voice pitched just above a whisper, as if reluctant to let praise linger too long in the open air. "Call Willow. We need to rule out some amateur predator waiting for an easy mark."

Color crept into Reeves's cheeks. He pulled his phone from his pocket and stepped away, already dialing. The faint buzz of his voice blurred into traffic and distant sirens.

Blackburn let herself slip sideways into thought, her body stilled but mind alive with possibility. Motives unfurled like blueprints behind her eyes. If someone hunted here knowingly, patiently, they'd bait the trap and wait for curiosity or habit to draw the prey close enough to snare.

A memory ghosted through her. Kendria in that cramped candle shop, wax and smoke thick in the air. One tilt of Blackburn's voice had unraveled Kendria's composure. Suggestion had become a compulsion with barely a touch. A blouse unbuttoned under soft light, all agency surrendered without protest or even awareness. The recollection sent a pulse along Blackburn's skin, a quiet surge beneath her ribs.

If she wanted to hunt, she could do it, and she wouldn't have to try hard at all.

That was what unsettled her most. How little effort true control required.

She exhaled sharply, as though clearing dust from her lungs, and flicked the thought away like ash from a sleeve. No use lingering on temptations she had no intention of indulging, not today.

"Willow will be here soon." Reeves's return broke through. The words carried promise and something else. Anticipation curled at their edges.

Blackburn let that settle. A small pleasure bloomed quietly at the thought of Willow coming when called. Perhaps there'd be time for an exchange before duty reclaimed her attention for the precinct meeting. She accepted the evidence bags from Reeves, plastic slick against her palm, and tossed them into her trunk with indifference. Compartmentalization rendered physical.

Movement caught Reeves's eye, a figure threading purposefully through thinning crowds down the block, neon sneakers flashing in the heat shimmer above pavement. He nudged closer to Blackburn without looking at her directly.

"Heads up," he murmured, chin angling subtly toward their approaching visitor. "Cassidy's inbound."

Blackburn straightened, not quite rigid but charged now with authority sharpened by expectation. Amusement, or maybe anticipation, skimmed across her features before settling into composure as she fixed on Brynn Cassidy's approach. A reporter scenting blood beneath civility.

"You're finding your own way back," she told Reeves without turning from Brynn's trajectory, her tone brisk enough to close doors behind him.

He grinned, rolling his shoulders as if shaking off tension. "No problem," he said easily. Then added with a crooked smile, "Just don't make me take one of those damned robo-cabs."

Their laughter was brief, a spark struck on flint, then gone beneath the oppressive hum of New Dresden pressing in around them.

She eased his exit with a gesture toward familiar territory. "Head back to the scene and pull whatever surveillance you can from those two shops." Her hand cut through the air, precise enough for instruction but loose enough to dismiss.

Reeves nodded once and melted away into the pedestrian flow, already plotting angles for camera coverage rather than risking entanglement with Cassidy's relentless curiosity.

Left alone on the curb, Blackburn allowed herself one small smile, the kind that barely disturbed her mouth but sent ripples inward, nonetheless. With distractions removed and Brynn closing fast, this became her arena again. Scrutiny sharpening every sense, control thrumming low under skin.

Brynn advanced, steps clipped through heat haze and exhaust tangling with perfume that clung stubbornly after late nights and whispered confidences. Her eyes were sharp-cut gems set deep with hunger. Not just for headlines but for whatever secrets Blackburn might yield under pressure.

"Detective Blackburn!" Brynn's voice sliced clean through traffic noise, a challenge wrapped in civility as she drew up short beside her quarry. Phone raised like a weapon, or perhaps an offering, she wasted no time. "Is this about the hit-and-run I tipped you off about?"

The device hovered between them like an accusation waiting for confession.

The city pressed close around them, sweat-slick concrete radiating heat, distant engines growling. Two predators circling in plain sight, each testing where power began and ended.

Blackburn angled her head, the faintest glimmer of amusement flickering across her otherwise impassive face. A ripple of light skated over porcelain. Her voice slid into the hush between them, silk drawn taut. "I am indeed investigating this autonomous vehicle incident." She let silence settle, a snare hidden beneath civility, before a slow smile curled at the corner of her mouth. "But you knew that already, didn't you? Always ahead of the curve, Ms. Cassidy. Makes me wonder what else you might know."

Her gaze pinned Brynn with the steadiness of a scalpel held in gloved fingers, half compliment, half challenge. To an outsider, it might have sounded like praise. To anyone fluent in subtext, the words shimmered with a razor's edge.

Light fractured across Brynn's cheekbone as she shifted, phone poised to catch every syllable. Blackburn tasted the moment, its tension, its latent heat, while behind her eyes memories flared. Jenna's image, sharp and cold as glass splinters under the light. A photograph surfaced unbidden. Jenna's smile caught mid-motion, questions webbed tightly around her like dust in forgotten corners.

Why had Brynn pointed her toward Jenna's death that morning? What invisible thread linked the reporter and the victim? What secrets had passed between them before Jenna vanished beneath steel and circuitry? Had Jenna whispered anything to Brynn in those final hours when truth trembled so close to the surface?

"This is it," Brynn thought, adrenaline threading through clarity. The story hovered just within reach if she dared hold on tightly enough.

She kept her tone crisp, professional veneer ironclad. "Could you comment on what happened here?"

The press pack pressed in, a low hum of anticipation vibrating through asphalt and glass. Blackburn stood at its center, spine straight as a blade. "An autonomous vehicle struck a pedestrian," she said, voice unhurried, each word falling like a pebble into still water. "The car malfunctioned soon after. It drove off before catching fire."

A muscle fluttered in Brynn's jaw. She'd expected more than recitation. Old news already cooling on city wires. "And the victim's name?" she asked, edging closer so that the glow from her phone lit Blackburn's collar.

"I can't release that yet," Blackburn replied, voice brushed with manufactured sympathy. "The family hasn't been notified." The lie tasted metallic. She could only hope Traffic had handled it by now.

Satisfaction pulsed just beneath her skin. Not triumph but something quieter. Possession of the narrative for these few minutes while bulbs flashed and voices waited for her cue.

Brynn's lips barely moved, but frustration darkened her eyes. A flicker there and gone as she recalibrated. "Detective," she pressed on, stance squared against Blackburn's advancing presence, "why return to the scene now? Hours after the initial investigation wrapped?"

Blackburn didn't blink. "The chief reassigned this case from Traffic Services to Homicide due to its complexity." She let the pause linger, a subtle assertion of dominance. "This is my first walk-through."

Not enough for Brynn. She leaned in again, question sharp as sleet. "Did new evidence prompt your visit? Anything you can share?"

"As I said," Blackburn answered evenly, her tone flat as polished stone, "this is my initial review. No new information yet. Standard protocol."

Brynn's eyes narrowed. A pulse at her temple betrayed effort, but she pressed forward anyway. "Any suspects or persons of interest at this time?"

A glint surfaced in Blackburn's gaze. Amusement warmed steel before vanishing into shadow. "There are no suspects until the medical examiner rules out accident and natural causes. And we're far from that." Her smirk hovered between invitation and warning.

Brynn changed tack without missing a beat. Questions flew like knives thrown by expert hands. "Do you suspect any ties to larger criminal activity?"

Blackburn exhaled slowly through parted lips. Even that breath felt calculated. "It's too early to speculate on connections or motives." The answer hung weightless, a door closed with gentle finality.

Their rhythm broke, not by design but by intrusion. Movement at the edge of vision drew both women's attention. Willow Adler drifted into view, a ghost at the periphery.

Opportunity flared in Brynn's eyes. Adrenaline surged anew as she pivoted toward it. "Detective Blackburn, can you clarify Willow Adler's involvement here?"

A subtle shift passed through Blackburn. Not quite visible unless one looked for it, but Brynn was always looking.

"Oh, that's right. You rattled her recently," Blackburn murmured, closing half the distance between them until Brynn retreated just a fraction. A dance they both remembered too well. The memory stung. Brynn dredged up old bruises in Willow during an ambush call. The echo of tears was still abrasive beneath Blackburn's composure.

"Ms. Adler consults on all tech-related aspects within Homicide," Blackburn continued, voice edged with something colder than professionalism. "Her expertise is indispensable when autonomous systems are involved."

Somewhere above them, neon buzzed against dusk. Somewhere behind them, cameras clicked and murmurs gathered mass. But here, between the detective and the reporter, tension hummed electric under skin and suit alike.

Blackburn held Brynn's gaze, a silent reminder of what was known and what remained just out of reach. Then Blackburn turned back toward shadow and chrome and all that refused to be named.

"Oh, Ms. Cassidy." Blackburn's voice cut through the quiet as she called over her shoulder. "Any luck finding out who slashed your news van's tires?"

Brynn stopped. Her shoulders tensed. Irritation flashed across her face and vanished. She steadied her tone. "No," she said, crisp and quick. "We filed a report. I figured it was just some bored kid with nothing better to do."

She met Blackburn's stare. Steady. Guarded. Blackburn smiled slowly and deliberately, as if the answer amused her. Brynn pressed her lips thin, slid her phone into her pocket, and turned on her heel with a small sigh. She chose not to engage further.

Blackburn watched her go, measuring the reaction and the timing. The detail registered and remained.

* * *

Reeves had no interest in Blackburn's games with the media. Let her deal with their prying questions and pointed microphones. He wanted no part of it. Answer incorrectly, and they made you look incompetent. He walked to Oak Street near Maple, where Jenna Langston had been struck and killed by an autonomous car. The morning hung close and gray. A light breeze carried the damp smell of asphalt and cut through his jacket. Traffic murmured in low waves.

He scanned the storefronts for cameras and opened his notebook. If the street yielded something, he would remain here for hours.

At Marge's Bakery, warm air and the smell of yeast and sugar drifted out as the door opened. The baker stepped out from the back with flour on her apron. Her expression shifted when she saw his badge and heard why he was there. "Oh, my word. I heard sirens but didn't know what happened." The concern seemed genuine. The camera had been inoperative for two weeks. Her husband kept promising to fix it. Reeves noted this and continued.

Coconut Glass Candles showed no visible cameras. The place smelled faintly of wax and smoke. The dark-haired owner drew the blinds and locked the door. Reeves documented this. Such details often proved valuable later.

Threads & Trends offered better prospects. Warm light spilled over racks of colorful fabrics. The hum of the HVAC mixed with the faint scent of fabric dye. The owner, with her precise pixie cut and meticulous makeup, waved him over when he asked about video. She displayed the footage. It showed Jenna at 6:25 a.m., phone to her ear, walking steadily along Oak. A silver Raider Straight Line followed at a consistent distance. Too consistent. Close enough to track. Not close enough to alarm. Reeves leaned in as both disappeared from the frame. Cold settled in his gut. He texted Willow to secure the footage and document the camera angles.

State-of-the-Art Security Solutions appeared polished. Their system did not. A lanky redhead greeted him with a nervous grin and an apology. "The cameras were installed last week. We're still resolving bugs in the system." He scratched his neck while speaking.

Reeves allowed the silence to work. He recorded the names on the invoice, the installer ID, the model numbers. He remained skeptical. He added another note for Willow to investigate this location immediately.

The coffee shop's manager maintained a clean setup that outshined the security store. Espresso hissed, and the grinder whirred behind the counter. "That place is sketchy. I heard they sell, uh, never mind," he said as he displayed crisp footage. Jenna passed at 6:31:23 a.m. The same silver car glided behind her. The distance remained constant.

"Do you think the car was following her intentionally?" the manager asked.

"Too early to determine," Reeves said. He captured a still of the license plate area, noted the lighting and angle, and flagged the clip for Willow. He documented the pacing pattern and timestamps.

Harry's Hardware had non-functional cameras. Wires hung loose during renovation. The owner, barrel-chested with grease on his hands, lifted a hand apologetically. Nothing useful here. Reeves moved on.

At Thompson's Pharmacy, the door chime rang thinly as he entered. LEDs buzzed overhead. The antiseptic smell permeated the air. They had footage. Jenna looked back over her shoulder. Her face tightened. He marked the time and wrote a note to request her phone records. If something or someone had contacted her, the reaction appeared here.

The Oak Street MiniMart provided the crucial element. Refrigeration cases throbbed with a low hum. The screen showed the autonomous car stopping. The feed glitched. A shallow stutter disrupted the image. Then the car surged forward. Reeves replayed the sequence multiple times. The timing remained consistent. The glitch occurred just before the movement. Possible data injection. Possible remote command. He recorded the exact timecode, the camera make, the number of dropped frames. He captured screenshots of the artifact and the movement vector. His notes remained precise and thorough.

The bookstore offered only apologies. The wiry owner fussed with a half-installed system, cables coiled like vines beneath the counter, his round glasses sliding down his nose. Dust hung in the air with the dry scent of old paper and binding glue. He tapped at a blank monitor and cursed under his breath when it refused to wake. Nothing to give.

At the flower shop, a kind-eyed woman pulled up a blurry view of an empty corner. Damp soil and cut stems scented the cramped space. Petals clung to her wrist as she tried to help. Nothing again. The pet store manager, a broad man with a beard and flannel, shrugged and admitted their cameras were more decoration than deterrent. The air smelled of kibble and wet fur. Across the street, a nervous toy store clerk confessed the same ruse. Plastic domes that blinked without recording, the kind meant to bluff shoplifters into better behavior. Tinny music tinkled from a speaker while the clerk avoided his eyes.

By the time Reeves reached Wooden Table Groceries, frustration sat hard in his gut. The door chimed, the refrigerated aisles hummed, and the floor was tacky in places where something had spilled and half dried. Here, finally, he got something. The balding manager slid over a thumb drive and pulled the feed on his screen. The car accelerated toward Jenna as she ran across its path. The same odd flicker hit the video just before impact, a brief shiver across the image that matched what Reeves had seen at the Mini Mart. He leaned in until his breath warmed the glass and ran her last seconds frame by frame. Jenna's shirt flashed white between parked cars. The grille lifted as the car surged. The flicker cut the moment thin.

He stepped back and reviewed his notes under faintly buzzing LEDs. Moths worried at the light covers. His pen dragged across the paper in neat lines while sweat gathered between his shoulder blades. Three usable captures told a clean story. Threads and Trends showed the initial stalking. Chicken Coffee confirmed the steady tail. The camera there caught the reflection of taillights in rain-dark asphalt even without rain. Wooden Table Groceries sealed it with grim finality. The aggressive surge of acceleration ended Jenna's run. Two feeds glitched at the critical moments. Both the Mini Mart earlier, the grocery now. It read like sabotage, not luck. Everything else along Jenna's route was conveniently offline. Broken cameras or amateur fakes, each one a blank square where a face should have been.

He tapped off a message to Willow, terse and precise. A soft vibration in his palm marked it sent. Blackburn's favorite tech savant would be inside these files before sunset if he knew her habits well enough, and he did. He imagined her at a desk with headphones on, eyes narrowed, hands moving in quick, efficient bursts. The image surfaced uninvited. He set it aside.

Too much lined up for coincidence. Too many outages, too many moments lost to malfunctions. Someone had engineered a blackout and stitched it across a single night. They hadn't stitched it clean. They had left threads for him to pull, and he had them. Three videos and two suspicious glitches would be enough to satisfy Blackburn when they next spoke. He could already hear her clipped questions and feel the pressure of her silence when he didn't answer fast enough.

Reeves closed his notebook and slid it into his pocket before stepping back into the heat. The door breathed out a cooler draft as it shut behind him. The first stop back at HQ would be spent drafting warrants for Jenna's home and for that shady security shop down by Oak Street that reeked of lies and stale coffee grounds. The place had a faded awning and a bell that never rang when you opened the door. He would make it ring.

This was not just an autonomous vehicle error. No machine acted this calculatedly without a human in the loop. Someone had gone to work erasing eyes from Jenna's path that night, deleting lines of sight and manufacturing blind spots. Not every eye was caught, and the mistakes mattered. He felt a prickle at the base of his neck that meant he wasn't the only one watching.

And now, they were being watched in turn.

Heat lifted off the pavement. The distance wavered like water. Reeves raised an arm, and two taxis angled in, horns snapping, nearly clipping each other at the curb. He took the cab with a human behind the wheel and slid onto vinyl warmed by the sun. The air conditioner sputtered and pushed out something almost cool that smelled faintly of pine. "Police HQ," he said. The driver nodded and pulled out. Time to let Willow bear the brunt of Blackburn's attention.

Chapter 5

The same heat that had dogged Reeves's investigation bent the afternoon light into wavering sheets across the crossroads. Blackburn watched her fellow detective climb into a taxi. The door thudded shut. She lifted a hand in a brief farewell and let him go. Her focus shifted to the woman rounding the corner.

Willow emerged from the crowd with a steadiness that cut through glare and noise. Familiar. Grounding. Even in the crush of traffic and sun, her presence found Blackburn with clean accuracy.

A different kind of warmth moved under Blackburn's skin, one that had nothing to do with the merciless sun.

"This way," Blackburn murmured, voice low and certain. She steered Willow east along Maple Street with a touch that lingered a breath too long. Intent resided in it. She let her fingertips graze Willow's arm, heat meeting heat. Brief. Controlled. Enough.

"Reeves didn't say why he wanted me," Willow said. Uncertainty threaded her tone. Her gaze flicked up as if hunting for more than an answer.

Blackburn let a small smile tilt her mouth, the expression an invitation with a bite. "What Reeves needs you for is far less interesting than what I want you for." She placed the words with care, each one set like a clean incision.

A live current moved through her. Kendria still burned in memory, a thin spark. Now Willow walked close, near enough to feel, not yet taken. The case lay beneath it all. Power. Risk. Desire. Blackburn refused to separate them.

Willow kept pace at her side, attentive and precise, eyes lifting in quiet checks, reading Blackburn for cues to follow.

The Lancaster Regent rose ahead, grandeur stubborn against the wear of years. Marble and steel. Ambition transformed into a facade and weight. She knew this hotel, its secret places and its hidden corners. Blackburn took them through the revolving door. Cool air pressed against hot skin as the lobby exhaled around them.

Inside, crystal cast a warm wash over marble. Leather, cut flowers, polished wood. A slip of high-end perfume under the cleaner's citrus. Money in the room and a hush that made voices fall.

Crossing the threshold steadied Blackburn's pulse. She tasted the change in the air, chilled and curated. Her gaze moved as they walked. Cameras above the concierge. Another near the bar. She knew them. Bell staff rotated on a preset loop. Elevators mirrored and bright. The fountain's soft murmur covered low speech. She cut toward a corner screened by a towering fern, where the sightlines bent and went blind.

The space was no stranger to either woman.

She guided Willow into the shadowed pocket. Their steps softened on stone. Her hand settled on Willow's lower back. She chose a seat that let her hold both the door and the mirrors in one glance. Control first, intimacy after.

She lowered onto the plush cushion with intentional economy. The fabric gave under her, velvet nap catching at her palms. She set her blazer across her lap and kept her gaze on Willow. Then she worked the clasp at her waistband with quiet precision. Metal clicked. The fabric slid past her hips and pooled at her ankles. Efficient. Unremarkable to anyone not looking.

"Come here," Blackburn said, almost a whisper but edged with command. She extended her hand, palm steady, the invitation impossible to refuse.

Willow's pulse flickered at her throat as she stepped between Blackburn's parted legs. The lobby's murmur ran beneath them. The fountain and the distant tap of heels on marble ticked a steady rhythm that tightened the air.

Blackburn's fingers threaded through Willow's hair. The slide met scalp, firm and exact, and she angled Willow's head. "Let me see how much you want this," she breathed, her mouth close to Willow's ear, her breath warm. The authority was quiet and unmistakable. "I need to feel it, Fawn."

Willow kneeled and inhaled. She set her mouth to Blackburn's skin with care, a kiss at the hinge where muscle met thigh. Heat. Salt. A faint note of clean soap. Blackburn's breath caught, a contained sound she didn't bother to hide. It landed like a reward.

Her grip tightened in Willow's hair. The coil of control drew taut and held. "Go on," she murmured, velvet wrapped around iron. "Narrate your devotion."

Willow's tongue found silk and seams. Her work was tidy, almost clinical at first. Damp lines marked a path. Every pass chosen. Every flick was measured to draw a response. Heat bled through the weave.

"Christ," Blackburn breathed, spine lifting a notch. Her free hand found the armrest. Leather creaked under her fingers. "Words, Willow."

"Tracing contours," Willow managed between shallow breaths. Her breath scorched through delicate fabric. "Slow circuits from front to back." Her teeth grazed lace to mark the count, and the sound above them sharpened into a tight inhale that threaded with the soft drone of the vents.

Blackburn laughed, rougher now. "Such a meticulous pleasure." She lifted Willow's gaze with a light tug. The control stayed gentle and absolute. Both of them held inside it.

Even through the heat, Blackburn kept the map of the room in the margin of her mind. Footfalls near the concierge. An elevator chimed at twelve second intervals. No curious glances toward the fern's shadow. That certainty anchored her. It sharpened everything between them.

Willow returned to her work without waste. She opened her mouth fully. Purpose ruled her movements. Heat spread where she set her lips, the fabric darkening under the steady build. Blackburn tipped her hips a fraction and felt Willow adjust without instruction.

Pressure rose in a quiet exchange, restraint wired to ingenuity. Sweat gathered along hairlines. The rhythm stayed contained, slight movements hidden. Willow's mouth drew heat through silk while Blackburn kept her hand in Willow's hair and regulated pace and sound with subtle shifts of pressure.

The fountain kept time. The lobby hummed. Their reflections ghosted across the elevator's steel, the secret both present and out of reach. Blackburn watched that blur, felt the line of the edge draw nearer in measured increments, and let it come.

"Yes." Blackburn's gaze drifted from the plush carpet to the ornate ceiling. Intricate patterns pooled in the dim chandelier light. A thin crack split the plaster like a quiet threat. Dirt and stale air hung close. Her hips lifted a fraction. Her grip eased. Permission formed as a command.

Willow obeyed. Her fingers tightened on a hard thigh. Her tongue pressed in, patient and relentless. Heat and salt cut through restraint. The faint taste of sweat sharpened her focus. Words dissolved into vibration against Blackburn's skin. Soft curses slipped out, low and tight, each one clipped by breath.

"Harder." The word scraped between clenched teeth. LED tubes buzzed overhead and threw a flat, unforgiving light. "Show me your best."

Teeth flashed. A brief flare of rebellion. Then Willow's mouth sealed with purpose and found a steady rhythm. Her moan bounced off cinderblock. The air smelled of cleaner and old dust. Blackburn's thighs closed around her. Containment by consent. The trap they both chose.

Release hit fast and leveled her. Muscle clenched. Breath caught. A tight crash became a long shudder. Thirty seconds held and broke apart. When it passed, Blackburn sank into the soft velvet chair. Her jaw cut a clean line. Her breath evened and cooled her lips.

She looked down at Willow, chest rising hard and fast. Swollen lips shone under the hard light. Blackburn lifted a hand, her wrist cool, her palm flat on Willow's cheek. "Up."

Heat climbed into Willow's ears. Blackburn's stare stayed sharp. It pressed against her sternum and pulled her upright. Willow rose. She steadied. Her feet found solid ground even as her pulse kicked, hot and unspent.

Blackburn wasted no time. Pants up, blazer on. Willow quickly lifted her t-shirt to wipe her face, but Blackburn leaned in first for a kiss. "So good," she praised.

They left the hotel in silence. The city absorbed them. Outside the Lancaster, a bus hissed and rolled through a wet light. Willow wiped her mouth with the back of her hand. Quick. Precise. The motion left a faint smear that she checked and erased. Her skin still burned where Blackburn had held her. Blackburn set her shoulders and scanned the street. Clean sweep. Traffic angles. Sight lines. Exits. Diesel exhaust tangled with the sweetness of a bakery vent. Her phone buzzed against her side. Reeves again. The scene still held. Evidence needed a chain.

"I need to tell you something," Blackburn said at last. Her tone was flat, but weight collected under it.

Willow turned, eyes careful. "What is it?" She touched the corner of her mouth, searching for proof of them.

Blackburn leaned in. Exhaust and her own heat met in the narrow space. Her breath skimmed Willow's ear and set the tiny hairs there on end. "There's something I have only told Chief Hayes," she murmured, and let the pause land. "The hit and run victim, Jenna Langston. I slept with her the night before she died."

The words settled. Heavily. A tight ache opened under Willow's ribs. She kept her face still. She didn't look away. The city roared around the quiet between them.

"And," Blackburn continued, brisk now, as if slicing an already frayed thread, "Jenna mentioned seeing someone outside my house when we went in together that night. I think someone has been watching me. Someone who didn't appreciate Jenna being there."

Her gaze pinned Willow. Hawk clear. Unblinking. "Anything you want to say about that?" Blackburn asked, the press of authority immediate and exact.

Willow swallowed. The movement showed in her throat. "It wasn't me outside your house," she said, softer now. A tremor edged the words. "Are you scared?"

Her laugh came low and cold. It cut cleanly through the air. "There's very little in this world that scares me," Blackburn said smoothly.

"Of course not," Willow said, quick to cover. Her voice fell again. "I'm sorry."

"Not yet," Blackburn said. The curve of her mouth barely shifted. Not warmth. Not mercy. A studied unsettlement that she wore like jewelry. Willow's eyes widened, then steadied. Panic receded under Blackburn's control.

The pull between them eased and reformed. Not gone. Redirected. Blackburn let it sit in her chest as a contained heat. Her shoulders lowered a fraction. Quiet returned, threaded with traffic noise and a distant siren.

Then she shifted. Command restored. Crisp. Useful.

"Reeves called you here for a reason," she said, as if the last twenty minutes had been a pause in traffic. Nothing more. "I need you to run scans of every business within range. I want a complete sweep for any Bluetooth or infrared signals that could interact with vehicle systems."

Willow's brow tightened. Her mouth flattened. "Interact with what exactly?"

"The autonomous car that killed Jenna," Blackburn said, her voice sharp and clipped. She stood square in the street as if bracing the city itself. Sun glazed the pavement, heat rose off it in wavering bands. Sirens murmured somewhere distant. "My working theory is remote interference. Someone controlled it, or tried to. I need you to find the evidence. Signal strengths, frequencies, anomalies. Whatever you can dig up. Document everything thoroughly and produce a complete report."

The scope landed hard. Willow swept the storefronts, each address a pocket of devices breathing in and out. Phones pinged invisible handshakes as people walked by. Bluetooth. Infrared. A stray Wi-Fi network bleeding onto the sidewalk. Consumer chatter. Earbuds pairing. TV remotes flicking pulses. Smart bulbs waiting for a voice. None of it was built to steer a car into harm.

"Three blocks," Blackburn added, cool as polished glass. She didn't raise her voice. It carried anyway. "In all directions from the scene."

Willow's stomach tightened. Three blocks would take hours. Days. She swallowed and forced her tone even. "Bluetooth and infrared only work at close range," she said, careful but unable to keep the catch from her throat under Blackburn's steady gaze. "Headphones and garage doors. Signals can't travel far enough for this."

Her words hung in the heat. Blackburn's expression did not move.

"One block," Blackburn said at last, firm and dismissive in the same breath. "Check Bluetooth, infrared, GPS."

Willow marked the last word.

GPS? Really?

Orders, not debate. She nodded and kept any reaction off of her face.

If Blackburn believed in this theory, then Willow would map it and test it. She would walk the perimeter and sweep for Bluetooth Low Energy beacons, note MAC addresses with timestamps, and flag anything that didn't belong. She would trace probable infrared lines of sight through each shop window and door. She would record Wi-Fi SSIDs with channel use and signal levels and identify equipment by type. She would request CCTV angles, reconcile the clocks, and chart the car's approach frame by frame. She would check local GPS conditions and pull a handheld receiver to look for spoofing or drift. She would write it cleanly and show what the data supported and what it did not. A careful autopsy of a thin idea.

Blackburn glanced at her watch, the screen flashing, then spoke without looking up. "Get going." Her voice struck like a stone. "Update the team tomorrow. In full."

Willow nodded, though Blackburn had already turned. Her heels clicked once and then faded as she took the corner without a backward glance. "And do not miss anything," she said over her shoulder, the words already receding with her stride.

Willow stayed where she was and watched the empty corner hold nothing. The street slid back into itself. Engines idled at the light, a bus sighed as it braked, footsteps passed, the grind of a skateboard wheel over a seam in the concrete. No goodbye. No lowered edge to the order.

Her arms hung loose. She waited for something she could not name. An apology. A gesture. A pause that might grant the smallest measure of softness. The only answer was the hum of traffic and the faint, metallic chatter of a loose sign chain tapping in a breeze.

Blackburn's car passed a moment later, dark glass catching the sun. No slowing. No wave. Willow felt a neat give inside her, a quiet break she had been bracing against.

A single tear slid down her cheek before she could stop it. She wiped it hard with the heel of her hand and drew a steady breath.

Then she hoisted her bag, felt the receiver and notebooks against her hip, and stepped off the curb to begin the work.

Chapter 6

Blackburn drove south with one hand steady on the wheel while her phone chimed at intervals from the cup holder. Three alerts in fifteen minutes. She let them sit. Curiosity pressed at the edges of her focus, a small itch she refused to scratch while the road demanded her attention.

Another tone cut through the cabin. She exhaled, signaled, and pulled into an empty lot behind a shuttered strip of storefronts. Heat shimmered off the asphalt. The phone lit her palm with a cold white glare. Petrović's name appeared at the top.

Text: *Microscopic glass fragments in Deonte Mills' pajamas. Embedded with traces of methamphetamine. Consistent with a crack pipe.*

Her pulse quickened, cleanly and steadily. Dawson had never mentioned drugs. If the father had smoked in the house the night the boy died, endangerment became possible. Perhaps more serious charges when paired with blunt force trauma.

"Thanks, doc," she said as she closed the app.

She shut off the engine and popped the trunk. The latch clunked, and the interior bulb cast a thin cone of light. A faint smell of rubber and warm dust wafted out. Her working box sat wedged against a crate of file binders and scene prints. Not evidence; not originals. She lifted the box, the cardboard rough against her fingers, and began sorting. Photo packets slid free, scene diagrams, notes with times and names in tight pencil. She arranged them in a quick grid across the trunk lining and the nearest portion of roof, paper edges whispering as they settled.

She located the Mills apartment shots and flipped through them methodically. Kitchen counters under cheap laminate. Sofa cushions with sagging seams. Baseboards by the makeshift bed, a thin black line where dust collected. Bathroom tile and sink with a hard water ring. Nothing obvious. No pipe. No scorched foil. No residue that would survive a warrant and a lab tech's scrutiny. No leverage connecting a pipe to a living room within reach of a five-year-old.

She returned the prints to their sleeves and packed everything into the box. Lid on. Box in. Trunk closed. Sound carried across the baked lot.

The kid died from blunt force trauma. The father claimed he left him alone. The mother remained missing. Blackburn wanted more than a clean homicide. She needed a charging theory that held under scrutiny. Special circumstances if the facts warranted. That was her reputation. Seeing what others missed. Not forcing evidence and not losing cases.

She settled behind the wheel again. The seat fabric retained the day's warmth. She merged onto the freeway as the afternoon faded into a pale wash at the horizon. A low hum filled the cabin. The vents pushed air that smelled faintly of plastic. Her thoughts drifted to Jenna's hit-and-run. Reeves's headlight analysis. The fragment angles.

She took the ramp and maintained sixty-five. Motion facilitated her thinking. The tires drummed a quiet rhythm over expansion joints.

A small shift at the edge of hearing. A slide and a light knock behind her. She dismissed it. One mile later, the gap in her mental inventory suddenly registered.

"Shit."

Rearview mirror. Nothing useful. She knew the roof was bare. Reeves's evidence bag was gone from where she had placed it. A two-pound package at most, now somewhere on the shoulder or ground into aggregate by passing vehicles. Chain-of-custody compromised the moment it hit the road.

She tightened her grip, then relaxed it. Options presented themselves. None favorable. Reporting the loss would trigger an audit, then Internal Affairs. Security camera footage from the lot outside the lab. Vehicle GPS logs time-stamped to the minute. Her name in the property ledger against a blank return. Every action scrutinized.

She continued forward. Not to the squad room. Not to the lab. Jenna's case already attracted attention. Any misstep would become leverage for others.

Home.

She left the freeway for familiar back streets. Lights and turns she knew instinctively. The stop signs appeared in a predictable sequence that calmed her breathing. In the mental space that followed, she organized her priorities. Triage first. Determine if anything from Reeves's bag had been copied, photographed, or duplicated on a lab server. Confirm the exact contents. Investigate if any of the components could be re-collected through alternative means that would withstand court scrutiny. Quiet calls. Favors without gossip.

She pulled into her driveway and stopped the engine. The sudden silence felt heavy. For a moment she remained still. The day weighed on her without drama, a simple burden she shifted off her shoulders one movement at a time.

She opened the trunk and checked the box. No trace but a few specks of grit, no stray shard of glass, no torn plastic seal. She closed it and stood, surveying the strip of lawn, the walkway, the gap under the side gate. The neighbor's maple leaves rustled in a gentle breeze. Nothing observed her except a squirrel balanced on a fence line, tail flicking. She felt an urge to strike something that would resist. She allowed it to pass.

The front door stuck before yielding with a scrape. She entered and closed it firmly. The sound marked a boundary. Work remained outside only theoretically. The house carried a faint scent of laundry soap and stale coffee. Floors creaked in the hallway as if the structure exhaled after her entrance.

Ten minutes later she pulled on running gear, tied her hair, and descended the concrete steps two at a time. The air had cooled; the sun hung lower, casting long shadows across the block. She found a rhythm that allowed her to think. Breath in through her nose, out through her mouth. Sidewalk seams clicked beneath her feet.

"Morgan."

Mary Margaret O'Sullivan's voice carried across the street. The older woman stood on her porch with one hand raised, a constant sentinel in a neighborhood that noticed everything. A porch light activated although daylight lingered.

Mary always had information to share. It could be a car idling suspiciously, a misdelivered package, or an unfamiliar cat. Blackburn acknowledged her with a raised hand without interrupting her pace. Not now. The evening air worked against the heat smoldering behind her sternum, and she surrendered to the rhythm of her stride.

Her feet found a steady rhythm on the asphalt as she cut through familiar streets. The image rose unbidden, the figure in last night's shadows. Watching Jenna? Watching her? Who could say. Heat gathered low and tight, not fear so much as readiness.

Deonte Mills stayed with her. Five years old, hollow-eyed, belly distended from neglect. Bruises mapped his small frame. The case had landed on Dawson's desk, but glass slivers and a chemical tang in his pajamas pointed to a father with a pipe and a temper.

She pushed harder. Her breath smoothed out as she set to the work of thinking.

She veered left past the park where kids on scooters carved the air. Wheels clicked over seams in concrete. Laughter carried thin and high. Another image surfaced. Jenna Langston sprawled beneath an autonomous vehicle, its safety protocols overridden by intent.

Jenna Langston, who had been lying on Blackburn's floor mere hours before her death. Blackburn clenched her jaw as her lungs burned. She would not slow. She needed a headlight.

Buildings grew older as she moved into worn streets where paint peeled and porches sagged. The air smelled of hot dust and old oil.

The compact car loomed ahead, a rusting relic hunched at the curb. Its headlight gleamed intact for now, pristine and vulnerable.

Blackburn slowed to a purposeful walk. Rusted, ready. She pulled on a glove. Her kick landed clean. Plastic burst in a brittle pop, and shards skittered across the concrete, ticking to a stop against the curb. Evidence for comparison, not for conviction.

She crouched and chose the largest fragment, grip steady while sweat traced her temples and darkened the cracks in the sidewalk. She slid the piece into a bag, took two quick photos, then ran.

On a longer route home, she let the noise in her head settle until the pieces lined up. Footfalls set a metronome. Air moved in and out. The city's hum faded to a workable quiet.

Someone had turned that sleek autonomous machine into a weapon, a weapon that killed Jenna Langston and left a trail she could read in code, scrape patterns and telemetry.

Blackburn would find them, whoever they were.

Chapter 7

Willow moved through New Dresden with the crowd, her gaze skating off glass and neon before moving on. Traffic hummed. Heat lifted from the street in wavering sheets. She tried to keep her hands still at her sides and failed. The twitch gave her away.

She checked her pockets and her bag again. No detector. No toolkit. Nothing she could trust in a clean room or on a curb. The absence sat low in her gut. She adjusted her pace and kept walking.

Blackburn would notice the gap in an instant. Willow pictured a look that meant more than words. Not anger. Not surprise. A small settling of the mouth, a silence. Enough to tell her she had fallen short.

She drew a slow breath. It steadied the shake, not the need. Showing up empty would cost her. Not just in the job. With Blackburn. That mattered. She put the thought back where it belonged and worked the problem.

She carried the city in her head. Not the bright storefronts. The places that kept parts in bins and cash under the counter. She cut two blocks without thinking. Gorilla Parts sat where the side street bent around a shuttered cafe that still smelled faintly of urine and bleach.

The sign needed paint. The window held a stack of towers that should have been recycled a decade ago. Good. The place was not for collectors. It was for people who built things because they had to. Like Willow.

She pushed the door open. The glass was heavier than it looked and sticky around the seal. Dust and warm plastic hung in the air. A trace of ozone indicated someone had powered a board within the hour. The city noise dulled to a muffled wash.

Shelves leaned. Boxes listed. Wires slept in gray nests. She moved down the aisle, counting lengths, form factors, power needs. The device in her head took shape with each shelf she passed. Screen, power, brain, antenna, housing. Keep the list short.

A clerk behind the counter lowered a magazine and watched her without interest. "You need help?"

She did not answer. A hand-lettered frequency range on a worn packet pulled her in. RF receiver module. She lifted it, weighed it, checked the pins by feel and sight. Good. On the next shelf, a narrow-beam infrared sensor with a removable lens sat half hidden behind a row of capacitors that had been sorted wrong for years. She picked it up and turned it into the light leaking through the front window. Clean.

The battery shelf had been raided. Two packs left that weren't swollen. She chose the lithium-ion with a decent discharge curve and set it in the crook of her arm. She worked quietly and quickly, not for show but because it was standard.

Willow crouched at a bin labeled DISCARDED. The floorboards creaked under her weight. Plastic cases, stripped boards, screens with spidered corners. One 2.5-inch LCD still wore its protective film. No scuffs. She set it with the other parts. On the next rack, a plastic enclosure the size of a paperback waited, scuffed but intact. It would take a hinge if she needed one. It would keep the rain off. Enough.

She brought what she had to the counter and lined it up. The order mattered. Power left, signal center, display right, housing last. She wiped her palms on her jeans and went back for connectors.

A soldering iron hung from a hook, its cord kinked and shiny with old flux. She heated the element in her mind and ran through the joints she would make. A strip of jumper wires. A small breadboard. Perfboard and standoffs would be cleaner, but speed came first. She reached for a Raspberry Pi and paused over the versions. She took the one with onboard Wi-Fi. Cheap. Reliable. It would handle what she needed if she kept the code lean.

The clerk looked up again. "What are you building?"

She kept her head down and checked screw sizes by eye against the enclosure. "A scanner," she said, her voice flat and precise. "Bluetooth, infrared, GPS signals. Handheld."

He blinked. He didn't follow. He didn't need to. "Right. Need anything else?"

She scanned the rack behind him. Electrical tape. Zip ties. She pointed with two fingers and waited until he slid them across. "Those." Her gaze shifted to the plastic bin he had pushed half out of sight. "Got a micro antenna?"

He fumbled under the counter and lifted a tub of mixed lengths. She laid them out from shortest to longest and checked connectors. SMA. u.FL. She ran her thumb over a dual-band stub with decent gain and light flex. It would manage crowded spectrum at short range. It would do for now.

The shop held its heat. A low thrum carried through the floor from something old and overworked in the back room. She let the noise sink behind thought and took stock of her pile. She added heat-shrink tubing, a ferrite bead, a cheap USB power meter. Small things that saved time later.

Her phone vibrated once in her pocket. She didn't check it. She pictured Blackburn instead. The way she stood over her and asked the one clean question. The one that cut through excuses. Willow put the last item on the counter and faced the clerk.

"Ring it up." She set her card on the scuffed counter, the LEDs humming above as she mentally rebuilt the project with cleaner lines and fewer weak points. "And plug this in, please," she added, handing over the soldering iron's cord.

"You're gonna do that here?" The clerk's voice climbed, then went flat when she did not answer.

He ran the sale while Willow mapped the sequence. Power. Ground. Headers. Antenna path. The board translated into a clean checklist. When he slid back the card and receipt, she split the packaging with her thumbnail. Plastic crackled. The smell of new electronics rose, sharp and faintly sweet from the antistatic bags. She arranged the parts precisely and wasted no movements.

She laid out tools on chipped laminate that had softened at the edges. Nothing fancy. The iron warmed until heat shimmered off the tip. She tinned it, the rosin flux releasing thin, sugary smoke, and set joints that shone tight and clean. She connected the antenna to the Raspberry Pi with the infrared sensor and receiver module. Short runs filled the breadboard in a logical pattern. The LCD slid into the front panel and snapped home with a bright click she deemed acceptable.

Fifteen minutes. Electrical tape secured stray leads. Zip ties held the heavier pieces to the enclosure to prevent rattling in the field. She closed the case and pressed power. The screen illuminated on the first try. A minimal interface. Readable. Only essential elements.

She tested the weight in one hand and watched the bars settle as the unit detected faint Bluetooth traffic nearby, including the clerk's smartwatch. The analyzer emitted a crisp, periodic chirp that cut through the low grind of the air conditioner.

"It works," she said flatly. She swept leftover parts into a plastic bag. The rattle of screws and headers barely registered.

As she turned to leave, the clerk muttered under his breath. "People are weird these days."

Willow stopped. Her boot squeaked on the linoleum. She looked back, not quite meeting his eyes. Her voice remained low and even. "Got any jammers I can test it with?"

The clerk squinted, curiosity and caution battling within him. "You a cop?"

She huffed a short laugh, the corner of her mouth twitching. "Hell no. Cops don't know this stuff." Not her cops, anyway.

Silence stretched for a beat. He let out a rough chuckle. "Fair enough." He ducked behind the counter, rummaged through dusty shelves, then placed a compact GPS jammer on the surface. "Get your baseline."

Willow raised the analyzer again. It gave a soft, affirmative beep. Ready. She set filters for L1 and L2, narrowed the bandwidth, and added averaging to smooth spikes. "Baseline acquired," she murmured, eyes fixed on the screen.

The clerk flipped the switch on the jammer. Numbers plummeted. Spurious peaks rose across both bands. A dirty, rolling hiss of energy filled the spectrum. The jammer radiated heat she felt when she leaned closer.

"How's it look?" he asked, amusement curling his words.

Willow's grin flashed, small and quick. "Like chaos," she said with satisfaction. Her eyes flicked to him. "Ever leave these running overnight?"

He shook his head and laughed under his breath. "Not worth dealing with crossband interference." He powered the jammer down. The room's ordinary hum returned, thin and stale.

She slid the analyzer into her bag, careful with the cable and screen. The work felt right in her hands. At the door, she pulled her phone and opened a spreadsheet template: Date and Time, Location, Signal Strength in dBm, Frequency Band, Interference Detected, Signal

Pattern, Signal Source Suspected, Analyzer Settings, Notes, Action Taken. The fields waited, bright and empty.

She entered the jammer test, then glanced out the door for Blackburn. No sign. Only traffic noise outside and the low whir of a ceiling fan inside the shop.

She stepped into the heat with the analyzer in her palm. The unit chirped occasionally. Clean GPS reads. Nothing significant.

She walked a methodical grid along the block and logged fixed points. Curb. Midlane. Doorway. Three readings at each, facing north, then east, then south. She noted bins and planters and the mouth of an alley where a device might hide unseen. The screen displayed stable numbers, steady as the tide.

The sun bore down on the broken pavement. Hot tar smell rose from the street. Storefront glass reflected harsh light at eye level. The beeps remained regular. Routine data without interference to investigate.

She checked logical hiding places. Overfilled trash bins. Planters with compact soil and space beneath. Alley gutters with sufficient cover for a battery pack. More noise. No signal worth pursuing.

Sweat formed on her brow. Flux clung to her fingers. She wiped both away with the back of her wrist and continued. She excelled more at fast pivots and clean hits than this slow, methodical search. The heat pressed, relentless and dull. Her patience held steady as she worked through the list.

Then it happened. A sharp beep cut through the monotony. Willow stopped mid-stride and turned toward the source: a coffee shop set into brick smeared with graffiti too faded to read. Chicken Coffee.

The glass door held a moment before yielding a cool weight against her palm. She kept her movements even. Inside, espresso machines hummed beneath low conversation and the clean scent of roasted coffee.

Her pulse quickened. Steady. The noise outside had broken into something traceable.

Willow moved through the shop with the analyzer in hand, eyes shifting between the screen and the room. The device maintained a soft beat, each tone accompanying a twitch of signal on the display. A businessman typed without looking up, keys ticking at a steady clip. A cluster of students bent over open tablets while the barista called names in a low, even cadence. Routine. The jitter on her screen suggested otherwise.

She adjusted gain and filters with small, precise motions. The spikes persisted but refused to settle into anything useful. Too much interference. Or someone deliberately stepping on her frequency. A quick glance toward the door caught a shift of shadow and a face turning away too quickly to identify. Her thumb paused over the controls. Static prickled along her skin. Nothing substantial.

She stepped back onto the street. Warm air greeted her. Traffic noise pressed in, a layered hiss of engines, voices, and brakes. The analyzer chirped against her palm while she logged into a crowded spreadsheet. Time, coordinates, frequency band, amplitude. She returned to the sidewalk and continued moving, letting the city's noise pass while she worked the grid.

Willow made a steady line down the block, incorporating cross-streets at regular intervals. Sunlight glanced off windshields and windows. The analyzer signaled when expected. She recorded every deviation and flagged the repeating ones. None exceeded background levels.

Time dissolved until the alert cut through her focus. Not a random spike. The readout surged, bright and clear. She verified it twice. It remained consistent.

She lifted her head and spotted the outlier. A storefront half a block ahead that she had completely overlooked. Glass and polished steel contrasted sharply against a row of tired brick. Above the entry, silver letters caught the last light: Alba Electrics.

She didn't recognize the name. Curiosity tightened, contained, as she crossed the distance.

The doors slid open with a smooth hiss and cool air met her face. Inside, rows of electronics sat in clean lines under cold LEDs that cast sharp reflections across a polished floor. The place smelled faintly of plastic and dust. With each step, the beeping intensified, drawing her deeper into the aisles.

She slowed when the pattern turned jagged. One shelf disrupted the store's order. Communications gear jammed into a single bay, pieces stacked without attention to fit or function. The rest of the displays appeared curated. This looked abandoned.

She approached closer. The air carried a weak vibration she felt more than heard, a quiver through teeth and skin. The analyzer's screen shook with it, patterns flickering too rapidly for any filter to smooth.

She identified the culprit immediately. A wireless repeater jammed into a tangle of wire and stripped insulation. It sat crookedly, pushed near the edge as if no one wanted to examine it closely. Whoever had installed it cared neither about concealment nor quality.

Willow leaned in and methodically assessed it. The chassis matched a common model. The board had been replaced with something else. Mid-range parts sat beside cheap components, connections tightened enough to function but not to endure. Solder spatter dotted the board. It was functional, barely. It could create interference.

Her display confirmed this assessment. Peaks and troughs cut across the band in a sharp, irregular pattern. The antenna was misaligned by several degrees. The unit had been configured to bleed across adjacent signals. It could severely affect GPS and nearby devices, pushing false data and disrupting timing. Spoofing was possible. Jamming was certain.

She took out her phone and entered the details. Make and model. Any visible serials. Screen glare forced her to adjust the device until the text became readable. She avoided touching the hardware. Willow sketched the wiring layout and noted the power feed and grounding points. She added photos to the record, wide shots first, then details of connections and labels. She tagged location, time, and meter settings. Last, she added a note to withhold contact until she had reason to escalate, and a better understanding of who owned the store.

As the data accumulated, the picture became clear. The build was sloppy but deliberate. It was positioned to appear as stock while contaminating the surrounding signals. Sufficient to corrupt, insufficient to provoke obvious complaints.

She checked the aisle. No clerk. No visible camera domes. Only her reflection sliced thin across a metal faceplate. She maintained an easy posture, as any customer might when examining a product.

She adjusted the analyzer again, ran a brief sweep, and captured a sixty-second sample for later analysis. The signal maintained the same angle. The drift was minimal. Not random.

She stood still for a long breath. Then she logged one final line, flagged it priority, and saved a local backup.

With a quiet breath of focus, she powered off the scanner.

"Excuse me," Willow said as she approached the woman behind the counter, adopting a disarmingly casual tone. The glass edge felt cool beneath her fingers. The air carried faint scents of dust and warmed plastic. "What's that weird-looking thing on the shelf over there?" She gestured toward the repeater with feigned nonchalance, uninformed. It was always easier when people underestimated you.

The woman tracked Willow's hand with mild disinterest, then fixed her gaze on the device. A squat metal box sat tucked behind a row of glossy routers, its paint scuffed, its antenna stubby and bent. A faint ring of dust marked the shelf around it. The woman tilted her head and shrugged. "No clue," she said. "One of the younger guys brought it in months ago before he got fired. It just sits there now. Does nothing as far as I can tell." Her lips quirked. "You want to buy it? I could dig up a price."

Willow laughed easily and shook her head. "Oh, no thanks. It looks kind of rundown." She waved a hand at the newer stock with their clean screens and unbroken seals. "Everything else here is so new and shiny compared to that thing."

The woman grinned, her laughter softening her voice. "Yeah. Looks like a platypus."

Willow blinked. A platypus. The comparison made no sense. It looked nothing like one. She offered a polite chuckle and nodded. "Yep," she said lightly. "A platypus."

"Can't blame you for passing," the woman added breezily. "Whatever it is."

Back on the street, Willow felt her pulse quicken as hot air pressed against her skin. The sun had set, but the heat lingered. Asphalt released the day's stored warmth. Traffic murmured. Voices rose and fell in snatches, a city settling into night. She activated her scanner without hesitation. Its low hum blended with the ambient noise. The so-called platypus stayed in her thoughts, a cleaner tag than repeater, and the use cases accumulated rapidly. GPS spoofing. V2X bleed. A dirty little box that could sit in plain sight and bend signals just enough to confuse New Dresden's autonomous cars. A drift here. A hesitation there. Nothing dramatic until it was.

Willow moved up the block. The handheld unit chirped at regular intervals matching her steps. She glanced at the display and continued walking. The readout revealed nothing she had not already mapped. She knew these systems. Their guardrails. Their blind spots. She could sense a pattern beneath the noise.

This was not about discovery.

Sweat prickled along her spine as she reached the corner. Her grip tightened. The casing creaked. Almost there. Close now.

Almost done. The heat would break toward morning, and her report would be on Blackburn's desk. She would log the spectrum sweep, attach timestamps, mark likely sources by block and elevation. By the book. It was about following orders. Blackburn's orders. If she were unhappy, Willow would get no rest.

Chapter 8

The neighborhood clung to the last of the night, quiet and unlit. Blackburn was awake and working on the problem. Willow's prelim, the hit and run, Jenna's destroyed body. She kept turning the pieces trying to make them fit.

She keyed a message to Reeves. "Don't forget the warrant for Jenna Langston's home. Between the targeted hit and run and the reversal, we should have enough to get inside." She added another line. "Once it's in hand, let me know. I want to be there."

She needed to be there. If Jenna's desktop was powered, if her BDSMessages account was still open, any delay invited a remote wipe. They would need a quick imaging, a Faraday bag, clean chain of custody.

Send.

The bowl on her counter showed the rest of her morning. Cold oats clung to porcelain. A blue streak at the rim. She closed her eyes and let the fatigue wash up and recede. A small, unhelpful wish for Willow. Then work again.

Outside, the air bit clean and dry. She paused on the stoop and filled her lungs. The street lay still and without traffic. The hour kept its secrets.

She checked the time. 5:42 AM. She accepted it and moved on. Driver's seat. Door sealed with a soft click. Ignition. The engine settled into a low hum. The steering wheel felt cold against her palm.

She reached for the gearshift. Movement caught the edge of her vision. A figure in the passenger mirror, coming slow.

She rolled back out of the driveway and eased to the curb.

Mary worked her way along the sidewalk. Small frame, big sweater, the gait of someone who knew how to move from one place to another without drawing notice. The trees made a dark arch over her.

Mary lifted a thin hand and knocked on the window. The sound landed cleanly in the morning.

"Morgan. Good morning, dear," Mary called warmly through the barrier between them.

Blackburn shook off the leftover thoughts and met her eyes through the glass. Her breath fogged up a small cloud that faded at once.

Mary leaned in until the light caught her thick lenses. Her look was direct. "Detective," she said again, urgency threading through gravelly tones worn soft by age.

Blackburn lowered the window halfway. Cold air slid in and took the warmth with it. "Mary," she said smoothly, her voice even while curiosity edged beneath her professional surface. "Good morning. What brings you out here so early?"

Mary pressed her lips together, then set them in place. "I remembered something," she said slowly and with care. "Something I saw last week."

Blackburn tucked a stray strand of hair behind her ear and gave a small nod. No rush.

"I saw you jogging yesterday," Mary added abruptly, as if connecting stray thoughts aloud. "I tried calling you over, but either you didn't hear me or you were focused." A faint chuckle, then the intent returned to her face.

"Come out here." Mary gestured firmly and tapped the metal frame of Blackburn's car.

Blackburn cut the engine. The low rumble faded into the cool stillness of morning. She stepped out with controlled economy. Shoes on gravel. A quick scan up and down the block. Mary waited by the crooked fence.

"Something wrong, Mary?" Blackburn asked, her voice steady and neutral.

Mary squinted up, one hand on her cane, the other open as if to catch the right words. "I'm not sure," she said at last, hesitant but insistent. "There was something. Last week."

Blackburn held the space and kept her face receptive. "Oh?" she prompted. *A dead body? A stray cat?*

Mary shifted a little, the cane ticking softly on concrete. A small breeze lifted a strand of gray hair and let it fall. "It was Tuesday," she said, eyes narrowing in thought. "About one thirty in the morning. You know I don't sleep well, not with this back of mine, and sometimes I sit by my window. Watching the street helps pass the time."

Blackburn unzipped one pocket with her thumb and started the memo on her phone. *Tuesday. 0130. Insomnia witness.* She pictured the sightlines from Mary's front window, the angles to the intersection, the coverage of the curb cut. She kept her breathing steady.

"Anyway," Mary said after a pause that stretched thin, "I saw these headlights sweeping across the street. Bright ones, like high beams." She lifted a hand as if to shield her face from the memory of them. "At first, I thought it might be one of those delivery trucks running late again. You know how they are these days. But then I realized it wasn't that at all."

She leaned in and lowered her voice as if sharing a secret. "It was a car, a fancy black one. Shiny as a mirror under those lights. Not your usual run-of-the-mill sedan, no ma'am."

Blackburn tilted her head. "And what did it do?" Her tone stayed even.

"Well." Mary's lips pursed. Her cane tapped a steady beat against the pavement, as if her thoughts needed a metronome. "It stopped right there, at the end of your driveway." She gestured down the street, palm open, then leaned closer. "A man got out. Sharp dresser. Suit and everything. Not many folks around here dress like that. Except you, perhaps."

Blackburn lifted a brow and waited.

"He gets out," Mary continued, voice gathering speed, "and he walks right up to your car. Not to the driver's side, but further back, passenger rear. He crouches like he's inspecting something, then stands again." She mimed the motion with jerky movements and tapped her cane twice for emphasis. "He stood there a good minute or two. Then he tapped on your trunk like this." She demonstrated with a quick double tap in the air.

"And then?" Blackburn asked.

"And then he got back in." Mary sounded almost offended by the simplicity. "Drove off like nothing happened. No rush at all."

Blackburn shifted. A faint smile held while a muscle tightened in her jaw. "Did you catch his license plate?"

Mary frowned and tried to summon it, her brow pinched thin with effort. After a few moments, she shook her head. "No, dear. I don't think so. My eyes aren't what they used to be. But I do remember him."

Her face softened with the memory. "Dark-haired. Young-looking, though everyone under fifty looks young to me these days. Confident sort. The way he carried himself said he knows how to handle things."

"I see," Blackburn said. Her voice remained steady. She inclined toward the neighbor, calm and patient. "Thank you for letting me know."

"Oh, anytime, Morgan. I thought you would want to know, with all the strange things happening in the world. You're such a nice young woman. Best to keep an eye out."

Mary's smile retained a tired warmth. Blackburn measured how much to entertain the story and decided any more possible detail wasn't worth the time.

"Thank you, Mary. You're absolutely right," Blackburn said. Her tone softened to match Mary's. "I appreciate it."

Mary nodded and turned toward her porch with an unhurried shuffle. Blackburn watched her go, then looked at her car under the streetlamp. Dawn had not yet shut the lights off.

Sodium vapor washed the vehicle in soft orange and dulled its lines. Mary had said black. But under the sodium vapor wash, nothing held true. The lamps turned paint into lies, her car's body into a dull orange shell. Blackburn knew it wasn't a black car.

But there had been a car and a man, and he touched her car.

She moved to the rear quarter panel and ran her fingers along the seam Mary had indicated. The metal felt cold and faintly dusty. Her nails clicked lightly as she slid lower. The air smelled of wet concrete and old leaves, the day not yet awake.

Jenna's voice cut through the quiet in her head, thin and insistent. "By the bushes. Tall, then gone." The same Jenna now in the morgue, tire treads pressed across her torso. A signature no one would mistake.

Blackburn crouched by the wheel well. Cold air found the back of her neck and slipped under her collar. She probed the inner lip with the flat of her fingers, slowly and methodically. Grit lifted under her touch.

There.

A small disc, no larger than a quarter, clung to the steel. Clean, low, and positioned to survive a car wash. Blackburn pulled a nitrile glove from her coat. The glove gave a soft snap around her wrist. She eased the device free with a fingernail and didn't smear the face.

She turned it in her palm.

One of their own trackers.

How disappointingly predictable. A muttered curse slipped from her lips. She lifted her phone and took a photo; the screen's cold light skimmed the metal. She slid the tracker her pocket, making a quick whisper. Blackburn set her collar against the chill, and stood. New Dresden was stirring. A truck braked at the corner. A dog barked twice and fell quiet.

Someone had been following her for days. Every stop. Every turn. She had missed it until now.

Blackburn got behind the wheel and checked the rearview. A loose strand of blonde hair had escaped. She tucked it back and let the mirror return to the street.

The amateur who thought this clumsy tactic would pass would pay for this.

The ignition caught under her hands, a low vibration running through the steering column into her palms as she mapped the route. Moves aligned in her head with clean edges: strategic stops designed to draw out whoever sat on the other end of the device's signal.

Let them think they were leading this dance; let them believe they had control. She would set the tempo.

A small current moved under Blackburn's skin as she merged into traffic. The car slid into the gaps cleanly. Horns rose and fell behind her, thin and impatient, then faded as she threaded forward.

Left onto Jameson Avenue. A pause at the narrow cut between Point Drive and Chata Avenue, where hedges threw a dark seam across the curb. She watched the rearview and counted beats with the click of the turn signal.

Next, the shopping center lot. Sodium lights hummed. Tires whispered over grit. Slow loops that tested a tail's patience. Then out onto Adelaide Street toward the office.

The precinct rose ahead, squared against the indigo before dawn. Light washed the stone and left the windows flat and cold. Imperfect symbol. Still standing.

Blackburn eased off the gas. Tension settled low and quiet, steadied purposefully by breath; this was no longer only evasion.

No, this was about reclaiming control over what someone else thought they had started.

Her heels clicked when she stepped out, the sound clean in the early hour. Cool air slid over her face. The glass doors gave way, and the sharp reek of disinfectant met the softer wax of freshly polished floors.

The desk sergeant looked up and smiled. "Detective Blackburn," he said, warm but unsurprised by her early arrival. "Good morning."

She gave him a brief, easy smile that hid the heat under her ribs and lifted two fingers in greeting. The badge reader chirped as she passed through. Her footsteps carried down quiet halls, past bulletin boards and scuffed baseboards, toward her office.

Inside, she shut the door and let out a breath she could not spare in public. Her room. Neatness made decisions simpler. Files squared to edges. Pens aligned. She took the chair and woke the computer. Blue light washed the desk as the system came online. The phone's message light kept its steady blink like a small metronome. It could wait.

She took the tracker from her pocket and set it down. NDPD insignia. Stamped serial number. Cool metal and scuffed plastic. It sat there like a dare.

Dawson.

Who else would risk this? The corner of her mouth tightened. She would handle him when it mattered.

She opened LisTrack, entered her credentials, and pulled up the search screen. Keys clicked. She typed the serial with care and hit enter. A status bar crawled. The fan gave a soft whir. She leaned close enough to read without pressing her face to the glow. When the screen refreshed, she captured a still of the result and saved it to a secure folder.

Sinclair.

She let out a thin breath. Not Dawson. Not surprise. Adjustment. She filed it where it would not get lost, both on the drive and in her head.

She shrugged out of her blazer. The weight slid from her shoulders and onto the stand; the cold edge of a button brushed her wrist. The red blink at the phone kept its rhythm. Voicemail.

She picked up the receiver and keyed in her code. The plastic felt cool against her ear. The timestamp read late last night.

"Detective Blackburn," came a voice over the line, clipped yet familiar, polished into composure. "It's Brynn Cassidy from New Dresden Today."

Irritation pricked the base of her skull and passed. Brynn Cassidy had a way of inserting herself where the seam was weakest.

"Detective. I've just spoken with Ms. Cindy Discart. She called our news line about the Homicide Division. Cindy claims you've stopped investigating her daughter's murder. I know you're tied up with the autonomous vehicle case, but I'd like to talk to you about your investigation. Please call me back."

Blackburn let a dry breath pass for a laugh and pressed delete. If Brynn wanted more, she could chase it.

Discart stayed with her. Monica Discart. The file had landed on Dawson months ago and sunk there. Blackburn had paired Sinclair with him on purpose, hoping energy might cut through inertia. The hope had been thin. It looked thinner now. She weighed what to pull first and whom to confront second.

Blackburn pulled open her desk drawer and sifted through the clutter. Paper clips rasped under her fingertips. Rubber bands stuck and snapped against her skin. A hotel keycard sleeve with a number she did not recognize slid to one side. Things she should have discarded. Her fingers found cold metal. Filing cabinet keys.

The bullpen maintained its quiet. LED lights hummed overhead with a thin electrical whine. An old duct complained somewhere above, the building's breath uneven. Detectives wouldn't arrive until eight or nine. She had the room to herself. Her heels marked a steady path across the tile to the gunmetal filing cabinets along the wall, each cabinet cool and faintly dusty to the touch.

Once, case files lay open on every flat surface. Notes, photos, half-formed theories left for anyone to read. That ended the night a cleaner was caught angling her phone at a spread of evidence. Security had watched the recording twice. Now everything resided behind locks.

At the cabinet marked D-G, she inserted the key and turned it. The lock answered with a clean click. She eased the drawer open. Steel protested under the weight. Manila slid beneath her palm until she found it. DISCART, MONICA.

The folder was thicker than it should have been. The kind of bulk that came from repetition, not progress. She closed the drawer with her hip and heard the soft bump of metal. The lock bit again when she tested it.

Back at her desk, her watch read 6:30 AM in hard green light. The morning waited ahead of her, open and quiet. Pale sun strained through the blinds and fell across the blotter in thin bands.

She sat. Paper smelled faintly of toner and dust. She let the room fall away and gave the moment to Monica Discart.

She opened the cover and read the summary written in neutral prose.

Victim: Monica Discart, 19 years old, female. Cause of Death: Manual strangulation. Location: Alleyway approximately one mile from residence. Time of Discovery: April 17, 04:38 AM. Evidence Collected: fibers, epithelial cells beneath fingernails, partial left shoe print. Men's running shoe size 10.

She stopped there and held the page by its corner. A skeleton of facts with no muscle.

The desk lamp cast a cold light on the autopsy report. Dr. Petrović wrote in clean lines, each entry spare and final. No sexual assault. No drugs or alcohol. No defensive wounds but three broken fingernails.

She lifted the clipped photograph. Glossy paper stuck for a second to her thumb. Monica slumped against a dumpster. Dark hair spread over greasy concrete that caught a dim shine from a streetlight. Bruising in bands across the neck. Large hands. Close contact. A note in block print below it recorded two empty cardboard boxes lifted off her by paramedics.

She turned to the boxes. Brown, stained, ordinary. Water marks feathered their corners. No labels. Nothing marked them as significant.

Next came the witness section. Dawson's uneven handwriting dragged across the forms in a slow slope. Three interviews. The parents. The delivery driver who found the body. No leads. The shoe print report remained unfinished. DNA from under the remaining nails still waited in a lab queue three months later.

Her jaw tightened when she reached the signatures. Sinclair had signed off on every page. No questions. No corrections. Dawson had rounded off his edges lately. It showed. The pressure of his pen cut into the top copy and dented the sheet beneath it.

She examined the scene photos. The alley from each approach, rain-dark asphalt slick around puddled oil. Debris clustered near the body. The contents of the dumpster spread out on a blue tarp.

Restaurant waste. Shredded paper. Damp cardboard. A bottle's neck glinting. She paused before the next sequence. The camera flash had caught the brief shine of a fly's wing at the edge of one frame.

The Discart house filled the frame. Two stories. White siding. Clean lines. Leaves gathered in porch corners, gray and papery. A small lapse in an otherwise maintained property. One photo isolated the number by the door. 1842.

The next photo showed the entryway. The security panel glowed green. System disarmed. A steady status light. No alarms noted in the report. The carpet by the door was flattened in oval patches where feet had paused and turned.

She turned to the bedroom. Unmade sheets on a twin bed. A white comforter dragged onto the carpet, one corner twisted under the bed frame. The air looked still in the photo, edges soft in the flash. Above the bed, a purple New Dresden Panthers poster. Cheerful color where it didn't belong.

A wider shot captured the mirrored closet. Two figures inside the reflection. Cindy with her arms folded tight against her chest. Her husband, Lewis, a step behind her, face drawn and tired under the flash, eyes half closed as if the light hurt. The mirror threw the bulb's glare back in a hard circle.

The last close-up focused on shoes near the bed. White Nikes. Small. One on its side, laces loose, scuffed at the toe. Set down fast and forgotten.

The surveillance photos covered Blackburn's desk in neat rows, glossy rectangles catching the overhead hum of stale LEDs. Each grainy frame held a fragment of the night. Pulled from nearby security cameras, they bore the usual flaws of cheap systems: blurred edges, warped shadows, dim light that turned everything to gray. One figure persisted. A silhouette threaded through the sequence, sometimes clear, sometimes lost in the dark.

She arranged them by timestamp. 2:17 AM: the shadow slipped out from behind Russo's Pizzeria, briefly etched against the alley where Monica was found. 2:19 AM: it moved across Third Street, indistinct yet steady. 2:22 AM: the figure reappeared, mid-stride toward the next block.

One photo caught her attention. The subject had come closer to the lens; small details emerged from the noise. A black hoodie. A build that revealed nothing. Average height. Average frame. It could fit half the city. And yet.

Blackburn leaned in until the cool varnish of the desk pressed against her forearms. On the right shoulder, a small mark, almost lost in the fold of fabric. Streetlight skimmed it for a heartbeat, enough to reveal its shape. A stain. No more than an inch or two wide.

Her hand hovered above the autopsy report, then settled. Paper rasped under her thumb as she paged through. She knew the findings, but she read them again. No lacerations on Monica's body. No punctures or abrasions beyond what matched a collapse against the dumpster. Bruising on the neck told the story. Strangulation, clean and sustained.

Which meant the stain could not be Monica's blood.

The photo slipped back onto the desk. Blackburn sat deeper in her chair, leather creaking as it took her weight. Her fingers drummed against the polished wood in a clipped pattern. Tap. Tap. Tap. Tap. Her thoughts moved with the rhythm, fast at first, tap. tap. tap. then slower as a connection formed. Tap. Tap. Her index finger paused, suspended above the surface.

Tap.

Her gaze shifted to another image, the family photo taken in the bedroom with Mom and Dad reflected in the full-length freestanding mirror behind them. Her back straightened. Dad wore a hoodie too, not black, but purple. A stain on the left. Not the right.

Wait.

Blackburn lifted the photo until the edges pressed into her fingertips. The mirror corrected her assumption. Not his left at all. Right shoulder.

She went still for a breath, then sat higher, skin prickling where the air cooled her collarbone.

She cleared her throat and pulled Lewis Discart's statement from Dawson's report. The staple bit the pad of her finger as she eased it free. She read clearly. She mentally underlined what mattered and let the rest fall away.

Asleep at home that night. Certain he had set the alarm. Cindy was beside him in bed.

She ran a finger down each line of the transcribed interview, feeling the indentations of the keys in the paper. She looked for inconsistencies.

The account was tidy. Too tidy. Routine phrases that closed doors. He called the day fine and normal. Soft language that said nothing while sounding complete. A defensive gloss was laid over each answer, structured to reroute questions.

What stayed with her was not only his wording. It was Dawson's note near the end. "Seemed shocked, though not visibly distraught."

Blackburn recognized that pairing. She had seen faces hold the shape of concern while the pulse stayed flat.

The note held. It sharpened her focus without raising her internal voice.

She raked the stack of scene photos closer, the paper sliding with a dry hiss. Then back to Lewis's statement. He placed himself at home all evening. The surveillance feed showed a figure with his unremarkable proportions, a hoodie with a right shoulder stain, moving through that corridor at 2:17 AM.

She checked her notes again, the pen leaving a shallow groove in the margin. Lewis said he'd heard about Monica's death on the morning radio. But the discovery call hadn't come in until 5:42 AM, and media never went public until next of kin were told. At that hour, there could have been no broadcast. The lie snagged and began to unravel.

Why had Dawson missed this? Why had Sinclair?

She reached for Cindy Discart's statement and slid it free of the pile. The details unfolded in Dawson's untidy scrawl. Mrs. Discart reports no unusual sounds during the night. States she was under prescribed sleep medication, Ambien, ten milligrams, and didn't hear the alarm system or any movement in the house.

Blackburn read the lines again, her fingertip steady on the page. The paper felt dry against her skin. The alarm had been armed that night. That fact mattered now. If Monica had stepped out, if Lewis had gone after her, the system should have tripped. Unless someone disarmed it.

She sifted through the photos until she found the shot of the security panel by the front door. The keypad's plastic caught a dull sheen in the flash. The system logs would show every arm and disarm, time-stamped with entry delays and user codes. Dawson hadn't requested them.

It made sense. Cindy, silenced by Ambien, would have slept through faint keypad beeps and the soft pull of a door easing against its seal. She wouldn't have awakened if Monica left, or if Lewis followed and returned to bed without a sound. The house would have maintained its silence.

Blackburn leaned back and glanced at her monitor. 7:30 AM. Blue light washed over her desk. The precinct would stir to life soon.

She opened a fresh spreadsheet and entered headers. Dawson, Sinclair, Cooper, Reeves, and one for Willow at the end. The cursor blinked in the first cell. Blank rows waited for assignments, laid out clean and verifiable.

This was Blackburn's domain, the structure behind her clearance rate, a system that held when everything else faltered. She visualized the layout of the work. Each variable had its place, each omission had a solution.

The cells anchored her attention. Dawson's column filled rapidly. Too rapidly.

He needed more. More work, more direction. Something to divert him from the sports section and lies on warrants. Her lips pressed into a thin line as she typed: follow up on Deonte Mills, drug residue, a warrant for Mills's residence could follow. Next task, assist Sinclair with re-interviewing crash witnesses in the Langston case.

Sinclair would take point on evidence processing for Jenna Langston. Better him than Reeves. If Reeves examined the plastic headlight again, he would start asking the right questions. With Sinclair maintaining custody, it would remain sealed in a bag pending review that didn't need to happen yet. No tests necessary, for now. An intentional choice, inconspicuous and firm.

Her jaw tightened at the thought of Dawson again, a distraction she could not afford. If not for that note on Mills's pipe earlier, she would not have allowed the headlight to slip from her grasp.

Cooper's name went next with a task. Trace the car's origin. A two-hundred-fifty-thousand-dollar vehicle leaves a trail. Someone logged it, sold it, spotted it. She added Monica Discart's follow-up interview to his list, a separate line connected by time and proximity rather than theme.

Willow received video review duty for Jenna Langston. Hours of camera feeds, motion triggers, dead zones, and clock drift. The fan on the server rack would hum and the images would crawl. The kind of work that rewards patience more than hope. Perfect.

The spreadsheet expanded under Blackburn's hand, a color-coded grid of intent. Green signaled progress made. Yellow marked tasks underway. Red flagged looming obstacles. She paused to assess the screen and what it revealed. The path forward existed if one maintained sequence and pressure.

She leaned back, a faint smile forming at the edge of her mouth. Almost time for her boys to start arriving. Footsteps would echo down the hall. Keys would clatter. Time for her boys to learn. And time to make them understand exactly how badly they had failed.

Chapter 9

Morning light slanted through Blackburn's office windows, revealing the controlled disorder she had arranged. Her color-coded spreadsheet sat atop the evidence spread across her desk. Every photo, statement, and map her team should have scrutinized properly the first time. Glossy paper edges caught the light, highlighter ink glowed in hard stripes. The faint smell of toner hung in the air. Her fingers struck the keyboard with crisp precision, each keystroke a clean note as she logged every oversight and missed detail that had nearly let a killer slip away.

"Morning, boss," Sinclair's voice cut through the tense quiet.

Blackburn didn't look up. She registered him in the doorway, his hesitation plain as his gaze skimmed the mess. Her workspace, normally pristine to an obsessive degree, now held the sprawl of an active review. The HVAC whispered overhead. Somewhere in the bullpen, a copier clicked and fell silent.

"Everything okay?" His tone hovered on the edge of caution.

"No." The single word snapped out cold and precise. Her eyes stayed on the screen.

Sinclair shifted his weight as if debating whether to ask more. Something in her rigid posture stopped him. He let out a quiet breath and retreated to his desk under her unspoken dismissal.

Moments later, Cooper appeared in the doorway with two cups of coffee. The rich, dark scent curled into the room. "Morning, boss," he said, offering one cup. His eyes moved over the scattered photos and notes, the scribbled arrows, the lines of highlighter stitching pieces together. He didn't flinch at the disorder. He stood and waited.

Blackburn lifted her gaze. Her expression softened by a fraction, a small shift that still registered. She nodded toward the chair opposite her desk. "Sit."

Cooper stepped in, set one cup down, and took the seat with ease. The chair creaked once as he settled. He watched as she picked up the coffee he had brought, both hands closing around the heat as if to steady herself. Steam rose in a thin ribbon. She took a sip and set the cup beside a stack of annotated reports.

"I've been reviewing Discart's file," Blackburn said, voice even and edged with resolve. "It's yours now."

Cooper stilled. His grip tightened on his cup, the cardboard giving beneath his fingers. "But that case is Sinclair's."

"Was," Blackburn said, firm and unhurried, as she pushed aside a layer of documents to reveal a highlighted witness statement at the center of the spread.

She leaned in and tapped a finger against a grainy surveillance photo near the edge of the desk, a hooded figure caught mid-stride beneath dim streetlights. The paper was cool to her touch. The image had the flat, washed look of cheap cameras and bad pixels.

"I need someone who can execute this properly," she said. Her gaze stayed on him.

She watched him carefully, not only his posture but every tightening muscle and flicker of his eyes. "First, contact Cindy Discart today." The name seemed to weight the air for a beat before she continued. "You're leading this now. Introduce yourself and set up a meeting."

He gave a small nod and reached for his notebook.

"And second," Blackburn added, her tone precise, "contact Public Works or whoever handles street lighting for New Dresden." She pointed again to the hooded figure under the streetlight. The tapping of her nail stopped. She looked back at him.

"Find out everything about those streetlights. Bulb types, maintenance schedules, power outages, any recent replacements. I want their full record."

"Streetlights? Because?" Cooper leaned forward, brow tight.

"I said."

He nodded again. A mental ledger of contacts flickered to life. "I've been fostering some solid connections at City Hall."

"Good," Blackburn said, the word sharpening. "Find out exactly what kind of streetlights they use in that area."

She traced the edge of the surveillance photo, her nail ticking lightly against the grainy silhouette. "If they're sodium vapor," she said, her voice dropping into the low register she used when dissecting evidence, "they distort color. This black hoodie could read as green, red, blue, even purple." She slid another photo into view, the bedroom shot. The gloss caught the light. She touched the faint reflection of Monica's parents captured in the glass.

Cooper's breath hitched. Blackburn placed the photos side by side with clean precision. Her finger moved to a subtle stain on the hoodie in the reflection, then to an almost invisible smudge on the shoulder of the figure in the surveillance image. The match was there if you knew where to look.

"Jesus," Cooper said, leaning back as the pieces aligned. The connection was undeniable now that she had laid it out, obvious once seen. He had reviewed countless surveillance photos in his career and had never considered how lighting could veil evidence so completely.

"Got it," Cooper said as he rose and squared the files into a neat stack. The paper edges clicked against his fingertips.

"Team meeting in twenty minutes," Blackburn said without waiting for him to turn.

Cooper nodded and tucked the folder under his arm. Paper brushed paper. He turned and left. His steps carried down the hall in a muted echo.

While Cooper wrestled with City Hall transfers, Blackburn cleared her inbox with quick, silent strokes and skimmed BDSMessages. Sent a quick message to Willow. The clock on the wall ticked in even beats. At the twenty-minute mark she pushed off her chair; the wheels gave a soft roll. She took her notes and went to the conference room.

"Willow says she will be here in ten minutes," Blackburn said, clipped. "We'll go ahead without her. She can catch us up later." Her tone remained even. Willow was often late, but less important than the detectives.

The room ran warm under the lights. Old coffee hung in the air, sour and flat. The whiteboard carried a thin solvent tang. Blackburn took the wall at the head of the table, loose stance, eyes sharp. The team settled.

"Sinclair," she said. "What do you have on Jenna Langston?"

Sinclair straightened and opened his folder. Paper rasped. "Got the VIN from forensics this morning. The tag on the engine block was still readable," he said. "Car is registered to James Zhang." He glanced up, found Blackburn's nod, and continued. "Zhang says he was about to report it stolen today, got tied up at work. He's coming in at fourteen hundred with counsel."

Across the table, Cooper snorted. "Convenient," he said.

Blackburn tilted her head. "Did Zhang say when he noticed it missing?" She stepped off the wall. The room tracked her without moving.

"Around zero five hundred," Sinclair said. "He said he had calls to make."

"Of course he did." Blackburn checked her watch. The second hand swept.

"Go on," she said. She folded her arms. Her fingers stilled against her sleeve.

"Traffic Services has nothing new," Sinclair said. He took a drink of water. The plastic creaked in his hand. "I reached the three witnesses. Piotr Swiatek, the cyclist. Anderson Keys, the truck driver. Both hold to the same account. No driver present. Same as their statements to Traffic."

Blackburn's gaze tightened. "And the third witness?"

"Mrs. Henderson from the flower shop on Lakeview," Sinclair said. "She reported the crash and called 911. Nothing beyond what we have."

Blackburn gave a short nod. "Cooper?"

Cooper opened his notebook and set a finger on the margin. He spoke levelly. "I canvassed Langston's family, coworkers, friends," he said. "Consistent picture. Quiet. Keeps to herself." He paused. "No boyfriend or ex anyone flagged."

Blackburn let out a small breath. The working theory held.

Reeves leaned in. The lines on his face deepened. His chair gave a tired creak.

"Nothing suspicious at all?"

"Not on the surface. Her friend Marla Sutton," Cooper said, then glanced at Blackburn. She stilled. Her face gave him nothing.

"Detective Blackburn already interviewed her," Cooper said.

"Yes, I—"

The door opened a few inches. Willow slipped in and took a seat at the far end. She set down her bag, lifted her laptop, and opened it. The screen lit her face in a cool wash. Her fingers found the keys and moved without looking up.

"Apparently, Marla showed up at the scene shortly after the accident," Cooper said. "Saw Jenna's body."

Sinclair straightened in his chair. "That is why that name rang a bell," he said. "I called, but never got a call back."

Blackburn inclined her head. "I reached out to Marla directly," she said. "Willow, nice of you to join us. Cooper, go on." The room settled back into quiet. The clock ticked.

Cooper nodded and adjusted his tablet. The glass caught a strip of LED light as he scrolled. "I dug into her digital trail." His voice stayed even. "Her JibJob profile lists her as a data entry clerk at Urban Plus Marketing. FamilyLynks is sparse. Basic info only. She used to post about yoga retreats, hiking trips, restaurants she liked." He paused. "Close to her parents and sister."

Blackburn stopped tapping the table. The soft rhythm died. "Anything else?"

"Marketing degree from the University of Illinois," Cooper replied, eyes still on his notes. "Active in creative industry circles. Marketing groups mostly. Kept a low profile online overall. No red flags. Clean criminal record. No controversial posts or affiliations."

Reeves hummed and rubbed his chin. "Sounds like your typical young professional." His eyes narrowed. "Almost too typical."

Blackburn glanced at Willow. The younger woman kept typing, eyes on her screen. Keys ticked in a steady run, blue light washing her face.

"And how are her parents taking it?" Blackburn asked as she shifted back to Cooper.

"Devastated," he said without hesitation. "They're flying in tomorrow morning. They said Jenna had just started feeling settled here in the city. She was starting to build a life for herself."

Blackburn moved her focus across the table to Reeves. "Reeves?"

He straightened. Frustration edged his report. "Filed for that warrant on Langston's place first thing this morning." He reached into his pocket, pulled a small notebook worn smooth at the corners, and flipped through thin pages. Paper rasped under his thumb. "Judge Harriman denied it. Said there was no probable cause since we have no direct evidence linking Langston to anything illegal. She's just the victim."

Blackburn's jaw tightened. She revealed nothing more.

Reeves continued. "At the scene earlier today, the one you and I cleared together, we recovered two items of interest. Some kind of metal shard and what looked like part of a headlight assembly." He looked up. "You took those into evidence."

Her face hardened. *The metal shard.* "Yes. Go on."

"Tracked down some surveillance cameras near where it happened," Reeves added. "Three angles total. I passed them along for review." He looked to Willow. She kept typing.

A bead of sweat tracked along Willow's temple. The room felt warmer than it should have, full of screens and terrible coffee. She continued at the keys.

"The scene was scrubbed clean by the time we got there," Blackburn said, her cadence even. "Traffic Services had cleared it as a matter of routine. I signed off on the release of the scene." She set both hands flat on the table and leaned in until her voice settled over them. "But I pieced together a theory. Someone might have found a way to hijack the car's autonomous systems, short-range tech like Bluetooth or infrared."

Reeves leaned back, arms crossed, and nodded. "Exactly. But they would need to be close. Think of it like a spider controlling its web from the center."

Silence held. The idea hardened in the air. An autonomous vehicle turned into a weapon.

"Willow is running scenarios to confirm its feasibility," Blackburn added, eyes moving across the team. "And the media is already circling. Channel 24/7 called twice this morning. Brynn Cassidy and New Dresden Today showed up at the scene."

"Willow? The security footage?"

Willow hesitated and swallowed. "No one handed it over yet," she said, voice thin at the edges. Her fingers worried the corner of her laptop. A faint tremor ran through them. "They're waiting for approval from their head office and IT staff."

Blackburn noticed the tremor and the strain. She arched a brow and fixed on Willow. Willow kept her eyes down.

"Reeves?" Blackburn asked evenly without looking away from Willow. "How many videos did you identify?"

"Three." He straightened in his seat and began to list them.

Blackburn barely listened. She watched Willow's eyes flick between the screen and her. It told her enough. She let the quiet press in and filled it with attention.

One.

Two.

Three.

Blackburn tilted her head and raised three fingers. Willow went still. Heat rose in her cheeks. She turned away from Blackburn's gaze.

The memory sat close, three fingers lifted in quiet reprimand, a sign of Blackburn's claim on Willow's body. Gravel in her underwear had been Blackburn's punishment last time. The thought tightened Willow's shoulders. She steadied her breath and braced for what was coming.

"Thank you, Reeves," Blackburn said coolly. She pivoted back to Willow with the contained focus of a predator drawing in. "What about Bluetooth? I instructed you to scan for Bluetooth and infrared signals at the scene." Her tone stayed neutral, with a clean edge that lifted the hairs on Willow's arms. The hum of the LEDs filled the room, thin and relentless.

"And GPS." Willow answered too quickly, speed covering uncertainty. Blackburn's expectation settled over her like iron. It pressed into her chest and made her breath short.

She fixed on her spreadsheet until the rows stopped swimming. The monitor's light washed the numbers flat. She filled her lungs, set her thoughts in order, and met the scrutiny from across the room without looking up.

With no cover left, she moved into the report with care, every word placed against Blackburn's unblinking stare.

"I completed a sweep of the site," Willow said, voice steady but quick. "I scanned for anything that could control or interfere with the autonomous car. Bluetooth, infrared, potential GPS jamming."

"How did you scan it?" Blackburn's question cut in, as precise as a scalpel.

Willow let a small, contained smile show and brought out the improvised scanner from her bag. Wires looped around a compact stack of boards, zip ties binding it tight. She described the build and the process, briskly and technically, until Blackburn lifted a hand for silence.

"What did you find?"

"Hardly anything." Willow's brief surge of pride cooled. "The biggest anomaly was a wireless Wi-Fi repeater at an electronics shop down the block. It was poorly assembled but could, in theory, cause interference. I flagged it as a false positive."

Blackburn's eyes slid to her, sharp and measuring. "Why?"

"The signal was consistent," Willow said. She glanced at Blackburn's hands on the table, nails short and crisply filed, catching the harsh light. "If it were interfering, we would have seen other systems act up while we were on site. Other vehicles misbehaving, devices failing."

She risked a look at Blackburn, gauging for an arched brow or the tightness along her jaw.

The results were thin. She counted on thoroughness to carry weight. "Apart from the booster, I didn't find significant sources of interference," she finished, voice dropping a register. "I flagged it anyway, in case the car's GPS had some sensitivity quirk."

Blackburn nodded once and tapped the edge of the desk with the side of a nail. The sound was soft and even. "Alright. The car owner—"

"James Zhang," Sinclair supplied from across the room, smooth and helpful.

"Mr. Zhang will be here at fourteen hundred hours," Blackburn continued, unruffled, "possibly with legal counsel. Sinclair, pull safety specs for me from Stan Raider Group, the whole suite of technical documentation if you can." Her gaze swept the room, cool and direct.

"I think we're making decent progress on Jenna Langston's case, given the time we have had," she added. Clipped, not unkind. "What else? Dawson?"

Dawson straightened. His chair scraped the scuffed linoleum. "Deonte Mills," he said quickly. "I'm working with Children's Services to determine if they were aware of him, and I'm still trying to track down his mother. She's supposedly in Florida, but we do not have an exact location yet." His voice held a defensive edge, almost a flinch before a blow.

Blackburn leaned back. Patience and authority sat easily on her. One eyebrow lifted. An expectant nod followed and offered no leniency.

"What?" Dawson blinked. The overhead light threw a pale sheen across his face. He shifted in his seat as if the air had narrowed.

"The M.E.'s report on the meth residue?"

"Uh, when did that come in?" He looked somewhere past her shoulder and found nothing. He didn't know.

"And what about Monica Discart?" Blackburn asked, quiet and tight.

Blackburn didn't look at him. She didn't need to. Under the LEDs' harsh glow, her expectation landed where she aimed it. "Either of you have an update?"

Dawson stared at the floor. The linoleum was worn to grey at the edges. His shoulders closed in. "I, uh, no leads," he muttered. The words thinned out in the silence she left him. Sweat gathered at his temple and tracked a slow line downward. He didn't move to wipe it.

Blackburn let the pause stretch until the room felt held in place. "Alright," she said finally, each syllable crisp. "Cooper is taking over the file. Let's see what fresh eyes uncover." The nails tapped once more, as precise as a metronome. The room exhaled around her. Willow kept still and took note.

The words struck Dawson. Heat climbed his neck as he straightened in his chair. "Why are you giving him my file?" His voice quivered with an emotion that teetered between indignation and desperation.

Because you're incompetent.

"Because you're overworked," Blackburn said instead. Her tone was unyielding. Her fingers tapped once against the edge of the table, a swift, even beat that punctuated her decision. "It's an old case. We'll let Cooper handle it from here." She shifted her sharp gaze to another target. "And Chandworth? What's happening there?"

A collective unease moved through the room. Fabric rustled. Chairs creaked. The air tightened as the detectives recalled the Chandworth debacle, the case that had cratered under Dawson's care. Ira Malone, arrested for Chandworth's murder but never extradited after a catastrophic mishandling of evidence. Only Blackburn, Dawson, and Chief Hayes knew how far Dawson had gone. He had falsified phone records to brace a failing theory. The lie collapsed at disclosure. The phone records were questioned. The DA backed off. The chief was furious. Dawson sat under Blackburn's scrutiny and drew a thin breath that scratched in his throat.

"No new leads." The admission slipped out in barely a whisper.

Blackburn's jaw tightened. Her lips pressed into an unforgiving line. "Reeves," she said abruptly. Her voice cleaved through the tension like an axe through wood. "You'll assist Detective Dawson with Chandworth."

Dawson exhaled as if granted a reprieve. Reeves gave a curt nod. The room eased with him, the taut atmosphere loosening without fully letting go.

Her focus swung to Cooper. "Cooper?"

Cooper leaned forward, consulting notes aligned at sharp angles. He responded crisply. "Currently working on CCTR-02399, a Jane Doe found in an alley behind Seventh Street shops. No ID, no distinguishing marks, no prints on record." He paused, his calm monotone unchanged. "Still waiting for Forensics to deliver their findings."

Blackburn offered nothing more than a minute nod before pivoting again. "Reeves?"

"On Langston now," Reeves replied evenly. "And assisting on Chandworth, as per your orders."

"Good." Blackburn pushed off from where she had been leaning against the wall with fluid ease. The scuffed conference table caught a slice of LED light as she moved, signaling the meeting's end without a formal dismissal.

Chairs scraped across the old tile as the detectives rose and filed out. The room's stale coffee smell lifted under a quick rush of footsteps and low voices.

Willow reached for her laptop amid the shuffle, then froze at Blackburn's sharp gesture. A single finger pointed directly at her.

"Not you."

Two words. Enough to stop her. She sank back into her chair. Her hands steadied on the laptop. She kept her eyes down. Passing detectives glanced her way, some with a flicker of sympathy, others relieved to be spared.

Blackburn ushered them out with slow purpose. Her heels clicked a steady rhythm against the linoleum until she reached the door and closed it firmly behind the last figure.

Silence settled. It was just Willow and Blackburn under the thin buzz of the lights. The quiet narrowed around them.

Blackburn's heels clicked again on the floor. Without breaking stride, she set a firm hand on the laptop screen and eased it closed. The soft click carried in the still air. Blackburn lingered, leaning against the table's edge. Her shadow cut a clean line across Willow's hands.

"Three stores," Blackburn said softly. The softness was razor-edged. "Three stores with surveillance footage you did not check."

Heat rose in Willow's face. Her fingers laced in her lap, knuckles blanching. She kept her gaze on the table. Blackburn's attention was enough.

"Look at me," Blackburn commanded. Her voice allowed no defiance.

Willow obeyed. Slowly. Reluctantly. She lifted her eyes and met the detective's stare. The room contracted to that single point. Blackburn held the moment. Then she plucked the closed laptop from the desk with almost casual precision, the metal warm under her hand and the hinge's faint resistance breaking the quiet like the tick of a clock.

"You won't be needing this for now," she said, voice cool and steady. "You will go to a store. You will buy one of those spiral notebooks adorned with cartoon puppies in bright party hats. You'll go back to basics." Blackburn's tone carried a thin strand of mockery. "Since you are behaving like a child, you will be treated like one."

Willow's hands went still in her lap. The low hum of the bullpen pressed in around them. Blackburn straightened to full height, a contained presence over her.

"You will handwrite this phrase: 'I will not neglect my duties again nor lie to the boss,' three hundred and thirty-three times," she said, each word precise. "You will do it here, where everyone can see."

Her fingers skimmed the edge of the laptop, a light, final touch. She let the silence hold for a beat. "And number every line." She set the laptop on the table. The soft thud carried farther than it should have.

Satisfied, she smoothed her blazer with crisp precision and turned away. The sharp clicks of her heels tracked each step toward the door. She paused on the threshold without looking back. "Get started," she said, and disappeared into the corridor.

Back in her office, Blackburn crossed to her desk and picked up her phone with unhurried economy. The room smelled faintly of paper and citrus cleaner. A small smile touched her mouth as she scrolled to a familiar name. Coconut Glass Candles. She held her pulse down beneath a polished surface. The thrill stayed tucked under control.

The line rang twice before a warm, honeyed voice answered. "Coconut Glass Candles, how can I help you?"

Blackburn let a breath pass and lowered her voice into something intimate and smooth. "It is me," she murmured.

Silence pressed for a moment, enough to cool her smile. Then Kendria answered. "I'm sorry, who?" The confusion was clean and plain.

"The voice," Blackburn replied, brisk now, a sliver of playfulness slipping through.

Recognition warmed Kendria's tone. "Oh, it took me a second to figure it out," she said, laughter threading each word.

Blackburn leaned back in her chair. The lapse still caught. Heat flickered low and unwelcome. Irritation, contained but real.

Her reply came cooler, stripped of amusement. "I need a new candle delivered," she said. "Today."

Kendria's voice stayed bright, untouched by the shift. "Absolutely. Is it for tonight?" Eager and light.

Blackburn's grip tightened on the phone. "Just deliver it," she said.

"I have a couple of customers right now," Kendria continued cheerfully. "As soon as they're gone, I'll send one over by taxi. It won't take long at all."

A muscle in Blackburn's jaw worked. Her free hand curled against the desk. Not being first in line pricked at her pride. The idea of a taxi landed harder. She kept her voice even, iron smoothing the edge beneath. "Something has come up. I have to go."

She ended the call with a firm tap. The phone hit the desk with a dull clatter that echoed in the quiet. She turned to her computer and woke the machine. The monitor washed the room in pale light as the fan whispered to life. Her fingers settled into a controlled rhythm on the keys.

The case file opened. Incident report, call logs, financials, interviews pending. Dates and times. A draft search warrant waited in her email for her signature. The clean grid of it cut through the residue of the call. The glow of the screen and the scent of warm plastic steadied her. Work would ground her and sharpen her focus. Kendria, and whatever game that was, could wait.

Chapter 10

The air carried stale coffee and warm toner without apology. Phones rang. Keyboards clicked. He crossed the bullpen with steady purpose, shoulders set.

Dawson hunched over his desk, his face washed in the flat blue of his monitor. He looked up as Cooper stopped at the corner of his workstation. Dawson's chair creaked.

"What's got you so upright?" Dawson asked, leaning back. His tone was casual, almost bored, but his eyes flicked to the file Cooper held close.

"Sorry about the Discart thing," Cooper said, the words deliberate and heavy. He rested a hand on the edge of Dawson's desk, fingers tapping an uneven rhythm against the cool metal frame.

The room tightened. Sinclair froze mid-note, pen hovering above paper. He looked up fast, drawn by the name. "She gave that to me first."

Cooper offered a small shrug that conceded nothing. His blazer whispered as he moved. "Orders are orders," he said simply, his tone offering no solace.

Dawson barked out a laugh, bitterness dry at the edges. "Classic Blackburn," he muttered, dragging a hand through his already disheveled hair. "She keeps us spinning like tops. Throws it to me one day, tosses it to Sinclair the next, now it's your turn." He smiled thinly and shook his head. "She loves this stuff."

Sinclair exhaled, the fight leaving his jaw. "Yeah," he murmured at last, his grip tightening on the pen before he set it down with care. "Guess she does."

Cooper turned and went to his desk. He opened the Discart file and arranged the pages in a clean grid. Crime scene photos. Witness statements. Forensic notes. Monica Discart's smile fixed on glossy paper, out of time with everything else.

The old desktop woke slowly. Its fan complained, then steadied, a thin current of warm air brushing his wrist. He signed in, kept his eyes on the work, and pulled up New Dresden Electricals' website. The home page loaded in corporate gray and blue, one square at a time.

He typed "street lights" into the search bar and hit Enter. The site turned over, then produced a response. A press release from March titled "Final Phase Complete: New Dresden Achieves 100% Sodium Vapor Street Lighting." Thirteen months ago.

He printed it. The machine coughed out paper and settled. The sheet came out warm, the faint chemical smell rising from the tray. He saved a PDF, labeled it Discart_Lighting, and filed it on the shared drive and a local copy. The drawer stuck, then gave. He backed up the hard copy.

"Smart move, boss," he muttered under his breath, admiration edged with irony.

He returned to the grainy surveillance still in Monica's file. A hooded figure under sodium vapor glow. Purple reads dark there. Often black. The detail had weight now.

Cooper sat at his desk, the screen reflecting off his furrowed brow. He opened the Emergency Production Warrant Request. He filled it cleanly. *Discart, M. Case CCTR 02781. Clothing items described as a dark hooded sweatshirt, including but not limited to hoodies, pullovers, or sweatshirt, matching the description of clothing worn by the suspect in the surveillance video recorded on April 17.*

He added the exhibits in order. The surveillance still. The lighting release. A brief note on sodium vapor skewing purple toward black. No flourish. Just enough to hold.

His cursor hovered over the Emergency Request checkbox.

Time matters. Evidence walks if you let it. He checked the box and sent it.

The email chimed almost at once. Judge Martinez's signature sat in the approval. He printed the order and set a copy aside for Records. The ink was still glossy when he stacked it.

Footsteps receded down the hall. Blackburn took the corner with her usual speed and gave a quick look back. Cooper raised a thumb. She nodded once and kept moving, expression contained and unreadable. He reached for the phone and hovered over Cindy Discart's contact in the file.

Three rings. A tired voice answered. "Hello?"

"Mrs. Discart? Detective Riley Cooper, New Dresden PD," he said evenly, his voice steady yet soft. "I'm calling about your daughter Monica's case."

Silence stretched. Paper-thin, close to tearing. He could hear the faint rasp of her breath.

"I thought Detective Dawson was handling Monica's case."

Cooper leaned back and set a quiet rhythm with his fingers on the desk. "I've been assigned to the investigation, Mrs. Discart," he explained gently. "I'd like to meet with you to go over the case file. I know you've reviewed it before, but I need to get up to speed."

"Oh." The single syllable lingered in the room, confusion edged with thin hope. "Yes, of course. When?"

Cooper straightened in his chair, his voice dropping. "As soon as possible," he said, smooth yet earnest. "I bringing one of our forensic technicians along." He allowed the pause to settle. "It is standard procedure."

"I do not understand." Her voice wavered now.

His tone softened but remained professional, each word precise. "It's just procedure," Cooper assured her gently with conviction. He let those last words register before adding more lightly, "This is actually good news. It means we are leaving no stone unturned."

Silence held. When Cindy spoke again, her voice came thin but steady, braced by months of waiting for answers. "Yes, please," she whispered, almost pleading. "Come by anytime. I'm home all day."

"I'll be there in ten minutes," Cooper replied, decisive yet kind. He ended the call with swift purpose and immediately dialed Forensics.

"Newton."

"Newton, it's Cooper. I have a residence to clear, warrant in hand. I am looking for clothing," Cooper said, fingers tapping the edge of his desk. He pulled on his jacket, the worn wool a familiar weight across his shoulders. "Parking lot in five?"

"On my way." The line clicked dead with Newton's characteristic brevity.

Cooper moved through the precinct corridors. LEDs buzzed overhead. The low murmur of phone calls and keyboards filled the hall. His badge tapped against his hip as he pushed open the double doors and stepped into the afternoon sun.

Newton waited by the exit. Tall. Composed. The white sweater and dark turtleneck looked clean against the concrete and glass. One hand held her kit. The other rested still at her side.

"You ready?" Cooper asked, signaling to his car with a press of the key fob. The navy sports car chirped in response, sunlight flashing over its hood.

Newton nodded once. She slid into the passenger seat without comment. Cooper took the wheel. The engine rose in a low, even rumble as they pulled away. Cool air flowed through the vents.

New Dresden passed in ordered lines and mirrored glass. Light strobed off windows. Foot traffic thinned as they cut toward the neighborhoods. Cooper maintained a steady speed, eyes on the flow. He glanced briefly at Newton's profile, neutral against the window glare.

He handed her the warrant. "Monica Discart homicide. Security video turned up clothing with a distinctive stain," Cooper said as he guided the car onto Maple Avenue. His voice carried just above the tire hum on warm asphalt. "I have a warrant for dark sweatshirts, hoodies."

Newton's expression remained steady. She scanned the warrant while her free hand checked the latches on her kit, inventorying by touch. Plastic clicked under her fingers. She glanced at Cooper. "So, I'm hunting hoodies?"

"Dark ones," he said. "Purple team sweatshirt if it's here. With a stain on the shoulder."

She gave a small shrug. "Makes my job simple."

They turned onto a quiet street of trimmed lawns and balanced facades. A sprinkler traced a slow arc, mist catching the light. The hiss was faint in the heat. Cooper eased onto a cracked driveway beneath a two-story colonial. Blue paint had thinned to chalk. The white trim curled away from the grain.

They stepped into the still heat. Boots scuffed the driveway on the way to the porch. The air was dry and carried baked dust. Cooper checked the doorjamb and window locks, then rapped on the peeling blue paint. The knock sounded dull against tired wood.

The door opened. Cindy Discart stood in the shade of the frame. Her eyes were red from crying. She met Cooper's gaze without blinking. The housedress hung too loose on her.

"Mrs. Discart," Cooper began, voice low but firm. "I'm Detective Cooper, and this is Tanya Newton, our forensics specialist." He indicated Newton. Newton gave a curt nod, her attention already mapping the entry and corners.

"I brought a warrant, ma'am," Cooper said, almost apologetically. He held it where she could see the seal.

Cindy stepped aside with politeness. Cooler air slid from the hallway, detergent underlaid by damp. "Please come in. What are you looking for, detective?"

Inside, lavender tried to cover the shut-in smell. The house felt sealed for too long. Dust hung in the angled light from the front window. A vent ticked as the system cycled. Newton shifted her weight and cleared her throat.

"It's all in the warrant. Can we sit and talk about it? Let Tanya do her job?"

Cindy looked at Newton, then took the warrant from Cooper. The paper crackled in her hands. "Monica's room is upstairs, on the left," she said. She waved Newton toward the stairs. "Mr. Coo— I'm sorry. I mean, Detective Cooper, let's go into the living room. Sit. Ask your questions."

Cooper sat with Cindy. The sofa gave under him with a tired sigh. "Tell me about Monica. What was she studying at university?" He watched Cindy's fingers work the warrant, dog-ear a corner, fold and refold until the crease held.

"Administrative Studies," Cindy said, eyes on Cooper as if confirming this was routine. "She had just started her first year. She even got a work placement at Lewis's hospital." Her voice thinned on the last word.

"Your husband works at New Dresden Medical, correct? A surgeon there?" Cooper kept his tone level.

"A brilliant surgeon," Cindy said. Pride surfaced and receded. "He has been there for over twenty years."

Newton's steps sounded on the stairs, measured and light, and caught Cindy's attention. "Are you in Monica's room?" she called up. "Last room on the left." She turned to Cooper. "What are you looking for, again?"

"Hoodies, sweatshirts, that kind of thing," he replied gently.

Cindy frowned. "What does her clothing have to do with anything?"

"Since I'm new on the case, I want to be thorough. Detective Blackburn asked me to be thorough," Cooper said as he shifted. A spring pressed into his thigh through the cushion.

"Oh yes, I called her the other day. She had Detective Dawson call. Why are you on the case? Is Detective Dawson okay?" she asked, holding the warrant out for Cooper to take back.

"Yes, ma'am. He's fine." Cooper watched how Cindy toyed with her wedding ring, turning it, letting it slip and catch against swollen knuckles. "And what was Monica doing at the hospital?" he asked. His gaze passed framed photos along the hall. Monica looked out from each one. Same smile, different outfits. A face held in one setting.

"Digitizing old personnel records," Cindy said, attempting a small laugh. "She hated it, said it was boring and repetitive. But I do not know what she expected from Administrative Studies." The humor didn't last. She smoothed the hem of her dress instead.

Newton came down the stairs, a large paper bag in her hand. The seal strip caught the light. Paper rustled against her thigh.

"What is that? What did you take?" Cindy said, rising from her chair. She reached out without thinking. Cooper angled his forearm across her path. He stopped her without touching.

"One dark hoodie. Collected from the primary bedroom. Documented, bagged, and labeled," Newton said.

"What does that mean? What was in our bedroom? Monica's room is on the left." The room went still with her. She pressed her hands together at her chest until her fingers trembled.

Cooper pulled a small receipt book from his pocket. The cover had a faint sheen of graphite from use. "I have to inventory the hoodie," he explained. "I'll give you a copy of the receipt." He nodded toward the bag in Newton's hand. "It's just procedure."

Cindy looked from the bag to Cooper and back again. Her fingers tightened until the joints went white. She gave a small nod. "Yes. Take it. Whatever it is."

Cooper wrote quickly. The pen scratched through the carbon, leaving a smudge on his thumb. Case number. Date. One dark hoodie. "Here you go," he said, tearing Cindy's copy from the pad and smoothing the edge before he handed it over.

Cindy took it, shoulders high and tight. "Detective Dawson never took anything."

Newton shot Cooper a look but remained silent. Cooper kept his voice steady. "We're making progress on the case. It might be nothing, but I need to make sure."

"Yes, yes," Cindy said as she turned back toward the living room. "I heard all about Detective Blackburn's need for procedure," she said. Her mouth flattened and then eased.

"Thank you for your cooperation," Cooper said. Warmth edged his words, and Cindy's face softened for a second.

Outside, the car smelled of old coffee and vinyl warmed by the afternoon. Heat rolled off the dash until the air started to move. Cooper started the engine. The fan whirred up from a low rattle to a steady push. Newton settled the bag across her knees with the seal turned up. Paper crackled under her palm. They traded brief smiles. It passed. The road took them toward headquarters, tires humming over patched asphalt while the sunlight flashed through the windshield in erratic beats.

The precinct sat flat against a darkening sky. Inside, noise ran constant. Phones rang. Printers clicked and fed paper. A TV muttered on mute. The air carried toner and stale coffee. They cut through to homicide down gray corridors under humming lights that flattened color and reflected off waxed floors.

Cooper stopped at Blackburn's office. He rapped on the glass and looked in. Blackburn sat over a stack of files, hair loose around her face as she wrote on a yellow pad. At the knock, she glanced up and waved them in with a flick of her fingers.

Newton came in behind Cooper, each step quick. Blackburn leaned back and looked from them to the bag in Newton's hands. One eyebrow lifted, the only question she allowed to show.

"Tanya Newton," Newton said, crisp, stepping forward with contained authority. "Forensics."

"Found this at the Discart residence," Cooper said evenly, satisfaction edging his professional tone as he set the paper bag on Blackburn's desk.

Blackburn's gaze held on the bag for a beat. Then she looked up at both of them, cool calculation behind vivid eyes that gave nothing away.

"Dark purple hoodie. Stain on the shoulder," Newton said.

Blackburn's eyes flicked over to the bag. Her face stayed unreadable. The office phone rang, a clean, insistent tone that cut through the room. With a curt flick of her hand, she dismissed them and reached for the receiver, movements crisp and precise.

Outside in the hallway, the air felt cooler. Cooper smiled. "Lab submission form will be in your inbox in ten," he murmured. "Work your magic."

Newton nodded. "I'll process this as soon as I can," she said, her tone firm as she pivoted toward the exit. Her steps landed with steady purpose.

Cooper lingered long enough to watch her disappear down the corridor. The precinct buzzed at a low hum around him, phones trilling, the smell of stale coffee threading the air. He turned and headed for his desk. The day weighed on him. The enigma of Lewis Discart pressed for attention.

He dropped into his chair. The cushion sighed under him. His fingers found the keyboard, the keys cool beneath his fingertips. First, the submission form. He ticked through the checkboxes with efficiency. Stains, tears, DNA, blood, standard toxin and drug panel. Send.

The New Dresden Medical site filled his monitor, clinical white spreading across the screen, stark and cold. He navigated the staff directory with economy. A quick search pulled up Lewis Discart's profile. A professional headshot showed a man in his mid-forties in surgical scrubs, his smile capable and controlled.

The bio underneath read: "Dr. Lewis Discart, MD, has served as an attending orthopedic surgeon at New Dresden Medical for twenty years. Graduated Wood Creek University Medical School in California at age twenty-six. Dr. Discart specializes in complex joint replacements and reconstructive surgery."

Next, Monica Discart. Her profile sat under Administrative Support Staff, still active. The photo showed a young woman with a bright smile that echoed her father's. The description read: "Monica Discart, Records Management Intern. Currently assisting with the digital conversion of historical records. Part-time position through university work placement program."

He paused. Odd that it was still live. He typed her name into the search bar again. Another link surfaced. He clicked.

The hospital's message appeared on-screen. New Dresden Medical Center mourns the loss of Monica Discart, a bright and dedicated member of our Records Management team. Monica's enthusiasm and attention to detail made her an invaluable contributor during her work placement. Her tragic passing leaves a void in our hospital community. Our thoughts are with her family during this difficult time.

Cooper exhaled, air leaking slowly from his lungs. He sent the page to the printer. The machine woke with a soft whir and fed paper, steadily and rhythmically. The notice was still up months after her death. He wondered if her father had asked for that.

A shadow cut across his monitor. Cooper looked up. Sinclair hovered near the corner of the desk, hands deep in his pockets, restless energy rolling off him. LED light buzzed overhead.

"Find anything good?" Sinclair asked, rocking back on his heels with casual interest.

Cooper rubbed his eyes, the skin gritty from hours at the screen. "I sure hope so," he muttered. "Blackburn is riding my ass on this one."

Sinclair leaned closer, voice low with a laugh buried in it. "Man, I wish she was riding my ass." His face fogged with the same haze he wore whenever her name came up.

Cooper snorted despite himself. The memory of Blackburn's ice-bright stare cut through it, the clean precision of her attention. "Trust me," he said, turning back to the screen. "Be careful what you wish for."

Sinclair's grin held, but he let it drop. Cooper's silence sent him on his way.

Cooper flexed his fingers and brought up Wood Creek University Medical School. The site loaded in fits, images arriving a beat at a time until a sunlit campus settled into place. He found the alumni search and typed *Discart*.

No results found.

The words blinked back at him, flat and final. He re-entered the name with care.

Still nothing.

A slow chill crept into his chest. New Dresden Medical stated the absence with certainty. It should have returned the record. Instead, it hung like a thread asking for a tug.

He leaned in, shoulders tight. He pushed deeper into Wood Creek's alumni database and began scrolling year by year. The lists were shorter than he expected. The class of 2007 had twenty-four students. 2006 had twenty-seven. 2005 had twenty-nine. Names clicked past under the wheel of his mouse, tidy and few, none of them Discart.

"That doesn't make sense," he said under his breath. He kept going. 1998 had twenty-three graduates. 1997 had twenty-six. 1996 had twenty-one. The neat rosters slid past, each one easy to sweep with a glance, and still no Lewis Discart.

The monitor's glow flattened the room. Cooper's eyes burned as he stared at the absence, a blank in the record that wouldn't resolve.

Cooper reviewed the sequence again, each detail clicking into place or refusing. Discart was listed as twenty-six at graduation. The age snagged. Even without a full grasp of the medical timeline, it read wrong unless he had been exceptional.

The LED lights buzzed softly. The monitor washed his desk in cold blue. He opened a new browser tab and pulled up the California Medical Board site, the dated portal he knew would produce results. He typed Discart into the search field and sent it.

Nothing.

He eased back and pushed a hand through his hair. The chair gave a small sigh. Discart's profile showed twenty years at New Dresden Medical and a degree from Wood Creek. No trail behind either. One detail kept cutting through. Graduation at twenty-six. It did not align.

He gathered his printouts. Monica's hospital profile. Lewis's staff biography. The memorial notice that had started this. Paper edges rasped against his fingertips as he squared them. He took the stack to Blackburn.

He knocked on the doorframe and waited. Through the glass, she finished a call without looking at him, her eyes already elsewhere, then waved him in.

Light came through the blinds in thin bars, laying stripes across her desk. Dust turned slowly in the beams. She gestured to the chair. Her fingers tapped once, then went still.

He sat. The leather cooled his back and creaked under his weight. He slid the stack across and watched her read. The quiet rustle of paper filled the room.

"Well?" she said as she reached the end of a sheet and lifted an impassive gaze.

"I've been tracing Lewis Discart," Cooper said, leaning forward as if closeness might confer weight. "According to New Dresden Medical's website, he graduated from Wood Creek University Medical School in California."

Blackburn raised an eyebrow. Interest contained. She kept turning pages.

"And?" she asked, voice cool.

"Nothing," Cooper said. Frustration edged his tone. "No records at Wood Creek, and nothing in the California Medical Board archives."

Her hand stopped on a page. She looked at the header, then back at him without comment.

"I went through a decade of alumni rosters manually," Cooper added quickly before she could cut him off. "Small classes, twenty to thirty students a year. Easy to scan thoroughly." He let the last word land clean.

She let silence do the work. The HVAC hummed, a low current beneath everything.

Her eyes stayed on him, sharp and steady. Her fingers stilled on the paper, possession established.

"What do you think is going on here?" she asked. The question carried an edge that made it something else, a test.

He shifted. Leather creaked. He ordered his thoughts. Clean options. No theatrics.

"First theory," he said, keeping his voice even though his pulse ticked under her scrutiny. "He could have changed his name. He might have gone to university under a different identity in California."

She gave him nothing. The pressure of her attention pushed him forward.

"Or there was a mix-up at New Dresden Medical," he offered, tongue dry. "Maybe they folded another doctor's credentials into his bio." Even as he said it, the idea felt thin. An error like that at a hospital of this size did not sit right.

He checked the top sheet again. No relief. Ink, dates, the same clean lies.

He leaned back, fingers tapping the armrest, and tried again. "What bothers me is his age when he supposedly graduated, twenty-six." He exhaled through his nose. "That's young for a surgeon. Most do not finish their residencies until their early thirties. Medical school and training take years." The pieces still refused to lock. Something in Discart's story was wrong.

"Another angle," Cooper said, momentum building as he spoke, "is that he's using someone else's credentials entirely. If that's true, the actual records wouldn't be in his name at all." His fingers tapped an idle rhythm against his thigh, a soft thrum in the quiet office, then went still under Blackburn's steady attention.

She leaned forward, not much, just enough to extend her reach across the desk. The lamplight cut a clean line across the papers between them. Her eyes held him in place.

"Borrow another identity," she murmured, voice deceptively calm, "without taking their name?"

The look she gave him stripped away his defenses. He felt opened up, as if every thought might spill into her waiting hands before he was ready to speak it.

He shook his head, backing off. "Okay. Maybe not that." He swallowed, tongue dragging over a dry mouth, buying himself a few seconds.

"But none of this explains why there aren't any Medical Board records," he muttered, half to himself, as if speaking could untie the knot inside his skull.

Then it hit. His thoughts shifted cleanly into place. A tremor ran through him before his voice could catch up.

"You know what's interesting?" he ventured, careful, testing the ground before he committed. The urgency bled through despite his efforts to control it.

Blackburn didn't blink. She didn't change her breathing. Something flickered behind her eyes, a small light he knew meant she had already clocked the change in him.

"Monica," Cooper said, slower now, setting each syllable between them. "Monica worked at New Dresden Medical, digitizing old personnel records."

He saw her sharpen at once. She didn't move beyond stilling her fingers on the stack in front of her, yet her focus narrowed like a camera lens. Paper rasped softly under her hand.

"At her father's hospital," Cooper pressed, throat tight as adrenaline rose under his skin.

"Tell me exactly what you're thinking," Blackburn said at last. Her tone made it plain she had already assembled most of the structure; she wanted to hear him build it out loud.

Cooper gestured to the printouts scattered between them. "It took me less than twenty minutes to find these discrepancies." His voice climbed a notch, conviction gathering speed; speaking faster felt like forcing light into the corners.

"Monica was smart. Probably," he pushed on, almost reverently, as if she might be standing just outside the door listening to what they were uncovering. "Detail-oriented. She was taking some Administrative Studies course, I think. She would have gone through decades of personnel files."

"And?"

"And maybe she looked for her dad's records. Or she did not find them and searched the way I did."

Blackburn leaned in, the dim light carving planes across her face. Her elbows settled on the desk; her gaze stayed level. "And what would she have found?"

"Nothing," Cooper said, the word heavy. The truth landed in his chest and stayed there. "Because maybe Lewis Discart never graduated at all. Monica would have seen that in the files she was digitizing. She would have realized her father was lying about everything."

Blackburn's eyes narrowed. Satisfaction sparked and vanished. She stayed very still; her presence filled the room without effort.

"Keep going," she said, low and smooth, an edge threaded through it that made his pulse beat faster. They were closing in.

His thoughts locked. "This is the motive," he said, urgency rising. "Lewis could not risk being exposed as a fraud. Monica pieced it together. She learned the truth in those records. And he..." Cooper paused, throat tightening. "He killed her to keep her quiet." He exhaled, forcing steadiness. "The purple hoodie with the stain could be enough physical evidence to make an arrest."

Blackburn's mouth edged into a thin smile; she contained it with ease. Her fingers drummed once, twice, each tap precise. "Excellent work, Cooper." She turned back to the papers. "Contact Wood Creek University and the California Medical Board. I want definitive proof of whether Lewis attended or graduated under any alias or name change. Keep it under wraps; we can't afford to tip him off."

A clean heat moved through Cooper. The strain and sleeplessness receded for a beat. Under her gaze, he felt seen, not just another cog but necessary to the machine she was building. He straightened.

"I'm on it," he said, voice steady as he rose.

The corridor air felt cooler as he stepped out of her office. Exhilaration lifted him, a current under his skin. Phones rang in distant bursts; the ceiling lights hummed; the faint smell of old coffee hung near the bullpen. He crossed the room with energy still crackling around him like static before a callout.

He passed Sinclair's cluttered workstation and let himself take a small, petty victory. Cooper stuck out his tongue in a quick flash. Sinclair's face tightened with envy; the look hit Cooper like fuel.

The hunt had begun again. This time, he felt unstoppable.

Chapter 11

Blackburn considered her call with Kendria, allowing irritation cool into aim. *But where?* She shifted in her chair. Leather creaked. Heat left her face in a slow drain. Now was the perfect time to deal with her tracker.

Her office sat in flat LED light. Shadows held their edges. The air was stale. The desk was ordered. Case files on the left. Laptop on the right, humming. The screen showed the last email from Dr. Petrović. The subject line pulled the warmth from the room. Homicide Confirmed: Jenna Langston. The matter was settled. No ambiguity remained. The case was officially hers.

She leaned back slowly, a pen loose between her fingers. It tapped against the desk in a deliberate rhythm. Sharp clicks punctuated the HVAC hush.

The door to the bullpen creaked open. Dawson returned and shuffled to his desk. The place carried the low thrum of printers and murmured calls. Blackburn had mapped out assignments to keep the case tight and her operation clean. Dawson and the others would follow without deviation. Except one.

Her gaze moved to Sinclair's desk. The GPS tracker from her car. Arrogance or stupidity. She hadn't decided. Either way, he would learn what it cost.

The pen stilled. The room tightened. She swept the bullpen. Everyone was present, heads bent to their tasks, paper whispering under their hands. A small smile cut across her mouth. She rose and moved toward Sinclair, heels marking the linoleum in clean beats.

"Gentlemen," Blackburn said smoothly, her voice cutting through the quiet with effortless authority. Conversations halted mid-sentence, every pair of eyes tilting toward her. "I've updated the task list for Jenna Langston's case. The details are live on the network. Review them immediately. She is officially a homicide."

Her tone was crisp, the undercurrent was steel. She moved through the bullpen with contained authority. The room adjusted around her.

At Sinclair's desk she paused, back to the others. He lifted his gaze, hesitating. Desire flashed and failed to hide. Blackburn tilted her head and slipped open the top button of her shirt with easy indifference. Every motion was calculated.

"Sinclair," she murmured, leaning closer until only he could hear. Her voice dipped lower, not soft but pointedly intimate, and carried a sharp edge of power disguised as familiarity. "I want you." She let the instruction hang for a beat. "My office."

Sinclair swallowed. His breath hitched at a closeness he had not earned. He reached without thinking. She let the reach die, then set something small and unmistakable on his desk with a flick of her wrist.

The tracker caught the light. Blackburn tapped it once with a manicured nail. The point landed.

"You have five minutes to get your act together."

She didn't wait for his reaction. She straightened and walked back to her office. Behind her, his silence and heat followed through the steady hum of the room. A prelude to what awaited him next.

Fun times were coming.

The tracker sat where she left it. Sinclair's infatuation tilted into unease. His pulse picked up as he replayed the edge in Blackburn's gaze. He knew that look. She was several moves ahead. This time he was the piece on the board.

In her office, Blackburn eased into the high-backed chair. The leather was cool against her shoulders. A small smile touched her mouth as she took in the room. Power suited her. She wore it with control. Her fingers rested on the armrests. No fidgeting. Across the room, Sinclair had five minutes to decide how he would explain a trespass that could cost him his badge. IA wouldn't need much to put him on the shelf.

Sinclair approached the office with hesitant steps. His reflection ghosted in the glass. His hand hovered over the knob, unsteady. The metal waited, cool against damp skin. Each breath was shallow. The nerves didn't settle. It was a losing battle.

The door creaked open. Blackburn's eyes lifted to his. The effect was immediate. She stayed seated behind the desk, posture exact.

Authority without raising her voice. Her fingers steepled. She looked as if she were laying out steps rather than threats.

"Sit," she said. Crisp, unhurried.

The word landed. Sinclair sat before he knew he had moved. Sweat gathered at his hairline and stung. His fingers worked against each other in his lap, small betrayals he could not stop.

Blackburn leaned forward, narrowing the distance in both body and bearing. "Why," she began softly, "were you tracking me?" Her voice held a deceptive calm, silk laid over razor wire.

His throat went dry. The prepared speech collapsed under her stare. "I was worried about you," he managed finally, weaker than intended.

Her brow arched a fraction, conveying disbelief without disturbing her composure. "Worried," she repeated slowly, each syllable measured until skepticism gathered at the edges.

Sinclair nodded too quickly. "Yes," he said, swallowing hard. "I've noticed strange things lately." He waved his hand at nothing. "I thought someone might be after you, or something wasn't right."

Something flickered across his face. A memory, maybe guilt. His hands fidgeted.

"I just wanted to make sure you were safe," he concluded weakly. His voice sounded thin beside her silence.

Her gaze didn't waver. It settled. "What strange things?" The question cut cleanly, leaving no room to drift.

He paused. The pause answered for him.

Something cooled in Blackburn. She marked his hesitation as a hunter marks distance. She let the room claim the space between words. No rush. No relief.

She leaned back. The chair remained silent. Air moved faintly from a vent above, a steady hum underscoring the quiet. She touched the tabletop once with her fingertips. The light in the corner lens glowed red.

"Were you outside my house?"

Sinclair's eyes widened before he could control them. "No, of course not," he stammered, his voice betraying him with a slight crack. "I would never."

Blackburn cut him off with a small motion. "You were outside my house to plant the tracker, so indeed you would," she said. Her tone stayed level, the way it did when she read incident reports into the record. "I think you're lying. I do not intend to waste time debating."

His mouth opened and closed. She saw it all. Not only the act but the motive wrapped around it. She would use that before anything else.

"You will write a report," Blackburn said coolly, folding her arms across her chest. Her voice carried inevitability. "A detailed one. I want every step you took and why you thought tracking me was necessary. Outline your reasoning, every strange little thing that concerned you and led you here." She tilted her head, studying him like a specimen pinned for display. "When it's done, it comes to me first. Then I'll decide how much lands on Chief Hayes' desk."

Color drained from his face. He could see the form number at the top of the page and the signatures beneath. "But that would—"

"Ensure there is a record of your misconduct?" Blackburn interjected, her lips curving into something neither smile nor sneer but chilling nonetheless. "Yes, Detective. It will. Cost you a job? That's not my call."

Sinclair scanned the room as if seeking an exit he had missed. The walls offered nothing. White paint. A clock ticking a slow, indifferent beat. Her voice did not rise. That made it worse.

Blackburn leaned in, close enough for the point to land. "Let me remind you," she said softly, deadly calm, "you used department resources to stalk your commanding officer. You didn't even bother to cover your tracks. You signed out equipment like this was another day at the office. You didn't even purchase an off-the-shelf personal tracker. Idiot." She let the word sit until the silence absorbed it. "You would be wise to salvage what you can before this turns into something that buries you."

He tried to lift his chin. It did not hold. His shirt clung to the back of his neck.

Blackburn straightened gradually. She gave him a path that looked like order and sounded like consequence.

"Beyond the report," she continued smoothly, "you will also be taking on special assignments for the next month."

Sinclair frowned faintly, confusion flickering in place of fear for a moment. "Special assignments?" he echoed, uncertain.

"Indeed." Her smile a neat flash of teeth with no warmth behind it. "You'll manage filing backlogs in Records. You'll handle a reorg in Evidence Room Three." She allowed the pause to linger just long enough for him to feel its weight. "And you'll run errands for the entire team."

It landed. Sinclair's shoulders dipped. He knew everyone in the room would notice. He attempted anyway. "But," he began.

Blackburn lifted her hand. No flourish. He went silent.

"If someone asks you to hold their dick while they piss," she said, tone flat and even, "you do it with a smile and say yes sir. Consider this your chance to reflect on your actions and their consequences."

He remained still. The hum of LEDs filled the space his voice did not. She observed him for one more beat, then turned away.

The point stood. He could bear the weight or break under it pretending he could not feel it.

Blackburn leaned in, forearms resting lightly on the desk. Paper pressed cool under her skin. Her voice lowered, precise. "Let me be perfectly clear," she said. "Any deviation from your assigned tasks, any further lapse in judgment, and disciplinary action will be the least of your concerns."

Silence pressed. She maintained it until his breath thinned. Then she offered a small, contained smile. "Do I make myself clear?"

Bravado drained quickly. He swallowed dryly and audibly. He gave a stiff nod.

"Good," Blackburn said, leaning back. The chair responded with a quiet creak. She flicked two fingers. "You're excused."

He stood too quickly, steadied himself, and kept his eyes down. He moved toward the door, slow under the room's scrutiny.

"Oh, Sinclair?" Her tone lightened. He turned with a thin hope that vanished from his face as she finished.

"Your first task," she said, drawing a plastic bag from her satchel and tapping it once against her palm, "is to deliver Reeve's evidence for the Langston case. After that, organize the file room, every last misplaced folder back where it belongs. Put them in the right drawer, alphabetically." She allowed the pause to linger. "I expect it completed by end of day."

She raised her voice to the bullpen. "Gentlemen? Sinclair is our office boy for the month."

Laughter rolled through, not loud, but enough to mark him. He turned away. His steps scraped the linoleum. The room smelled like old coffee and copier toner. Colleagues watched without commitment; some smirked, others kept their faces tight. He avoided both.

At his desk, he dropped into the chair. Dawson stared. Heat saturated the look.

Dawson leaned closer, breath sharp with mint and stress. "What the hell did you do?" His voice came thin and cutting. Sinclair remained slumped, color gone. His mouth opened. Nothing emerged. He glanced at Blackburn, then looked away.

Blackburn settled back, one ankle over the other, energy contained rather than spent. Control left a clean aftertaste. The room still carried the echo of Sinclair's retreat. The flush at his throat. His late understanding of the trap. Not a triumph. Necessary. The sensation flowed through her, cool and steady. Authority returned to its channel.

Her fingers tapped an even rhythm on the desk; her pulse remained level. The office was hers to shape. So was the case.

A knock clipped the air. She looked up.

"We're set up in Interview Room Two," Sinclair said from the doorway, one hand on the frame. "Mr. Zhang and his lawyer are ready whenever you are, boss." He sounded composed. She trusted he would hold the line.

She nodded once and stacked the files she needed under her arm. Kendria could wait.

She stood. She smoothed her blazer with a quick pass. James Zhang would get the version of her that never missed. She gathered her notebook and moved toward the hall. Shoulders squared. Purpose clean.

"Who's his lawyer?" she asked as she collected the bag and a pen.

Sinclair scratched his chin. "Jacob Schwartz?"

Blackburn paused and let a brow lift. The corner of her mouth turned in mild amusement. "Schwartz? The estate guy?" It clicked. A careful man in a dark suit, a speech at Charles Roche's memorial gala not long ago.

She bent over her keyboard, the plastic keys clicking under quick, economical fingers as she entered his name into a state database. The screen's pale light washed over her face. The state bar list of certified criminal law specialists loaded with a soft whir from the tower. As expected, Schwartz's name wasn't there. Nowhere near qualified for this kind of work. A small grin pulled at one corner of Blackburn's mouth as she straightened, the expression gone as soon as it appeared.

"Well," she said under her breath. Amusement flickered across her sharp features and vanished behind cool professionalism. "This ought to be fun."

* * *

Blackburn stood behind one-way glass. James Zhang eased into the hard plastic chair. Its edges bit at the fabric of his tailored Italian suit. The room was utilitarian, a cluster of cheap furniture under LED lighting that hummed overhead. The light flattened everything it touched and carved deeper lines across Detective Reeves's weathered face. The table's surface was scuffed and sticky at one edge, a faint ring where a coffee cup had once cooled. James wore his smile like armor. Sly, polished, impenetrable. The same expression that had disarmed boardrooms and derailed negotiations many times before.

"Your autonomous vehicle was involved in a fatal accident," Reeves said evenly. He slid a manila folder across the table. Paper rasped against fake wood. The air was close and stale, tinged with old coffee and disinfectant.

James's fingers touched the knot of his silk tie, a tiny adjustment that would have looked like nothing if someone had not been watching. Reeves watched. His gaze settled on James with quiet intensity, taking his measure.

"These things happen," James replied, voice smooth and detached, every syllable trimmed to neutrality. "That's what insurance is for." Each word sat inside a carefully built calm meant to deflect.

Reeves let silence fill the room until the buzz of the lights and the steady click of the wall clock stood out like separate sounds. The second hand ticked forward with fussy precision. James resisted the urge to loosen his collar or signal to his lawyer waiting just outside. Any crack in the facade would be a tactical mistake.

"A woman died," Reeves said finally. He didn't soften the words.

James leaned back in the rigid chair, projecting ease. "And that is tragic," he said. He paused, letting the word sit. "But these vehicles have safety records far beyond those of human drivers. One incident does not negate that."

The LED hum pressed against the quiet. It matched the low thrum in James's chest. None of it showed on his face. He met Reeves's stare head-on and called up what he had practiced in mirrors. Confidence without arrogance. Empathy without culpability. The same balance he used to shape markets and ease investors through bad news.

Sweat gathered at James's hairline. He refused to lift a hand to touch it. His smile widened instead, curated to read as ease, as if they were speaking about the weather rather than a death.

The facade wavered when Reeves stood. The detective moved with an unhurried purpose. "Shall we head to the interview room now?"

The words landed hard. James blinked. "I'm sorry, what? Wasn't this the interview?"

Reeves laughed, warm and genuine enough to cut the tension. The sound bounced off the near-empty room. The corners of his eyes crinkled. He glanced back at James. "No," he said easily, shaking his head. "This is where we have people wait. The real interview room is down the hall. You will meet the boss."

James nodded, the motion stiff. His poise faltered. His Italian leather shoes pinched as he stood and followed Reeves into the corridor. LED lights ran in a straight line above them, each fixture buzzing a fraction out of sync with the next. The air smelled like floor polish and old paper. Their steps echoed off painted cinderblock, each one scraping a little more at the confidence he had built layer by layer over the years.

As soon as they left, Blackburn left the observation room and headed to the other interview room.

Blackburn heard the heavy metal door open. James hesitated, expecting the detective to go first.

Reeves let out another quiet chuckle and set a firm hand between James's shoulder blades. "After you," he said. His voice stayed even. The pressure was subtle and not negotiable. He added with a faint smile, "It's just the two of you."

The room was spare and bright in a harsh way, a metallic table taking up most of the space. The light flickered at the edges of his vision, faint but insistent. The air felt colder here, processed and dry.

What stopped him wasn't the table. It was the single occupant.

Detective Morgan Blackburn sat with her hands poised loosely on the tabletop, her posture easy yet exact. Her presence settled into the room and made it feel smaller. Her gaze locked onto James with unnerving precision, sharp and unrelenting, as if light narrowed and found only him.

James froze for the briefest moment. He searched for a routine gesture. A handshake. A polite introduction. Anything that would restore a familiar script. Nothing came. Silence spread out and then pressed in.

"Detective," Blackburn said at last. Her voice was cool and edged with authority. Her eyes flicked toward Reeves, still in the doorway. "Move those chairs for me."

James watched Reeves stack the last chairs against the wall, his hands efficient, his face blank. Metal legs scraped and then settled. A quick look. There was nothing more.

Reeves slipped out. The latch clicked with a clean metallic bite. The room sealed. The sound pinned itself in James's ears and lingered.

Blackburn lifted her pen and pointed to the chair across from her without commentary or welcome. James took the seat. The metal felt cold through his trousers and gave nothing back.

Even in a suit cut to flatter and priced to signal authority, he felt exposed under the overheads. LED light carved hard lines across Blackburn's face and rendered the cinder blocks behind her a flat institutional gray. She didn't blink at the brightness or shift for comfort.

She leaned in, pen poised above a notepad already lined with tight script. The point hovered without touching paper. James kept his hands on the table where she could see them. His throat tightened. He left it alone.

A red dot glowed on the small camera in the corner. The recorder at the edge of the table showed time running in steady blue digits. The vent breathed cool air that smelled faintly of disinfectant. Process moved forward regardless of his preferences.

"Thank you for coming today, Mr. Zhang." Her voice remained even, letting formality do the work. Her pen moved in a slow circle that left no ink. "Let's cut to the chase. I have questions about your missing autonomous vehicle, the Raider Straight Line."

He shifted once, then stilled. The movement was barely perceptible, more breath than motion. He touched the bezel of his Rolex with one knuckle. The fluted edge bit lightly at his skin and steadied him.

"Of course," he said, keeping his tone level. His face remained neutral. "That car is a niche luxury item. Easy to afford while overseeing Nexus Realm." He let the title hang and waited to see if she would look impressed. She did not. "One of a dozen high-end cars I have."

Her eyebrow lifted. Nothing else moved. James filed that reaction with a low burn of unease and maintained his open posture.

"Hard to notice when those kinds of vehicles go missing. When you have so many cars," he said. A short laugh slipped out, too thin for the room. He let it fade. Blackburn watched him without filling the silence. The clock on the recorder ticked. The quiet persisted.

He adjusted his feet. The leather of his shoes rasped softly against the tile. The movement bought him a breath and revealed more than he intended. He pulled his shoulders back and met her eyes.

"Most people would notice if a six-figure asset disappeared into thin air," Blackburn said, her tone remaining mild though her words were not. "Don't you think they would?" She paused just long enough for the question to settle. "Especially after what they've been saying about that girl on the news."

He felt it land. He kept his hands flat. His fingers twitched toward his tie and stopped halfway. He left it crooked.

The light overhead buzzed. He heard it now that she had given him something to notice. The chair seemed harder. The table colder. None of that mattered to the camera.

The door opened a few inches. Hinges whispered. James turned his head without moving his shoulders. A detective he didn't know stepped in, tall, blazer rumpled, attention focused on the table. He slid a single photograph in front of Blackburn and withdrew without a word. The door closed again. The red dot continued glowing.

Blackburn looked at the image. Her face remained unchanged except for a small line setting at her jaw. Her pen stilled above the page.

"What is it?" The question escaped faster than he intended. He leaned forward involuntarily, drawn by habit and need. His pulse ticked at his neck. She did not answer.

She studied the photograph. Seconds stretched thin. She let them. The room held steady around her. The air felt dry in his mouth.

James eased closer. His tie touched the edge of the steel. The LED panel lit the glossy surface and turned it blank until he shifted, searching for clarity.

The glare slid. The picture resolved. And then he saw it.

"Know her?" Blackburn's voice cut through the room.

Zhang answered too quickly. "No."

Something flickered on his face, anyway. Recognition skimmed across his eyes before he dragged them back to her.

The LED lights hummed overhead. Blackburn studied the photograph between them. Jenna Langston stood centered under a hard flash, phone lifted for a selfie at what looked like a corporate celebration. Glasses raised, blurred movement. In the background, out of focus but certain, Zhang appeared with a purposeful set to his shoulders, his face turned away from the camera.

Zhang swallowed. His fingers tapped the table once, a small, hollow sound on wood, before he stilled them.

"Curious, isn't it?" Blackburn said. She let quiet settle until it drew sharp lines around them. "How little you seem to know about someone you were supposedly so close to."

His composure cracked. Sweat beaded at his temples in the cold light. When he reached for words, they came uneven. "We weren't close. I meet a lot of people at these events." He paused, then tripped again. "It's easy to forget."

The stumble cut through his usual polish. Blackburn raised an eyebrow and watched the muscles in his abdomen tighten beneath his shirt.

"Your parties," she said evenly. "Open invitation? Anyone walk in?"

"No." The word snapped out. "Invitation only." Another pause, telling. His voice tightened. "Corporate event."

"And her place of work? This mystery woman?"

"A marketing firm." The words tumbled. "One we hired."

Blackburn did not move. Her stillness did the work. A muscle jumped in his jaw before she could ask her next question.

"Her name?"

The pause stretched long enough for her to count his fast blinks. "Jenna Langston," he said at last.

Too easy. Far too easy.

"Both first and last name," Blackburn murmured. "For someone you claim not to know."

He reached for fraying excuses, his hands worrying the edge of the table. "I was mistaken."

Her mouth curved in something that looked like a smile and felt like a warning. "Yes, Mr. Zhang. You certainly were."

He reached for his water with a slight tremor and set the rim to his lips. The sip didn't steady him. Condensation left a wet ring on the table.

"Where were you when the car disappeared?" Her tone stayed casual. She watched the weight land.

His fingers twitched against the glass. He held still the next instant. "Home." The beat before the word landed too long. He tried for steadiness. "Alone." Another pause, defensive now. "Busy working."

Blackburn tipped her head with an air of understanding that didn't reach her eyes. A quiet mockery edged her expression. "What time was that?"

"I don't know." Too fast again.

She lifted her chin a fraction. "Then how do you know you were home when the car disappeared?"

He froze for the briefest moment. It was enough. "I've been home since Thursday afternoon."

Rehearsed. The words came out stiff and drilled.

"And yet," Blackburn replied, smooth as glass, "you have no proof?"

"I was alone." His tone sharpened, all edges, as if volume could keep her out.

"Online? A purchase? A post?" She set each question down with surgical precision, watching his defenses loosen with every one.

The lights buzzed. Somewhere, a vent sighed. He exhaled and played his last card. "I was playing Nexus, R.I.P. Driver." He hesitated. "My gaming log would show that."

"Game logs can be pulled." She let the phrase cool the air, then moved on. "And home security footage? A man like you will have a home security system."

Color thinned from his cheeks. "Of course."

Blackburn rose and kept her voice procedural. "We will need both immediately, Mr. Zhang."

"Yes," he said. The word barely cleared his throat. He straightened in the chair as sweat darkened his collar. "I did nothing wrong."

It broke as it left his mouth, caught on his teeth.

Blackburn brushed her fingers through the air as if sweeping away lint. "Intriguing," she said, amusement held at a polite chill. "It's unusual here to hear someone boast about doing the right thing. Almost refreshing. You did the right thing, didn't you?"

She focused and pinned him there. "Tell me, Mr. Zhang, are you good at gaming?"

He didn't hide the spark. Pride lifted his spine. "Yeah," he said. His shoulders squared. "I beat people all the time." His chest rose.

Blackburn lifted a brow. "It's a driving game."

He nodded before restraint returned. Too late. "R.I.P. Driver is amazing. It's about scoring points by running over..."

He stopped. Her stare held him. Comprehension hit. His eyes widened. His mouth parted. He grabbed for a lifeline. "I wasn't in the Straight Line when it hit her!"

It came out ragged, pitched by panic.

Blackburn leaned in just enough for the table to cut the light between them. "In this age of autonomy," she said, quiet and plain, "is that even necessary anymore? To be in the car?"

Steel lived inside the softness of her next words. "Someone like you, fluent in games where screens blur into streets, might test the edges. The simulation lost its charge. You wanted the reality." She let the words settle. "'I wasn't driving, I was home.' A tidy denial from someone who understands the systems."

His breathing shortened. A bead of sweat worked from temple to cheek. His grip on the table went hard enough to blanch the knuckles.

"No." The word burst. "I didn't do anything. You're twisting my words. You can't just... just..."

The sentence broke. His pulse jumped at his throat.

Blackburn didn't look away. "Or perhaps," she said, "this was a tragic accident. And yet." She tightened the quiet. "You've failed to file a report. Doesn't that strike you as careless?"

He leaned back an inch. Space as retreat. "I..." He fumbled. "I didn't kill her."

Too formed. Too steady. Blackburn let it sit unacknowledged.

"I didn't even know the car was missing." The words dropped into the quiet. Another gap. "How could I..." He let the rest die.

She waited. She let him listen to his own collapse.

He swallowed. The motion climbed and settled. "I wasn't even there." Each word landed with weight. "I want my lawyer."

Blackburn's smile barely moved. "Mr. Zhang, You're not under arrest. You can't request a lawyer."

"He's here in the lobby."

"Jacob Schwarz?" Blackburn asked, mild in tone. "The estate lawyer. I spoke with him days ago at the Charles Roche Memorial Gala. Lovely man. Very adept with trusts and inheritance disputes." She leaned a fraction. "Criminal law, however, is not his strength."

"I'm not a criminal," Zhang shot back.

"Of course not," Blackburn said, easing into her chair. "No one is until convicted."

He flinched. His eyes pulled toward the door. "Am I free to go?"

Blackburn inclined her head. "You always have been."

Reeves filled the doorway without a sound and waited. Zhang rose slowly, joints reluctant, as if each needed persuading.

Blackburn watched them in profile as they moved down the corridor. No words passed. The hallway smelled faintly of old coffee and lemon cleaner. In the lobby, Jacob Schwarz stood with a fixed smile and anxious eyes. Reeves stepped aside, then slipped back into the precinct, leaving client and counsel in a quiet that pressed close.

Chapter 12

Silence followed Blackburn out of the interview room. LED lights hummed overhead. She paused to steady her breathing, then entered the observation room with a water bottle secured in her gloved hand.

The team gathered at the one-way glass. No one spoke. All eyes tracked Zhang. Hayes leaned forward in his chair, drawing a faint squeak from the vinyl.

In the corner, Willow clutched a fresh notebook against her ribs. Her glasses fogged with each uneven breath. Three hundred and thirty-three lines of neat script filled the pages. Both busywork and penance. She stood ready if Blackburn requested to see it. Graphite dust marked the heel of her hand.

Blackburn surveyed the room once and raised the bottle. It retained Zhang's warmth through her nitrile gloves. The implication required no explanation. Trace evidence. Chain of custody. A clean retrieval.

Reeves approached with an evidence bag already open. Plastic crinkled as Blackburn placed the bottle inside and sealed it with an audible click. The adhesive caught and held. Reeves uncapped a marker. The sharp scent of solvent cut through the stale air as he noted the time and his initials on the flap.

Cooper placed his hand on her shoulder, the weight and heat penetrating the fabric. Reeves murmured, "Excellent work." She allowed the praise to pass through her and realigned her posture. The precision of the interview still coursed through her system, creating a steady rhythm that calmed rather than agitated.

"Sinclair." Her voice sliced through the room. "The photo you presented during questioning showed perfect timing. Where did you find it?"

Sinclair straightened. His tie hung askew from leaning against the glass. "Not me," he replied after a pause. "Willow found it."

All heads turned simultaneously. Willow froze under their collective gaze. Color rose in her cheeks.

"I, um." She adjusted her glasses with a nervous gesture. "I saw James Zhang post online about his homicide interview. I ran facial recognition on my archive of Jenna's photos, using Zhang's profile pictures for reference." Her voice grew steadier as she described the technical process. "The program identified a match from the New Year's party within minutes. I printed it immediately." She swallowed. "The resolution was sufficient to make an impact."

Blackburn maintained her focus on Willow. Contained approval surfaced in her expression. "Quick thinking," she said, her tone edged with respect. "Very quick thinking. Good—" Blackburn barely held back "girl."

She turned from the glass and tapped a slow rhythm against her thigh with two fingers. Tap, tap. The room shifted with her movement. Everyone awaited the next directive.

"Willow," she said, keeping her attention on the analyst, "could those gaming logs Zhang mentioned verify his alibi about playing R.I.P. Driver?"

Willow's shoulders tensed. Light reflected off her lenses. "I'm not a gamer," she admitted, fidgeting with a loose thread on her sleeve. "I wouldn't know."

"I play some online games," Sinclair offered, stepping forward with renewed confidence. "Most platforms maintain detailed match records. Login times. Opponent information. Some games track every action. Moves, kills, item collection." He shrugged once but met Blackburn's gaze directly. "I'm unfamiliar with R.I.P. Driver specifically, but it likely uses similar systems."

Blackburn considered this. "Since Zhang owns Nexus, could he alter those logs?"

The room grew quiet. The ventilation system hissed. A printer in the bullpen clicked briefly before falling silent.

Willow cleared her throat. "Yes," she stated quietly but with certainty. "Most technical support staff can access logs for security purposes or to prevent cheating." She pushed her glasses up again. The motion remained the same, but her jaw had set firmly. "From what I've observed of James Zhang, he appears to maintain tight control over his systems."

Hayes shifted, already reaching for his phone. Reeves checked his watch and pressed a finger along the evidence bag seal, testing its security.

Blackburn maintained momentum. "Reeves," she instructed crisply. "Go to Zhang's house. Secure those gaming logs before he has an opportunity to modify them. Collect the home security footage while You're there." She looked toward Willow with a single nod. "Take her with you."

Chairs scraped against the floor. Reeves capped his marker and handed Sinclair the evidence bag. Willow hugged her notebook once before setting it down, her fingers lingering on its childish cover. Blackburn observed the small ritual without comment. The hum of the lights filled the space as everyone moved into action.

Reeves grabbed his keys and cut for the door. Willow fell in behind him, her steps quick and neat in the hall.

Blackburn remained in the observation room, steady and controlled. Passing clouds varied the light across her face. The overhead LED hummed. The glass reflected a faint image of the room back at them.

The room carried the smell of hot coffee. Chief Hayes's chair creaked as he shifted. Frustration carved deeper lines into his face.

"Why did you let Zhang walk out of here? We had him," he barked, his voice sharp enough to cut steel.

Detective Blackburn leaned against the wall, composed. Her suit remained crisp; the fabric maintained its line even as she folded her arms. The low thrum from the interrogation room underscored her reply.

"Because right now we have too many threads and no clear picture. I need clarity before I can identify Zhang as our suspect."

Hayes's mustache twitched. His growl remained low. "Not good enough."

Blackburn raised a finger. "Consider it this way. Zhang could have driven his own car there, parked nearby, and used a remote to send it after his target."

Cooper stepped from the corner into the spill of overhead light. His voice was cool but clipped. "Or someone else stole the car outright. Hit Jenna and fled before anyone knew what happened. Sent the car off by itself afterwards. The fire destroyed any DNA we might have collected."

"Exactly," Blackburn said with a short nod, her gaze unwavering. "It's also plausible, assuming Zhang's story checks out, that he didn't know the car was gone and someone staged the entire thing." A faint smirk touched her mouth. "And there is always door number four. The car acted on its own."

Sinclair stood near the surveillance monitors and cleared his throat. The screens flickered across his eyes. "We do not even know for certain if Jenna was the intended target," he said, quiet but weighty in the still room.

Blackburn tipped her chin. "Which is why we untangle their connection and reconstruct every second of that vehicle's path from Zhang's house to the crash site." She allowed the thought to settle. "There's more ground to cover before we corner anyone with charges."

She wanted the car's event data recorder and the complete navigation history. She wanted every street camera pull, toll ping, and any over-the-air updates. A clean chain of custody. Warrants if necessary. No gaps.

Hayes stepped closer, finger jabbing the air as color rose in his face. "More?" His voice elevated, hard and near. "We have their connection. We have means. We have opportunity. What more do you need?"

"Proof," Blackburn said evenly, the word precise. Her dark eyes held his. "Concrete proof that holds up in court. Proof no defense attorney can dismantle piece by piece."

Hayes turned away and took two hard steps toward Cooper. His jacket brushed the wall. He spun back to face them, his fist grazing the edge of the drywall. "The press hounds me every second. The mayor's office won't stop calling. This autonomous car nightmare has everyone terrified."

"And acting prematurely will only intensify that fire," Blackburn said, calm as she crossed her arms again. The light glided across the clean line of her sleeve. "Zhang's lawyer will dismantle this case faster than we can file paperwork if it isn't airtight."

"Do not lecture me on timing." Hayes snapped the words and slammed his palm against the wall. The faded drywall produced a flat crack. Dust shook loose. Cooper jolted despite himself, while Sinclair watched, expression reduced to essentials.

Blackburn stepped forward and closed the distance. Her movements remained contained. She stopped close enough to hold him in place with her gaze.

"You want a headline tomorrow or a conviction six months from now?" she asked softly. Her tone cut the heat momentarily. Her mouth lifted, neither smug nor mocking; certain. The old light flickered once over the glass. "You can't have both. Rushing gives us neither."

Chief Hayes stared at her, his jaw clenching and unclenching. A pulse jumped in his temple. Without a word, he spun on his heel and stormed out. His curses trailed low as he proceeded down the hall. The door shivered back into its frame behind him.

The detectives lingered. Cooper looked at Sinclair, then at Blackburn. They exchanged brief looks and departed one by one. Chair legs scraped. Footsteps faded into the corridor's cool echo. Somewhere down the line, a copier activated and clicked back to sleep. The room settled, the coffee turning cold in the cup by the monitor, the glass still preserving the ghost of their faces.

Blackburn walked to her office alone.

With the door closed, she let out a long breath and pushed a hand through her hair before taking the nearest chair. Heat from the interview dissipated in slow increments, leaving a steadier center. She opened the case log, tagged the audio, marked the time the suspect shut down. Waiting remained. She hated waiting more than noise.

Two hours crept past. A cautious knock. Willow appeared in the doorway, a quiet outline against the darker room.

"We're ready for you," she murmured, her voice barely above a whisper.

Blackburn did not look up immediately. When she did, her gaze held firm. The room measured her temperature and cooled around it.

"No one is ever ready for me," she said, her tone clean and final.

The chief's email still sat open on her screen. The phrasing was careful. The doubt was not. Do not question him again. She shifted her eyes to the notebook on the desk. Three hundred and thirty-three lines in Willow's compact hand. Neat. Precise. Almost flawless. Almost. The order had been simple. Compliance hadn't been.

Blackburn kept her voice level. "Why did you not follow my instructions?"

Willow paused, then moved a step closer, as if proximity itself might steady her. Her chest rose and fell too rapidly. One hand pinched a fold of her shirt, a small anchor.

"I did everything you asked," she said hurriedly, her voice thinning under the fear between them.

The desk lamp cast a clean circle across the blotter. Blackburn leaned into its light, the line between them narrowing. She drew the notebook closer with a slow drag. The cover was scuffed at the corners from use. Her tone remained even.

"I told you to write 'Lying to my domme is a direct violation of my submission.'" She held the silence a beat, then indicated the page with a small tilt of her chin. "That is not what you wrote."

Willow's fingers tightened around the pen until the plastic clicked. "I wrote, 'I will not neglect my duties again nor lie to the boss,'" she murmured, each word coiling tighter around her throat.

Blackburn stood. Arms folded. There was no need to raise her voice. "Are you challenging what I said, Willow?" The question was cool, weighted with threat.

A flicker moved through Willow. Heat touched her face and then receded. She kept her eyes down.

"No," she breathed, barely audible, cheeks burning. "I must have been mistaken."

The lie settled between them. Mutual, understood. Blackburn had made the rule harder than the instruction had been. Willow had chosen not to name it. The decision itself carried weight.

Blackburn let the silence expand until the room returned to ordinary sound. Outside, phones rang. Someone called out a warrant number. The printer ticked and paused. Work continued, indifferent to how any of this ended.

Willow steadied the notebook with both hands.

"Your initiative with the Zhang photo has earned you some clemency," Blackburn said at last, her mouth barely shifting. "But boldness without submission is chaos." Her finger tapped the notebook, each tap considered. "Three hundred and thirty-three lines. 'Lying to my domme is a direct violation of my submission.'"

Blackburn observed her. Willow's grip tightened until color drained from her knuckles. The Zhang image had cracked the timeline on their primary lead. A reflection in a storefront window. A glove with a stitched seam not sold locally. Willow had seen it and flagged it quickly. Correct. Useful. Not permission to deviate.

Blackburn slid her chair back. She stood and looked to the door.

"Follow me," she said without looking back. "We are not done."

Her heels counted the hallway in steady beats. The bullpen's hum pressed at their shoulders. Detectives hunched over monitors, faces washed in blue light. A courier signed the chain-of-custody sheet at the front desk. Someone laughed once and then stopped. Willow kept pace, half a step behind, silent.

Blackburn chose the single occupancy women's washroom at the end of the hall. Neutral ground. No curious eyes. Beige walls. Old LED hum. She turned the lock. It clicked and held.

The room was small. Clean enough. A mirror. A sink. A paper towel dispenser that tore along a serrated edge. The air carried a faint lemon disinfectant. Blackburn's presence filled what space remained without theatrics. She met Willow's eyes in the glass. Not a contest. An instruction held until received.

She washed her hands as if they had just left a scene. Water on. Water off. The sound was controlled and spare. She dried them slowly and folded the towel once, then again. On the counter, she set the notebook and opened it to the last page. The lines ran uniform all the way down, each sentence a small surrender.

Blackburn looked at Willow's reflection. This was not a public correction. This was course adjustment, not display. She kept her pulse out of her voice. The case board would advance if they made the right calls before the hour turned. The chief would expect a briefing the moment she stepped out.

Blackburn closed the notebook and tapped the spine once with her fingertip. Willow stood very still. The tiled room amplified small sounds. A breath. The light's thin buzz. The quiet count of a woman deciding what obedience required and what it did not.

When Blackburn finally spoke, her voice was low and weighted. Menace carried not by volume but by restraint as it moved through the quiet between them.

"You've crossed a line," she said evenly, each syllable precise. "That calls for a reminder. One you will not forget." There was no rage in her tone. Only control.

She lifted her hand with quiet care and tipped Willow's chin with her knuckles. The touch was a calculated claim.

"Here," she said, her fingertip following the shallow curve of Willow's collarbone with unhurried focus, "and here," she added, pressing beneath Willow's ear where heat pulsed against her skin. Her words wrapped velvet around steel. "You are mine to do with as I see fit."

Her voice sank lower, edged and possessive. "I own you, Willow. I always will. And you will always belong to me. Do you understand?"

Willow swallowed hard. Her breath hitched in the charged air. "Yes."

Blackburn did not pause. Her mouth found the first promised point, warm breath brushing bone before the kiss landed. "Here," she murmured, then moved to the soft place beneath the ear and sealed it again. "And here."

Her finger rested on Willow's pulse for a beat, taking the rhythm there as if counting it into memory. The room thickened around them. Willow's chest rose and fell in tight measure. Goosebumps lifted along her arms as Blackburn traced the map she had drawn with touch.

When Blackburn's hand closed around Willow's throat, the hold was firm and almost tender. It felt less like restraint and more like a given. A collar made of skin and trust. Then Blackburn took Willow's mouth. The kiss was hard and sure, purpose stated without a wasted second.

It ended at once. Blackburn pulled back as if cutting current mid-surge, leaving heat and hunger stamped on Willow's lips.

* * *

Blackburn turned and left without another word. Her heels set a confident rhythm down the corridor, the echoes hard and clean. Willow faltered, then followed, legs unsteady as if unsure they could carry what had just been placed in them. She touched her fingertips to her mouth and felt the heat Blackburn left behind. Then she pushed herself into motion.

By the time she reached the bullpen, Blackburn had already stepped into the meeting room without a glance back. Conversation thinned and fell away as heads turned, attention angling toward the evidence board across the far wall. The board read like a working map of leads assembled piece by piece. The case still unfurled, players shifting their positions, but Willow moved through the doorway altered by those few stolen minutes beyond its edge.

She slid into her chair near her laptop and steadied herself against the cool metal rim. She risked a glance through lowered lashes. Blackburn stood at the front of the room, calm and magnetic, a point the room leaned toward.

The evidence board was a patchwork of fragments, each tile carrying its own fact. At the center, a photograph of Jenna held a quiet light, hazel eyes alive with unspoken plans, unaware of what waited. To the left loomed the scorched frame of an autonomous car, once sleek, now reduced to a skeletal silhouette of soot and warped steel. Below it, a glossy studio portrait of a Raider Straight Line gleamed with untouched promise, its silver polished and sterile beneath controlled light. A thick safety manual hung beneath like a command no one had heeded.

Across the board, surveillance stills froze Jenna's final movements. In one, she walked a crowded street, hair lifted by a wind the camera could not hold. In another, the Raider Straight Line cut through pre-dawn dark, its headlights carving pale corridors out of the gloom.

A second board carried time itself. A line of small photos ran alongside notes in urgent ink; the dates stacked like ribs. Next to it, printouts of data logs spilled over their pins, edges curled, their dense columns of jargon legible only to those who knew how to read them. The final board held witness statements in spare bullet points, tidy lines set against the disorder they described.

* * *

Blackburn stood rigid before it all, gaze honed and cutting. Silence settled because she willed it. Even the hum of ventilation receded. Around her, the team's restless energy leaked through tapping fingers and jittering feet, but no one spoke.

Her mouth flattened into a thin line. Without looking away from the board, she tilted her head toward Reeves. "Quick work," she said at last, her voice smooth and heavy with authority. "Walk me through it."

Reeves straightened. "We secured the gaming logs and the home surveillance," he said, then gestured toward Willow. "She isolated what matters."

Willow's voice came clear and steady. "I want to start with a few anomalies in the video," she said, simply and firmly, confidence threaded through the quiet. Chairs creaked as attention shifted. She stood, the edge of her palm brushing the cool lid of her laptop as she rose.

She took off her glasses and wiped the lenses on the hem of her shirt. The familiar motion steadied her breath. She slid them back on and stepped close to the screenshots pinned to the corkboard. The paper edges lifted where the pushpins bit in.

Willow traced the silhouette of the car on the grainy printout, fingertip following the hazed outline. "Here," she said, her voice settling. "The car is parked in the driveway at an angle that hides the front from view. The bushes here block visibility almost entirely." She paused, eyes narrowing at the obstruction. "It could be deliberate, like someone was trying to avoid being seen."

Her gaze moved to Blackburn. Blackburn nodded once and gave a slow wink. It was enough. Willow let a tight smile show and continued.

"I combed through footage starting at four in the morning," Willow said, bringing up the timeline on the screen. "No movement until the engine turns over."

Sinclair leaned toward the table, voice testing the space. "Could it have been started remotely?"

"And?" Blackburn pressed, tone sharp enough to bite.

"And." Sinclair faltered for a heartbeat and then steadied. "That might mean the headlights could have blinded the camera when someone got inside. You wouldn't see the interior lights turn on."

Blackburn's mouth flattened. She did not do maybes. "Does that happen? Do we have footage of the camera being blinded?" Her words were clipped, direct.

Willow met her gaze. "No," she replied, shaking her head once. "There's nothing like that. The headlights stay off until the engine starts. All we get is a flicker across the frame when it happens."

She pivoted to the monitor and called up a second angle. Her fingers moved with clean economy across the keys. The new frame filled the display. The monitor's hum undercut the room. "This one is from another angle," she said, pointing at an indistinct shadow behind glass just before the car inched forward. "It's subtle, but there might be someone in the driver's seat."

She rolled the clip. The feed stuttered, then held. Timestamps ticked in pale digital numbers. Exposure juddered and steadied. The room quieted. Faces picked up the cold wash of the screen as eyes tracked her hand through the frames.

The detectives leaned in. The shadow behind the tinted glass stayed stubborn, uncooperative. The room tightened by inches, a quiet that belonged to concentration. Stale coffee, old paper, and the dry tang of electronics filled the air. Nothing else competed.

"Can you sharpen it any more?" Cooper asked, tone even but threaded with urgency.

Reeves eased back in his chair and crossed his arms. "We have run every filter we have," he replied, voice flat with finality. "Whoever or whatever is in that car wasn't moving for hours. Maybe some dumb kid messing around, poking buttons until they got the thing running. But let's be real, not even an idiot would hang out failing for that long."

Blackburn let out a short sound that passed for a laugh. "No movement inside the vehicle. No one climbing in. No lights flickering on. Nothing to suggest anyone sitting there waiting."

Cooper's fingers tapped a slow beat on the table. He did not look away from the screen. "What if it's James himself? Say he drove home drunk and did not make it past the driveway, passed out behind the wheel. Maybe he did not want anyone knowing he had been drinking."

Reeves tipped his chair farther back. A thin smile. "A multimillionaire crashing in his own car? Please. The guy has staff willing to carry him to bed if he yawns too hard."

Cooper turned toward him, jaw set. "Money doesn't change everything," he said, defensive heat in his tone. "When I used to drink, I would pass out in my car all the time. Sometimes you just do not make it inside."

Reeves shrugged and pointed his chin at the screen. "There's no evidence James is a drinker, let alone enough to get wasted in his own driveway," he said, gesturing at the footage like it held answers only he could see. "His social media shows him champagne-toasting at black-tie events, not pounding cheap whiskey at a corner dive."

"Champagne can get you drunk too," Cooper retorted. "Maybe he had too much of the high-end stuff and did not make it past the driveway."

"Or maybe," Reeves said, tone slick with sarcasm, "instead of spinning out wild theories, we focus on actual evidence."

Blackburn raised a hand. The room cut off mid-breath. "Gentlemen." Her voice sliced through the tension. She scanned the table with contained impatience. "Let's recap. A drunk millionaire snoozes in his car, wakes up, drives off, hits a woman, gets out undetected, and somehow leaves behind a blazing wreck. Any other brilliant ideas? Aliens teaming up with Sasquatch to settle old scores with Jenna?"

Willow advanced the video one frame. The flicker turned into a thin band of light along chrome and was gone. She marked the time-code with a neat note. She circled angles where hedges obstructed the view and recorded heights and distances. Procedure made the air breathable.

Cooper stopped tapping. Reeves let his chair legs meet the floor with a soft thud. Sinclair studied the keyboard as if it might help.

The temperature in the room felt different. Dawson's face flushed red. He had been quiet too long. His palm hit the table with a sharp crack that bounced off the walls. Several heads snapped toward him. Then the room went still again.

"This is ridiculous," he barked, his voice cutting through the sterile room. LED lights buzzed above them, cold air pressing against skin. "What does it matter if he's drunk? It doesn't change a damn thing."

Blackburn's gaze snapped to Dawson. Her expression emptied out, controlled to a fine edge. "Watch your tone," she said, voice low enough to settle the room. "You're not assigned to this case. You're here because I allow it."

Cooper cleared his throat, the sound soft against the hum of the vents. His eyes moved between them. "Apologies," he said carefully. "We let things get out of hand."

Dawson snorted, holding his anger tight. "This whole thing is a waste of time. Just arrest the guy and let him prove himself innocent in court."

Reeves leaned in, jaw set. "That isn't how justice works," he said evenly. Case files lay open in front of him, photos clipped to a report that still needed signatures and a charging decision.

Sinclair shifted in his seat, eager to pivot. "What if James Zhang is angling for money? Think about it. Arrested but innocent. He sues for defamation later. Loss of reputation equals financial payout."

"Are you suggesting he murdered someone to orchestrate his own arrest, manipulate a jury into acquitting him, and then sue for damages?" Blackburn asked. Her tone remained flat; disbelief carried the edge.

Cooper leaned back, palms up. "Admittedly, it sounds worse when you say it out loud," he said. The attempt at a smile died before it formed.

Reeves tapped his pen against the table, mind already on the vehicle sheet. The click punctuated his words. "Or what if he tampered with the car? Made it look like a malfunction to score a massive settlement from the Stan Raider Group."

Dawson flushed and slapped the table once. The sound cracked through the room. "This is insane," he said, louder than necessary. "You are all just making crap up now. What if it was a malfunction? Or someone hacked its system?"

Willow pushed her glasses up. Her fingers steadied only after a breath. "Hacking is nearly impossible," she said, pointing to the spreadsheet taped to the board. "I checked for any signs of GPS jamming in the area. There was nothing."

Blackburn took in the room, then settled back on Dawson. "Dawson," she said, each word restrained, "that theory holds no water. The car was too damaged to recover usable data."

Sinclair nodded fast, seizing the lane. "Exactly. We stick to what we have. The owner's motive is the clearest lead right now."

"He has no motive," Dawson said through his teeth. He gripped the edge of the table until his knuckles went pale. Muscles jumped in his jaw.

"Wait," he said, refusing to yield the floor. "What if this was sabotage? A rival company trying to discredit autonomous vehicles by staging something high-profile?"

Blackburn looked at him, unimpressed. "Corporate sabotage of a gaming CEO by hacking his car and not his game?" Her voice turned dry. It cooled further. "You're proposing that without a sliver of evidence. That isn't just far-fetched. It's ridiculous."

The room held its breath for a beat. Pages rustled. The wall clock ticked. Coffee went cold in a paper cup near the case binder.

Dawson stared back, eyes bright with irritation. "You're all too quick to back your own crazy theories and dismiss mine," he said. Spit caught the light as he leaned in. "There is always more beneath the surface."

Blackburn did not rise to it. "You're letting paranoia cloud your judgment. We need evidence, not conjecture. Stick to what we can prove."

Dawson shook his head. His voice jumped and caught. "My imagination? You're the one throwing out bullshit about Sasquatches and aliens."

"Enough," Blackburn said. The word was plain and final.

The chair scraped across the tile as Dawson stood. Heat rose off him in waves. "You are always undermining me!" he bellowed, the sound bouncing off the glass walls. His fists curled. He leaned over the table. "Every goddamn time!"

Blackburn tilted her head, the movement slight. Her mouth tightened into a smile that did not reach her eyes. She chose the angle of attack and took it. "Maybe if you had anything worthwhile to contribute, anything at all, you wouldn't feel so threatened." Her next words dripped with disdain, soft but razor-sharp. "Save your tantrums for something within your expertise, like figuring out how long that coffee pot has been sitting there."

The hit landed. Dawson lunged. No warning. Papers lifted and skittered. His chair slammed the floor. The tendons in his neck stood out, his face set hard. "You fucking—"

Sinclair and Cooper were already moving. Years of control tactics clicked in. Cooper took Dawson's right wrist and turned it down. Sinclair secured the left and stepped to the outside, weight low. They braced and pulled him off the table edge, shifting his balance without causing injury. Dawson fought the hold, breath rasping, spitting words that broke apart in the noise. His shoes slid on the polish as they walked him back toward open space by the wall.

Willow's notebook slipped from her hand and knocked softly against the floor. She froze, eyes on Blackburn. Reeves moved to Blackburn and set himself between her and the threat. One step. Shoulders square.

Dawson fought hard.

Chairs squealed. Voices overlapped. The room tightened, then held. Cooper and Sinclair adjusted their grips and kept Dawson contained, inch by inch. Blackburn did not move. She watched Dawson as if gauging a storm line, face composed and unreadable.

"Let me go!" Dawson bellowed, his voice fraying at the edges with raw fury.

"Stand down!" Sinclair barked, straining to maintain his grip on the thrashing detective.

Cooper's sharp voice sliced through the chaos. "Cool down, dude!"

Blackburn's posture did not change. A hint of humor touched her mouth, quick and cold. She tested the line again. "Is that all you have got, Dawson?" Her tone was light, almost lazy, but each word carried a razor's edge. "Flailing about like a child denied his candy? No wonder your solve rate is an embarrassment."

Color climbed Dawson's face. The veins at his temples beat hard. He snapped toward her with whatever he could find. "You bitch! You think you're untouchable? You're nothing but a—"

"Enough." Blackburn's voice sliced the air cleanly, its chill freezing every movement in the room save for Dawson's trembling outrage. "One more word out of your mouth, Detective," she warned, her gaze piercing through him like a scalpel, "and you will find yourself suspended before you can blink."

He kept fighting the line. Spit flecked his lip. "Bitch!" The rest turned to noise. Sinclair shifted his grip to a shoulder tie. Cooper dropped his weight and anchored the wrist. White knuckles. Controlled pressure. Dawson's boots squeaked as they edged him farther from the table.

Blackburn's eyes hardened. The call was made. "That is it," she announced coolly, her words clipped and decisive. "Go home, Dawson. You are done here. I will be reporting this directly to Chief Hayes."

She held his stare for a beat. Enough to register consequence. Then she turned and left the room. Her stride was even.

Behind her, Dawson's shouts carried into the corridor and thinned. Sinclair and Cooper kept him in the corner until his breathing dropped a gear. Reeves stayed with Blackburn's chair, staring. Willow picked up her notebook, mouth agape, and shook her head.

Chapter 13

The meeting room kept its air refrigerated. Down the corridor, Blackburn's heels clicked a steady count toward the door. Dawson hunched at the sleek table, throat scraped raw from shouting, shirt wrinkled where Sinclair and Cooper had pinned him. His arms still remembered the press of their hands. The LEDs hummed at a thin pitch. He held his fists on the polished surface until the blood left his knuckles. The rage that had burst out of him.

He tracked Sinclair, Reeves, and Cooper with restless eyes. They traded quick looks and kept their voices low. Willow glanced over once, briefly. The air ran tight. Recycled cold clung to his collar. A vein beat at his temple, a count he could not slow. The room felt smaller than it had a minute ago.

"You think I don't see it?" Dawson's voice cut the quiet. It trembled but held. "You're always whispering behind my back," he snarled. A fleck of spit caught the light, then nothing but the compressor's thrum and the scrape of a chair leg.

His fist hit the table hard. Coffee cups rattled. Pens jumped and rolled. The sound carried and then died in the vents.

Sinclair's flinch was small. He met Dawson's eyes and kept them there. Cooper did not move. Jaw set. Gaze flat. Reeves sat down and crossed his arms, relaxed in his posture, alert in his eyes. He offered almost nothing, then a thin smile as if to let gravity do its work.

Time stalled. No one gave ground. No one said the thing that would push it past the point of return.

The chair creaked when Dawson let himself fall back into it. His chest rose and fell unevenly. Sweat gathered at his temples and ran to his jaw. He raked a shaking hand through his hair and made it worse. He tasted salt and the metallic edge of a throat gone raw.

Blackburn was not in the room, yet she occupied it. Dawson felt the static of her approach and the control she liked to keep. He had seen how she ran a case chart, how she stood near the door and waited until silence did the work. The thought iced his skin.

"She's behind this," Dawson said, low and tight. The words held. He looked from face to face, hunting for a tell, any sign of collusion. "Blackburn always has it out for me," he spat. "Hell, I wouldn't put it past her to kill someone just to mess with us."

Sinclair shifted, suit seams pulling at the shoulders as he leaned forward an inch. He kept his voice even.

"Let's not say things we'll regret later," he said.

Dawson cut him off.

"Spare me," he snapped. The edge in it was raw. "You don't get it. You can't get it. The cases keep piling up around me like rubble, and where is everyone? Nowhere. I'm drowning here while you all sit back and watch."

Cooper's jaw ticked. He leaned in, eyes narrowing.

"Cut the self-pity," he said, voice low. "We're all dealing with our own shit. I'm tired of hearing you pretend you're the only one who's suffering."

"We shouldn't be suffering!" Dawson screamed. "It's her! She's toxic. Guys?" He held his hands out to Sinclair first, then Cooper, and then Reeves.

"Blackburn," Dawson said again, quieter and harder. "She's behind all of this. Pulling strings just to watch me unravel. To humiliate me." He fixed on Willow. She sat near the end, notebook tight to her chest. She had stayed clear of the crossfire. The edge of the paper marked a line in her palm. He looked to her for a verdict he could live with. "You understand, don't you? What it feels like to be humiliated?"

Willow adjusted her glasses and looked away. Her breath caught. She tightened her hold on the laptop, its warmth steady against her forearms. The memory of writing so many lines surfaced like a bruise just under the skin. No reason given. The lesson had been humiliation.

"Leave her out of it," Reeves said. At the edge of the table, he leaned in with quiet authority. The overhead lights carved tired lines into his face. His voice remained even. "Dawson," he said gently, "you're out of line. Blackburn isn't like that. She's tough, that much is true, but orchestrate this? Or kill someone? No way."

"She absolutely would not," Cooper shot back. He sat up, shoulders set, jaw tight. His voice cut clean. "You've got it wrong. Blackburn's trying to help you. You're too wrapped up in your own paranoia to see it."

A chair scraped. Dawson stood fast, eyes gone hard. "Fuck all of you!" he shouted. The room held still after the echo. He left. The door slammed into the frame and the framed commendations rattled against the wall. He returned long enough to snatch his blazer, spat near the table, then disappeared.

The detectives exchanged a look and released the same tired breath. Routine. They broke apart and returned to their desks. His mood lingered behind, a film clinging to the air.

Willow remained where she was a few seconds longer. She closed the laptop and tucked it under her arm. She said nothing. Then she moved. The basement lab would be quiet.

Down the stairs, away from raised voices. Concrete underfoot. The smell of dust and cold metal. Evidence racks, humming servers, softer light. The temperature dropped a few degrees and steadied her as she went below.

* * *

The sun came through the blinds in Hayes's office and drew hard lines across the room. Heat pressed at the glass. Blackburn leaned against the desk, composed, still. Leather creaked when Hayes shifted. The light caught on his scalp. His mustache twitched, a warning that he was already done with the day.

"Sir," Blackburn began, her voice smooth, each syllable considered, "we need to address Dawson's latest outburst." She let the words settle.

Chief Hayes exhaled, leaning forward. The chair protested again as he brought his clasped hands onto the desk. "What now?" he asked, his tone edged with weariness.

Blackburn kept her face still. "It happened in the meeting room not long ago," she said. "I left to take a call in my office, and while I was gone, he exploded. Accused other detectives of ganging up on him." She paused, the hesitation almost imperceptible, then continued. "He even suggested I orchestrated some sort of conspiracy. Went so far as to accuse me of having Jenna Langston killed just to, in his words, mess with him." Her tone remained even. "His behavior has been unraveling for weeks."

Chief Hayes's eyes hardened. The skin around them pulled tight. "He said you killed her?"

Blackburn shifted just enough to re-center the exchange. "Yes, sir." The last word landed as intended.

Commendations glinted behind Hayes in neat rows. The room felt close. Dawson's accusation had found its way in and sat between them.

"He's a liability," Blackburn added after a beat, tone limited but resolute. "His paranoia is escalating. He's lashing out at colleagues and missing deadlines. Last week he lost control during an interrogation and nearly wrecked it entirely. And there's Malone. He faked evidence for that extradition order, and he manipulated you into signing it."

Color drained from Hayes's face. His fingers tapped the desk, tap tap tap without rhythm. "Christ," he muttered under his breath. "If

Dawson starts flapping about that extradition order..." He loosened his collar. Sweat shined at his temple. "We should have handled this sooner."

Blackburn remained where she was, composed, hands light against her arms. "And who do you think will listen to Dawson right now?" she asked, voice smooth as glass. She tilted her head a fraction. "You have seen him lately. Paranoid. Unstable. The squad is already watching him come apart."

"Doesn't matter," he muttered, tension tight in his voice. "Even a madman can cause damage if he talks to people who will listen. What if he tells someone I did not check the paperwork? What if he does?"

"Sir." Blackburn's voice cut through his tirade, low and steady, control held tight. "I never saw you sign it. It's just Dawson claiming you did. If it comes up, we deal with it then." She leaned back against the desk, palm on polished wood, posture relaxed by design. "Right now, it's noise. Dawson has not said a word, and be honest, who would believe him? You are the chief. Decades of clean service don't crumble over one allegation."

Hayes stopped pacing. He pressed his fingers into his temples as if he could knead the headache out. "You don't get it, Blackburn," he said, the years evident in his tone. "People don't remember decades of good work. They remember the screw-ups. And when those stick, they erase everything else." He shook his head once, a dry scrape of breath in his throat.

"It won't stick," Blackburn said softly, calm threaded with resolve. "Not unless we let it. Dawson is flailing. It's bluster. He's not stupid enough to set himself on fire just to scorch you." Her gaze held steady as she continued. "He knows the cost. Pension gone. Benefits gone. If he overplays this, he loses everything."

Hayes turned toward her, skepticism shadowing his features. "And what if he doesn't care?" His voice was quieter now but no less tight. "What if burning everything down is exactly what he wants?"

Blackburn tilted her head and shrugged, composed and unruffled. "Then we deal with it when the flames start," she replied evenly. "Right now you have bigger problems to tackle, like keeping the mayor off your back while I get us what we need. A damn arrest."

Hayes exhaled through his nose and sank into his chair. He studied her for a moment, eyes narrowing against the lines of light cut by the blinds. When he spoke again, his voice carried resignation more than resolve. "You always make it sound so simple."

"That's why you brought me in." Blackburn pushed off the desk with easy control. The smallest smirk touched her mouth, confidence held close. "Let me clean up this mess while you handle the politics." She paused and met his eyes with steady focus. "My name will come up in this. I trust you will keep me covered."

Hayes hesitated before he nodded. "Fine," he muttered, gruff, unease still lingering in his expression. "But if this blows up..."

"If it does," Blackburn interrupted smoothly, tone firm yet restrained as she moved toward the door, "I'll handle it, just like always." She glanced back over her shoulder, spare and direct. "We can't let our guard down."

The office air felt heavy. The fan hummed, dull and constant, and the clock ticked slow on the wood-paneled wall. Dust hung in the thin bands of light. The smell of old coffee lingered with furniture polish and paper.

Blackburn sat across from Chief Hayes, composed and in control. Sunlight filtered through half-drawn blinds and striped the room in pale lines that broke across his desk.

"I'm concerned about the team, sir," Blackburn began with an undercurrent. "Morale is already fragile, and Dawson's outbursts are fracturing it further. He's juggling three open cases. I have had to pull others in to compensate for his lapses." She let it settle. "If this continues, it could jeopardize our investigations."

Her expression softened a fraction, calculated and contained, as she leaned forward. Her fingers rested lightly on her knee, stillness held on purpose. "I've already sent Dawson home. He needed space to cool off."

The clock kept time in the quiet. Hayes's mustache twitched, a tell she watched for. A faint red rose in his cheeks as he absorbed the cracks in his department. He nodded slowly and leaned back in his chair; the leather answered with a small creak that sounded like a decision made.

"Good call," he said finally. "We can't let him spiral any further." His gaze dropped to the desk, skimming the polished surface for answers that weren't there. The light caught in the grain. "Mental health is paramount in this line of work. We have lost too many good officers to burnout."

"Completely agree," Blackburn replied, professionalism threaded through restraint. She straightened, presence contained but unmistakable. "This job demands more than most people can handle long term."

Hayes's fingers drummed a brief cadence on the desk, a crisp tap that marked his thinking. He spoke as the rhythm stopped. "First thing tomorrow, I'll meet with Dawson directly." His eyes lifted to meet hers, set with purpose. "We need to tackle this head-on. Counseling, reassignment, whatever gets him back on track."

Blackburn nodded once, then pressed. "I recommend involving HR immediately," she said, firm without crowding his authority. "Out of caution, for him and for us, consider placing him on leave while ensuring he gets proper help." Her gaze held on Hayes while she laid it out.

Hayes regarded her for a moment before he inclined his head. "You're right." His voice lowered with weight, acknowledging the stakes. "Thank you for bringing this to my attention." He cleared his throat and smoothed a hand across the edge of the desk, the movement small but final. His tone stayed resolute, edged with gratitude.

"We can't afford to lose good detectives like Dawson, but compromising investigations isn't an option either."

"Of course not," Blackburn said, her voice even, warmth smoothing the room without ceding control. She eased back into her chair, allowing the strain of the briefing to bleed off in slow degrees.

"I'm only doing what's best for the team," she said.

The statement settled between them. Hayes turned toward his desk, lamplight skating over stacked files as he began to chart next steps. The wall clock kept a steady tick behind them, unhurried and precise.

Blackburn rose. The carpet muted her steps. She closed the door on her way out. The latch caught with a quiet click. A restrained smile touched her mouth. Satisfaction moved through her like a cooled current. The board sat where she wanted it. Day shift edged toward evening, and she had one more piece to place.

She headed for the elevator. The corridor smelled faintly of toner and stale coffee. In the mirrored doors she caught her own calm reflection before the panels slid apart. The car hummed on its descent, numbers winking down. Metal and chilled air surrounded her. She knew exactly where to find her next target.

The basement offices waited, low-ceilinged and LED bright, where Willow would be closing out her shift.

Chapter 14

The basement hallway was bare and utilitarian, a stark contrast from the polished corridors upstairs where career-altering mistakes had just been made. Cold LEDs flickered in patches, creating hard shadows across bare concrete. The air smelled of dust and recycled chill. Willow's footsteps echoed in the emptiness. Thud, thud. Each dull impact fell out of rhythm with her pulse.

Her fingers trembled as she found the keys at her side, their metallic jangle loud against the quiet. Dawson's voice threaded through her thoughts, fragments of his tirade replaying on a loop, etched into memory. Each word tightened her chest and dried her mouth.

She pushed open the office door and stopped mid-step. Her breath caught. Detective Blackburn stood at the room's center, her presence controlled and unmistakable. The glow from the monitors cut planes across her face, sharp and precise. LED light from above framed her in stark contrast, tension contained rather than displayed. The hum of electronics thinned the silence to a fine wire.

"You certainly took your time getting here," Blackburn said. Her tone was low, edged with amusement. A smile curved on her lips, neither gentle nor kind. It belonged to someone who played with fire because they could.

Willow's pulse quickened. Heat rose as anger steadied the initial shock. She lifted the thin spiral-bound notebook like a shield, its childish cover jarring against her simmering frustration. "I needed this. Something new for the updated lines," she said, defiance trembling in her voice. "Why are you here? I have work to do."

Blackburn raised one brow, unbothered by the tone or the flare in Willow's eyes. If anything, she looked entertained. "Relax," she said smoothly, as though daring Willow to do anything else. "I'm here to go over some surveillance footage with you. There are a few things I need clarified."

Willow slammed the notebook onto her desk with more force than intended. The sound cracked through the room like a gunshot. Its weight stayed with her as if it had landed on something more fragile than wood, a warning she could not quite name but felt, nonetheless. Her fingers jabbed the power button on her desktop with careful aggression. The machine groaned to life. The login screen blinked up, then the camera index, timestamps lining the monitor in neat rows. A startup hum filled the tense air between them like static awaiting discharge.

"That doesn't give you the right to barge into my space," Willow muttered. There was no conviction in it. Reflex, not rule, against Blackburn's dominance.

Blackburn tipped her head a fraction, silent. The computer's whine climbed until it felt like a third presence in the room.

"Oh, come on," Blackburn said, her voice a sinuous thread winding through the charged air, a low purr that sent a small shiver down

Willow's spine. "I've been so deep in your spaces I could map them blindfolded." From the pocket of her tailored jacket, she drew an object that caught the room's flat light. A plastic gold pen, its polished surface gleaming with a cheap, inviting charm. "I even brought you a peace offering."

Willow turned. Her eyes narrowed at the pen, its shimmer a small lure set just beyond casual reach. Something coiled under her sternum, desire and unease knotted tight together. The gift unsettled her. Blackburn did not bring peace. She set terms, then noted who fell in line.

"A gift," Blackburn murmured, her smile caught in the dim office. "To help you write your stories." Honey laid over steel.

With care, she set the pen on the desk between them. Her fingers grazed it an instant too long before retreating. The gesture hovered like a challenge or a promise. She nudged the door shut with her toe. The latch clicked with quiet finality. The air drew in around them. Silence thickened until it felt tangible. Each heartbeat sounded larger than it should.

Blackburn dragged a chair closer to Willow's desk. Metal legs screeched against concrete, a scrape that grated across Willow's nerves like ground glass. Every move landed on purpose. Each inch taken. Blackburn slid into the space beside her. Their shoulders brushed. Heat pooled where they touched.

Blackburn leaned in and pressed a kiss to Willow's cheek. Soft, possessive, precise. It lingered just long enough to mark proximity and control. When Blackburn pulled back, Willow's gaze slid to the pen on the scuffed desk. A knot cinched tight in her chest. Something about it felt wrong.

She focused on faint branding etched into the barrel. Coconut Glass Candles. A frivolous name she knew from an artisan shop near Jenna's crime scene. The plastic caught the light and revealed a thin smear of wax along its surface. It glinted like a residue from other hands. A pale sweetness rose from it, coconut and paraffin, almost imagined and yet there. Secrets clung to its innocent sheen, restless and alive under the gloss.

Willow lifted the pen into the light. Her fingers trembled once and steadied. The residue at the tip caught and shone, a thin skin of tacky shine. "Why, why is there wax on this?" Her voice remained thin but steady enough to carry.

Blackburn watched her, face contained and unreadable. The room hummed with low electricity, a quiet that allowed the question to sit between them while Willow tried to make the pieces align.

"It is exactly what you think," Blackburn said at last. Her tone was even, without apology. "There is a woman who owns a candle shop. She keeps these at the counter. I guess that one was used." She observed the small shifts in Willow's expression, tracking what landed and what did not.

Willow tapped the pen against her notebook. Quick. Precise. The crisp beat steadied her more than it shook her.

"She owns a shop near the hit and run," Blackburn said, as if logging an update. "She makes candles for wax play, you know. Special blends that melt at lower temperatures. Very nice work." The words were clinical in content, charged in effect.

The tapping stopped. Willow searched Blackburn's face for a softer read and found none. The curve at Blackburn's mouth was small and sharp, a tell that could pass for a smile.

"I, I do not." Willow tightened her grip on the pen until the plastic clicked. "I'm not into fire. It's dangerous."

Blackburn stepped closer to the desk. She set one palm flat on the surface and leaned in just enough to claim space without crowding it. The move conveyed control more than comfort.

"Do not worry," she said, voice lowered. "I would never let you near an open flame." She left the words there. A beat. "But Kendria. Now she is another story."

Willow's breath caught and went shallow. Her hand did not move. "Kendria?" The word rasped.

Blackburn smoothed her cuff with two fingers and did not hurry. "Dinner tonight," she said, calm and decided. "Kendria is curious. Adventurous. Absolutely stunning. Those eyes, sharp as glass. Thought she might shatter with a touch of heat." She glanced at Willow. The smile returned, quick and cleanly. "But you. You aren't ready for that, are you?"

Color rose in Willow's cheeks. She shook her head. "No. I'm not."

Blackburn tilted her head and weighed the answer like any other data point. "I thought as much," she said. The edge eased a fraction. "And it is fine, Willow. Really. You don't have to be brave all the time." Two taps on the desk closed the topic with a small sound.

"Besides," she added, thoughtfully, "Kendria. I think she enjoys a little burn."

The brief smile that followed tightened Willow's stomach, anyway. Blackburn let it fade and shifted back into work.

"All right then," she said. The pivot was clean. "Let's focus on the security video instead. Any chance someone else was in that car for hours before it left?"

"No." Willow set the pen down and faced the monitor. Her hands found the keys with familiar economy. Cold light washed her face.

Blackburn took the chair beside her and folded her arms. She focused on the paused frame. No commentary, just intake.

"It starts here," Willow said. She scrubbed back until the time stamp slid into view and pressed play. "Twelve thirty-two in the morning. James Zhang arrives." Her cadence followed the footage.

A car slid under a porch light. The sensor tripped and poured a pallid wash over the driveway. Hedges blocked the far side. The engine settled into a soft tick as the vehicle eased in and stopped.

"There," Willow said. She pointed as the driver's door opened and the cabin light came up. James Zhang got out, keys in hand.

"See?" Her tone stayed contained, excitement checked. She marked it anyway. "He exits here, locks up. Watch for yourself." The headlights double-blinked, and James moved toward the door while the light threw him in and out of shadow.

The monitor cast a cool rectangle of light across Willow's face. The hum of the CPU under the desk filled the small room, steady as a metronome. Her fingers moved over the keyboard with quiet certainty; each click sounded clean and deliberate.

"It's motion-activated," she said, voice even. "The porch light comes on when someone pulls into the driveway or walks past the sensor. After that, it stays off for the rest of the night."

Blackburn stood beside her, arms crossed, gaze fixed on the screen. The pale glow sharpened the lines of her face. Her brow ticked up a fraction. "And the car?"

Willow scrolled the timeline back. The time stamp rolled to 5:54 AM with crisp jumps. Outside, dawn thinned the darkness to a flat gray. Headlights cut through it, hard and white. A vehicle eased out of the driveway, backed into the street, and slid into the darker strip of trees beyond.

"There," Willow said, stopping the frame. "If anyone had gone near the car before it left, the light would have tripped. It did when he got out of the car." Her focus remained on the controls. "This shows no one entered that vehicle from the moment he parked it until it drove away."

Blackburn straightened, face composed; her attention held the image precisely. "Which means," she said, low and sure, "the car was operating autonomously when it left."

Willow nodded once. "Exactly. And if it was programmed to leave without him..." She let the quiet complete her thought.

Blackburn's mouth curved, small and contained. "Then we're one step closer to proving that Zhang was just an unlucky bystander."

Willow glanced at her. Curiosity edged past caution. "Is that why you let everyone in the meeting spin their wheels with theories?"

Blackburn's answer came clipped. "It wasn't time to steer them."

Willow shifted in her chair, the vinyl creaking as she moved. "Do you think this is enough to clear James?"

"Not yet," Blackburn said. She stepped back into the dim, as if distance helped her see the whole board. "It's part of the puzzle, but not all of it." Her eyes cut to Willow, then back to the frozen frame. "We need his gaming logs analyzed. If he was playing at 5:54 AM, if there's no sign he left his home during that window, then we can start clearing him."

Willow's fingers tapped a brief rhythm against the keys, more purpose than nerves. "I've checked the gaming logs," she said, steady again. "They're recorded in five-minute increments. At 5:50, he was playing. At 5:55, same thing. It's definitely him. We can confirm it through the chat convers—"

The door banged open, the strike plate catching with a sharp crack that halted her mid-word. Chief Hayes filled the frame. His face was flushed, collar too tight for his thick neck. He brought the smell of damp wool and hallway air with him.

Blackburn turned in her chair without hurry. "Chief," she said, calm threaded with steel. "What brings you to our doorstep this time?"

Hayes's gaze slid between Blackburn and Willow. Suspicion. A trace of worry. He shifted his weight, half in and half out, then started to retreat like a man who realized he had stepped somewhere he shouldn't. Blackburn stopped him with a single word.

"Wait."

She rose, smooth and controlled and closed the space by a calculated step. Close enough to claim it; not enough to cross it. Her voice dropped. "Why is it," she asked, almost conversational, "that you always show up angry when we are alone? I'm starting to sense a pattern here."

Hayes flinched. His eyes tracked anywhere but her face. The floor, the blinds, the wall clock with its faint tick. "I, uh, I got a call," he said. "Someone said, well, there was... something going on in here."

Blackburn let a quiet laugh out on the exhale. "Oh, chief," she said, mild on the surface. "The only thing going on here is my job. Willow and I are reviewing surveillance footage for the Zhang hit-and-run case." She tipped her head, studying him the way she studied a problem. "And guess what? The footage shows he didn't drive away after all." Her mouth curved, pleasant enough to pass. "Surely that's no cause for alarm?"

Hayes's color deepened. He tugged at his collar without effect, the fabric refusing to give. "From now on," he said after clearing his throat, the command rough around the edges, "leave the door open when you're in here."

"Chief," she said, unhurried. "The door was closed for a reason."

Willow remained at her desk, eyes fixed on the monitor. The cursor sat motionless. Screen light illuminated the side of her face. A faint flush climbed her ears. She didn't look up when Blackburn spoke. Her shoulders remained just a little too tight.

"Why was the door closed?" he asked.

Blackburn straightened her back but lowered her head. As if addressing a child. "Chief."

Chief Hayes's face softened, guilt settling in the room. The hallway's noise diminished at the threshold. Blackburn observed the shift and seized it.

"I can't leave the door open, chief," she said, voice level. "It compromises the investigation. Confidential content. We both remember the cleaners who walked in once without a knock."

She leaned a shoulder against the frame, posture relaxed, eyes steady. "I've got a better option. Move Willow upstairs to homicide. Let everyone see us work. No rumors. No side chatter. Full transparency."

Hayes shifted. His mustache twitched. He kept his eyes on the floor, on a scuff in the tile. The air carried faint traces of burned coffee. "That won't be necessary," he said, voice thin under the pressure in the room.

Blackburn stepped into the hesitation. "You know, chief," she said, light on the surface, controlled underneath. "What makes someone keep tabs on me? Call you about things that haven't even happened?"

He glanced up. A furrow, then retreat. "I don't think it's personal," he said, but without conviction.

"I do," she said, mild. She held his gaze. "You won't tell me who it is. I can only guess at the angle."

She released a small breath, nothing that registered as humor. "I've had Sinclair tracking my movements and Dawson calling me a murderer." Her voice lowered. "Chief, I've been nothing but honest with you. About everything, even Jenna."

"Sinclair?"

"You'll hear from him before the end of day."

She allowed the words to linger. The HVAC hummed. Willow's keyboard remained silent. Then she pressed the point carefully. "Someone's running at me from the side, and you're stuck with the fallout. Maybe they're setting up an HR complaint. Failure to act. Noise now, paper later. Truth optional."

Her tone cooled. "Maybe they want a clean payout off the department. Say you didn't address harassment and let it stand. Let that hang for a day and they're in position."

She paused, letting silence complete her argument. Footsteps passed in the hall and faded. Blackburn moved closer by a fraction, the proximity pointed, not warm. "Have you considered something larger? Someone trying to move you off the board? Build enough HR paper, get your name in the wrong file, watch the pressure build until you step aside." Her voice dropped to a quiet aside. "Ambition uses convenient tools."

She gave him time to consider. She watched doubt appear, then take hold.

"No," he said finally, but without conviction. "He's a nobody."

"Nobodies report to somebodies, chief," she said. "Bottom feeds up. That is the point."

Her eyes moved to the door, then back to him. "Chief, take a beat. Review your options. Let this settle. Meanwhile, Willow and I need uninterrupted access to this footage." She straightened. "With the door closed, for the integrity of the investigation."

Hayes remained still. His shoulders tensed. His hands trembled, then stopped. He nodded once.

"Alright," he said. He stepped out and pulled the door until the latch clicked.

As soon as the door closed, Blackburn let her composed exterior fall. The shift was stark. She crossed to Willow and sat beside her. Blackburn cupped Willow's face in both hands. Her palms were warm. The pressure was firm, contained. A quiet directive.

Willow went still. Heat gathered under Blackburn's fingers, a steady thrum. Before thought caught up, Blackburn leaned in and pressed her mouth to Willow's. The kiss held for a breath, enough for a current to take hold.

"Maybe we should be doing something else entirely," Blackburn murmured against Willow's mouth when they parted, her voice rich and low, velvet over stone. Her dark eyes traveled Willow's face with a predator's patience, deliberate and unhurried.

Willow held Blackburn's gaze. Her pulse filled her ears. Want and need pressed tight in her chest. "I would like that," she murmured, her voice a fragile line laced with anticipation.

The space between them tightened. Willow leaned in. Her lips parted. She caught the heat of Blackburn's breath.

Blackburn pulled back, her dark eyes glinting with an intensity both electric and unnerving. "The analysis was useful," she said, her voice low but firm, nearly a growl. Her thumb brushed Willow's lower lip, lingering just long enough to leave a spark. "Write up the report and send it to me and the chief before you head out. Your work has been exceptional, critical, even. And I want those lines tomorrow."

On the computer, the video was still open. The pen sat rough against her fingertips. Willow could already see the report headers, the summary of findings, the pull for call detail records, the routing to the chief. The monitor's glow washed the paper in a thin light. The building's air hummed through the vent.

Without warning, Blackburn dipped closer, her breath warm at the hollow of Willow's throat. Her teeth grazed Willow's neck with sharpness, a pinpoint sting that bloomed heat, then she stepped away.

The imprint of Blackburn's presence held on her skin. Her heart was fast. Breath thin. The chair pressed against the backs of her legs. The room steadied around the open file and the quiet movement outside her door.

Willow watched through her office doorway as Blackburn's figure disappeared down the hall, the detective's purposeful stride eating the distance. The soft strike of heels faded. A trace of her cologne hung in the air. Blackburn was moving toward her next destination, a dinner with another woman.

Chapter 15

The clock's chime carried through the candle shop, a clean strike at eight. The brass note skimmed the glass and settled over the faint sweet of wax and smoke. Kendria had been tracking minutes since Blackburn's text earlier: *Finishing up at the station. Still on for tonight?* She set the last inventory slip aside and glanced to the window.

Blackburn leaned against a black car at the curb. The red dress was simple and exact. Evening light thinned along her legs and vanished into shadow. The effect was spare and intentional, like a line drawn once and left to stand.

Kendria lifted a hand before she could think better of it. Her fingers shook as she counted the cash in the till. Paper edges rasped against her skin. Coins clicked cleanly. She slid the money into the safe and turned the dial, not lingering on tomorrow's numbers. Coat, keys, lights. She felt the coat along her bare arms, the lining cool at first, the weight practical and steadying. The shop smelled of dye and warm paraffin.

The bell above the door chimed as she locked up. The click settled the shop behind her. She dropped the key into her bag and checked the door once more. The night air brushed her face, cool and a little metallic. The streetlights flattened the block into orderly pools of gold as she headed toward Blackburn. Her pulse climbed on a contained beat.

Blackburn watched her approach, composed, a controlled read of the scene. Their eyes met. Kendria's open. Blackburn's measuring. A brief lift at Blackburn's mouth suggested she'd already decided what came next.

Kendria let her fingertips touch Blackburn's arm. The contact was no more than a trace, warm skin under smooth fabric. It traveled fast. She felt it in her chest and low in her abdomen, a quiet ignition she did not display.

She leaned in and kissed her. Soft. Deliberate. Their mouths met without hurry, warm and sure. They held it long enough to say what needed saying without spectacle.

"You're stunning tonight."

Blackburn's smile turned precise. She drew a thumb along Kendria's cheekbone and the small ownership in it registered. The touch left a faint heat.

"I know," she said. "I always deliver what's promised."

The city's noise hung back. A bus sighed at the corner and faded. Blackburn stayed close, then straightened. The night had a direction again.

In the car, Kendria felt Blackburn's attention move over her with the same thoroughness she applied to handcrafted candles. The seat's leather cooled the back of her thighs. She fastened her belt. Heat gathered anyway. She shifted once and stilled. Her confidence pushed against the impulse to anticipate and please. The engine came alive and held steady as Blackburn eased into traffic. Tires rolled with a low, constant hum.

Blackburn drove with neat hands and eyes that kept a disciplined sweep. Mirrors, intersection, speed. Indicators clicked once, then silence. The habit of someone who liked to control variables. Her fingers tapped a light cadence on the wheel that stopped the moment an autonomous patrol car glided past in the opposite lane. Sodium light cut angles across her features and made her look more severe.

"So," Blackburn said. The sound of her voice trimmed away the rest. "Tell me something about yourself I wouldn't know just by looking."

Kendria pinched the hem of her coat between her fingers and eased it free. The wool rasped softly against her nails. The question sat squarely between them. Not small talk. A check of sources.

"Something you wouldn't guess?" She heard the stall and let it pass.

The corner of Blackburn's mouth moved, not a smile so much as an acknowledgment that this, too, was a test she expected to score.

"Yes," she murmured. "Something unexpected."

Kendria held Blackburn's profile and made a choice toward disclosure rather than charm. She kept her voice even.

"I used to be a competitive gymnast," she said. "Back when I was younger, before candle-making became my thing."

Blackburn's eyebrow lifted a fraction. Her gaze flicked to Kendria and back to the road.

"Gymnast," she repeated. "Useful information." She let that sit, then allowed it to turn. "That explains the precision in how you move."

Kendria felt heat touch her face. It wasn't the compliment. It was the cataloging of it. She lowered her eyes, not to hide but to put the feeling away.

"I stopped because of injuries. But I don't regret it."

Kendria watched her work the road. The restraint, the attention to exits, the casual way she covered more than one reason for any move. The air from the vents touched Kendria's knees and slipped past. It was attractive. It was also a warning.

"Injuries are just data," Blackburn observed after a beat of silence, her voice dipping into something that sounded almost philosophical but felt oddly detached. "They tell us what we can survive and what we need to avoid."

The quiet between them lengthened with purpose. Not discomfort. Anticipation. The cabin held a faint flow of cold air. Kendria noted the neat angle of Blackburn's jaw and the intentional economy in her movements. Precise. The kind of posture that came from long hours observing scenes and people, measuring what mattered and discarding what didn't. Kendria tried to imagine what it meant to live there, on that edge, cataloging the worst and choosing where to cut in.

They turned onto a side street. Gravel ticked against the undercarriage. Blackburn took a slow loop before pulling into a narrow lot, choosing a spot with a clear sightline to the entrance and a clean exit.

No wasted movement. She shut off the engine and looked over, gaze locking on Kendria with efficient force. Control was the point. Still, Kendria felt her pulse skip.

"Tonight follows my preferences," Blackburn said, her tone leaving no room for negotiation. "I choose the food, the wine, the pace. You adapt. Clear?"

The question felt like an assessment. Kendria's instinct kicked against it, then settled. Something deeper, something that both excited and unsettled her, made her nod. "Clear," she murmured.

A small, satisfied curve touched Blackburn's mouth. She stepped out, moving with clean lines and no excess. The night air held a trace of rain and city metal. She circled to Kendria's side and opened the door. Cool air slid under Kendria's collar as she rose. Blackburn's hand grazed the small of her back for a breath. Too brief to claim space. Clear enough to set it.

Inside, the hostess greeted them and led them through warm light and low sound. Exposed brick. Soft jazz threaded through conversation. The clink of small plates. Olive oil and garlic lifted into the air. Intimate without the performance of romance. Refined, with an edge. A restaurant chosen rather than found.

They took a corner booth. Leather gave a muted sigh under them. Blackburn slid in where she could see the door, the bar, both exits, and the kitchen swing. Kendria felt herself tip forward and try to steady. The ground was familiar, but Blackburn shifted its lines by inches.

Blackburn settled into the seat as if she belonged there. Calm authority in her shoulders and hands. She checked the small menu without looking away from Kendria for long, eyes skimming and returning, a steady cadence of attention.

"Allergies? Medical restrictions?" Blackburn asked, voice smooth, clinical. Intake questions.

Kendria glanced down. The blur of choices didn't hold; the paper felt thick under her fingertips. "No allergies," she said softly. She kept her voice even under Blackburn's watch. "What do you recommend?"

Blackburn's smile was sharp as winter. "I'll handle it." She flagged the server with a small flick of fingers that read as command rather than show. "We'll have the charcuterie board, the stuffed dates, and the garlic prawns. And bring the lady a glass of Albariño."

The server nodded and moved off, the pen tucked cleanly behind one ear. Kendria sat with the mix of gratitude and irritation that came from being directed well. Competence had its pull. So did ceding ground to it. Her shoulders eased, then tensed again as if catching themselves.

"You're very sure of yourself," Kendria observed, looking for footing.

"Confidence comes from preparation," Blackburn replied, easing back an inch. "I researched this place. I know what's good here." Her gaze held. "Just like I know what I want from tonight."

The wine arrived with tidy timing. A pale, chilled pour set in front of Kendria. She took a sip. Crisp. Clean. Peach and saline at the edges.

It steadied her more than it warmed her. Blackburn's attention didn't waver, and heat rose along Kendria's skin.

"Tell me about your family," Blackburn said, the request sounding more like gentle interrogation than casual conversation.

Kendria cleared her throat and chose her path. "I have a daughter. Marilyn. She's seventeen, in her second year at UND."

Blackburn's head tilted by degrees, the information stored where it needed to go. "Seventeen and in her second year of college. Accelerated."

"She tested into Mensa at fifteen," Kendria said, pride and another note threading through. "Brilliant kid, but sometimes I think all that intelligence just feeds into other things."

"Such as?" The word sat light. Nothing in Blackburn's face was loose.

Kendria set her glass down and watched the condensation slide toward her fingers, cool and insistent. "Ultra-conservative religious streak. When I told her I was bisexual, she went silent on me for a month. It was like living with a disapproving ghost who haunted the kitchen at midnight." The memory brought back the hum of the refrigerator, the square of light on tile, the sound of a spoon against a mug that never acknowledged her.

"Interesting pattern," Blackburn observed, her voice as cool as a case consult. "Gifted children often seek rigid frameworks to contain their intensity."

Small plates arrived without fuss, ceramic whispering against wood. Thin slices of cured meat, a wedge of Manchego, a few dates with goat cheese, prawns slick with garlic and oil. Orderly. Efficient.

"This looks incredible," Kendria said, taking a date. The bite balanced cleanly, sweet and tangy. "Excellent choices."

"I research my investments," Blackburn replied, lifting the Manchego with steady fingers. The word made Kendria pause. Investments, not interests. It fit the way Blackburn approached everything, including tonight.

They ate methodically. Blackburn sampled in sequence, noting, then moving on. Kendria watched the quiet control in her hands, the placement of knife and fork. Attractive. Also a little cold.

"So what about you?" Kendria asked. "Any family skeletons rattling around?"

Blackburn's smile thinned. Not warm. Precise. "I prefer to focus on the present. The past only informs it." She took a prawn and set the tail neatly aside, fingers clean. "Your situation interests me. A business rooted in candles and handcrafted work, a daughter with conservative leanings, a personal life of unconventional choices. Situations like this produce tension."

The way she said "tension" pressed on a nerve. Kendria felt it like a shift in air pressure.

"Some days I wonder how I managed to raise someone so different from me," Kendria said. She took a sip of wine and set the glass down with care, stem cool against her fingers. "Here I am, marching in BLM protests, registering voters, building a business around alternative spirituality, and somehow I've got a kid who seems determined to become the poster child for religious conservatism."

"Perhaps that's exactly why," Blackburn said. Her tone dropped a notch. "Children sometimes define themselves in opposition to their parents. It's a way to control outcomes when the world feels uncertain."

Control sat between them. Clean, unadorned.

"Speaking of control," Kendria said. She leaned in. "There are things you should know. Before this goes any further."

Blackburn's attention tightened. She didn't change her posture. "I'm listening."

"I have hard limits," Kendria said. Her voice stayed even. "No master-slave dynamics. Ever. I won't use that word or participate in anything that evokes that history. And absolutely no racial language or race play of any kind."

"Understood," Blackburn said. Crisp. "Those aren't my preferences anyway." She studied Kendria without staring.

"No permanent marks. No photography. No water sports, no blood play, and no other fluid exchanges. Saliva stays above the neck."

"That is a lot of 'no'. What if someone crossed those lines?" Blackburn asked.

"Then they'd discover this switch has a very dominant side, and she doesn't handle disrespect quietly," Kendria said. Soft words. Steel underneath.

Approval flickered, clean and brief. "Good. You're not naïve." Blackburn took the last prawn and placed the fork down parallel to the plate's edge. "That makes you more interesting, not less."

The server moved in and cleared the plates. Blackburn gestured for the check with minimal motion. Kendria felt her pulse quicken. Not panic. Anticipation under control.

"My safe word is 'apple,'" she said quietly.

Blackburn's smile sharpened. "Interesting choice. Innocent fruit with hidden complexities." She signaled the server again. "Actually, could we get an apple for dessert? Just a simple red apple."

The server blinked, then nodded. When he returned with the fruit on a small plate, Blackburn paid and palmed the apple with a light, proprietary touch. The skin held a soft sheen. She turned it once in her hand as if weighing it.

They stepped into the cool night. The street was quiet, air clean with a faint trace of exhaust. Kendria considered her next move, feeling the pull of structure against the tug of her independence.

"Your place or mine?" she asked. She already knew the likely answer.

"Mine isn't an option tonight," Blackburn said. No elaboration. No apology.

Kendria checked herself. Breath in, breath out. Planning edged into arousal. "My place," she said. "A converted office space. Completely private. Soundproofed."

Blackburn's look held. Satisfied. Certain. "Perfect," she said. "Allow me to get the door for you."

They drove through low traffic and dark storefronts, signal lights cycling over empty intersections. Kendria stole brief looks at Blackburn's profile. The set of her jaw. The focus on the road. It felt less like a date and more like an operation with moving parts.

The shop came up on the right, its sign washed in streetlight. "Park around back. No security cameras back there."

Blackburn parked with clean alignment and cut the engine. Silence settled. Kendria felt resistance, then something gave way, quiet as a lock turning.

"Are you ready for this?"

Kendria's breath hitched. "I think so. I know so. Yes."

Blackburn nodded once. She slipped the apple into her coat pocket. "Good to know."

They crossed to the door. Kendria keyed in her code and listened for the soft click, the keypad's muted confirmation. She could feel the shape of what might happen settle around them. Not heavy. Precise.

Whatever Blackburn had planned, it would be controlled. It would test boundaries without crossing the lines they had set. Kendria stepped into it with intention.

Even if part of her suspected she might not emerge unchanged.

Chapter 16

Ahead lay what had once been Kendria's office, now a space now transformed into something intimate and exacting. Burgundy walls cloaked the room in warmth, their rich tones deepened by low, strategic lighting that bathed every surface in an inviting glow. At its center stood a restraint table of unmistakable luxury, its black leather shimmered faintly beneath carefully positioned lights. Three brass D-Rings hung along each side.

Along one wall hung an array of impact tools. The floggers, crops, and paddles were immaculate, arranged in flawless precision from smallest to largest. Their placement spoke of care. The discipline appealed to Blackburn.

Opposite this display was a solitary armchair upholstered in smooth leather that caught the light just so. It was positioned perfectly for observation and flanked by a small table bearing an assortment of massage oils and candles. Nearby, steel rings were mounted securely into another wall at varying heights. Functional yet unobtrusive fixtures that told their own story without preamble or explanation.

The air held a medley of leather and sandalwood, underscored by the faint sweetness of coconut wax. Each surface gleamed under subdued lighting, pristine and orderly, a dedicated statement of

Kendria's meticulous nature. In one corner stood a discreet cabinet, its contents concealed but unmistakable in purpose. Nearby, a compact mini-fridge hummed softly, a quiet promise of refreshment for later.

Blackburn stepped further into the room, her gaze sweeping over its details. Kendria watched her closely, noting the slight lift of an eyebrow here, the slightest tilt of an approving nod there. Every element of this space mirrored its owner: precision balanced with subtle sensuality, an invitation cloaked in restraint.

Blackburn's eyes surveyed the open cabinet. Restraints organized by function. Implements arranged by intensity. Leather and steel rested in orderly rows, cool beneath the room's consistent light. Someone here understood control, though not with her precision.

She selected a black silk blindfold. Soft enough for comfort. Opaque enough to eliminate light. The fabric glided cool across her fingers before warming to her touch. Control begins with manipulating what the subject can and cannot perceive.

"Come here," she said, her voice conveying quiet authority.

Kendria moved forward, and Blackburn observed the slight tremor in her hands, the quickening of her breath. Fear and anticipation in perfect balance. The height difference served a purpose. Kendria tilted her chin upward to meet her gaze, a subtle submission. A pulse flickered at her throat.

The blindfold slid over Kendria's eyes. Silk settled against skin and sealed at the edges; Blackburn adjusted it until no light penetrated.

Pressure gathered at the temples and crown. Sensory input narrowed to only what Blackburn permitted.

"I'm in complete control now," Blackburn declared, noting how Kendria's shoulders tensed at the words. "Do you trust me?"

"Yes." The single word carried significance, vulnerability.

Perfect. Trust provided the entry point.

From the cabinet, Blackburn retrieved a cloth gag. Nothing elaborate, merely effective silencing. Clean cotton, sturdy weave. "Open your mouth."

She noticed the brief stiffening in Kendria's posture. The small intake of breath. Compliance followed. The gag positioned firmly, a solid presence against tongue and teeth. Speech diminished to a muted hum. Speech reduced to tone and movement. Another layer established and documented.

Blackburn placed a hand on Kendria's shoulder and applied gentle pressure. Warmth, then compliance. "Stand straight."

The response was immediate. Spine aligning. Chin raised. A gymnast's response. Subtle adjustments revealed their own narrative. Kendria was already interpreting Blackburn's rhythm and attempting to anticipate it.

Moving deliberately, Blackburn unbuttoned Kendria's blouse. Each button a clear removal of protection. Plastic clicked in a soft rhythm. Fabric whispered as it separated. She monitored Kendria's changing breath.

"I'm going to expose you completely," Blackburn said, her voice clinical. "You belong to me now."

The impact registered. Breathing deepened. Muscles yielded toward vulnerability. A flush appeared and receded. Arousal intensified in steady progression.

Blackburn circled. Assessment, not impatience. Footsteps calculated to keep Kendria uncertain of position. The soft scrape of her soles defined the room for Kendria yet revealed nothing. She unfastened the final button and removed the blouse with the same methodical precision she applied to a scene. The fabric brushed warm skin, then left a slight chill in its absence. Nothing wasted. Everything accounted for.

She folded the blouse and placed it on the table beside the leather chair. The wood's texture was smooth beneath her palm. The chair carried a clean, oiled scent. Order maintained.

Kendria's skin registered the change. Gooseflesh along the arms. Sensitivity heightened by the blindfold's steady pressure. Air flowed across her exposed skin, and every touch would register clearly.

Blackburn moved leftward. Kendria's head followed the sound. Seeking information. Blackburn offered none.

"Straighten out," Blackburn commanded.

Kendria attempted compliance. The line of her shoulders wavered. Uncertainty compromised her posture. Unacceptable.

Without warning, Blackburn located Kendria's nipple and applied firm pressure. Two fingers, precise and unyielding. The reaction was immediate and genuine. A caught breath, a small restrained sound against cloth. Perfect. Pain as instruction, correction as control.

She adjusted Kendria's posture with precise hands. Shoulders back, hips forward, spine aligned. Warm palms pressed and withdrew. Each touch claimed another fraction of stance and breath.

"Remember who's in control," Blackburn said softly, the steel in her voice unwavering, close enough for Kendria to feel the whisper against her ear.

The bra came off with a quiet snick. Another barrier gone. Another step toward exposure. Cool air passed over newly bared skin, drawing a fine shiver. Kendria responded as expected. Compliance first. Then the small betraying shifts she could not contain. A swallow. A tight inhale. Heat rising along her chest.

From the cabinet, Blackburn retrieved leather cuffs linked by a short strap. The leather carried a faint scent of oil and long use; the hardware offered a clean, metallic bite. She secured Kendria's hands behind her back efficiently and tested the fit with care. Edge checked. Flex checked. Two fingers between strap and skin. No pinch. No numbness. The buckles clicked into place with quiet finality.

The remaining clothing came off methodically. Fabric whispered down Kendria's legs. The room's cool air kissed damp heat from skin. Blackburn noted each detail. Breathing quickened to a faster cadence. A fine tremor at the thighs. A set jaw holding pride in place beneath exposure. Vulnerable yet maintaining form.

Each piece of clothing was folded and stacked, edges aligned, weight settling into order. Control made visible. Agency reduced piece by piece. The room narrowed to the ritual of removal, the quiet scrape of fabric, the soft click of hardware, the faint hum of air through the vents.

Blackburn selected a thin metal rod. Not for pain. For precise sensation. The tip touched Kendria's shoulder without warning. Cold met warm skin. Breath spiked. A step edged away, heel skimming the floor.

"Trust me," Blackburn corrected, her voice carrying gentle menace. "Don't move away from what I give you."

Kendria nodded. Acceptance. Blackburn gave a light pat. Reward clean and spare. The small exhale that followed confirmed her timing landed.

Neck, breast, stomach, cheek. With each flinch came a pinch. Earlobe, nipple, lip.

Rewards had to be earned. The next correction came sharper. A test of commitment under restraint. Each response provided data. Range. Threshold. Yield. Blackburn noted it as she would log evidence. Sequence, reaction, recovery. The ledger built in her mind.

The rod touched again. Command explicit: "Don't move."

Blackburn took the leather chair and went quiet. Darkness held. In absence, suggestion worked. Minutes stretched without input or guidance. No sound of movement. No hand at her back. Only the air system's steady breath and the faint scent of leather and skin.

Kendria held steady initially. Then the search began. A slight turn of the head. An ear tilted for a cue that never came. Weight shifted off one heel, then back. Tongue pressed to the roof of the mouth seeking moisture that had thinned. Isolation pressed in and did its slow work.

When Kendria turned her body, seeking orientation, Blackburn spoke.

"Stand still."

The effect was immediate. Kendria froze. Her breathing seemed louder in the quiet.

"You're not obeying," Blackburn observed, disappointment refined to a thin line. "Do you really want this?"

The nod came quick. Desperate. Eager. Perfect.

"Then you must pay for disobedience. Bend over."

Kendria complied and braced. Expectation tightened every muscle along her back. Fingers flexed against the cuffed grip. Pain would have been simple. Blackburn chose control.

Instead of striking, she lifted Kendria over her shoulder in one smooth motion. Center of gravity shifted. Her body tilted out of frame. Legs kicked. Body squirmed. A startled sound caught in Kendria's throat. Disorientation hit hard.

"You're safe," Blackburn said firmly, her voice the anchor. "Stop resisting."

She adjusted her hold and kept the carry balanced, one arm locked around Kendria's thighs, one hand secure at the waist. The cuffs stayed clear of pressure points. Breathing remained open. Blackburn felt the warm thud of a heartbeat against her shoulder and counted the beats. Three breaths. It started again. "You're okay." Five breaths.

The struggling continued, instinctive fight-or-flight responses overriding judgment. Blackburn waited, patient, listening to

Kendria's breath rasp and catch, allowing the panic to crest and settle before speaking again.

"You're okay. I have you."

The cycle repeated twice more. Each time, Kendria jerked, then stilled a fraction sooner. Finally, her body went slack, resistance draining from her limbs. The shift revealed itself in her hands, in the slight unclenching of her jaw, in the shiver that released from her shoulders.

Blackburn checked the cuffs with the same methodical precision she used for evidence seals. No give. No rub. Warm skin beneath cool leather.

She turned them in a slow circle, creating disorientation while her voice remained constant, the only fixed point in the room.

"I will keep you safe," she repeated, steady and low. "Relax into it. Let me carry you."

When Kendria's weight released fully, Blackburn felt the clean snap of resolution she experienced when a case broke open. Everything aligned. The sensation settled in her chest, precise and right.

"That's it. Let go. I have you."

When Kendria surrendered completely, body soft and resistance gone, Blackburn set her back on her feet. "Beautiful." She maintained a hand at the elbow, thumb steady on bone. The room still spun in Kendria's darkness; sweat cooled along her hairline.

Aftercare commenced without delay. "You did so well." Blackburn's tone softened as she unlocked the cuffs, palms careful as she slid the straps free and examined her skin for marks. She lifted

Kendria's wrists and rubbed warmth back in with efficient strokes, the quiet rasp of skin on skin steadying the air. "So good. You handled that with grace."

The gag came out slowly, and Blackburn noted with satisfaction how thoroughly soaked it was. Physical evidence of Kendria's complete surrender to the experience.

"You did beautifully," Blackburn said, meaning it. The performance had exceeded her expectations.

The blindfold was the last barrier to fall. Blackburn shielded Kendria's eyes with one hand as she lifted the fabric, allowing light to seep in a sliver at a time. Even this return proceeded on Blackburn's terms. Control held, then released. Kendria blinked against the soft glow until her pupils adjusted. "You're okay."

Kendria reached out to Blackburn's hips, to steady herself. Blackburn allowed it.

"I need to lie down," Kendria said, her voice hoarse but satisfied.

Blackburn guided her to the padded table and pulled a soft blanket from the cabinet. The fabric whispered as it unfolded. She tucked it around Kendria with the same methodical care she had shown in removing her clothes. She smoothed the edge at the shoulder, and placed a bottle of water within reach, condensation beading against plastic.

Blackburn's eye caught her phone vibrate on the table, but she had something better in front of her.

"That was..." Kendria paused, searching. "Transcendent. Like a spiritual experience."

Blackburn nodded once. The psychological arc had landed. Kendria had found meaning in giving over. Blackburn had achieved what she had intended.

She watched Kendria's breathing even out, counting the beats as they slowed. The tension on Kendria's face smoothed; her mouth softened at the corners. The evening registered as a clean result. She reached out and brought the apple to Kendria's hands.

"Rest," Blackburn said softly. "You've earned it."

"Th—"

"Shh. Kendria, I have to go. Will you be okay by yourself?" Blackburn asked.

"What?"

"I have to go. Cop life."

Kendria cleared her throat and nodded. "Yeah. Yes, I'll be fine."

Blackburn gathered her things without noise. Keys, phone, shoes. She headed out the back door, the automatic lock engaged behind her as she stepped into the alley. The sound was final and satisfying. Cool night air carried damp concrete, oil, and the distant hum of traffic.

In her car, Blackburn allowed herself a small breath of genuine satisfaction. Another successful acquisition. Another person who now understood their proper place in her world.

She started the engine and drove into the night, already planning their next encounter. Headlights cut a clean path. Kendria was hers now. Perhaps forever.

Chapter 17

Blackburn reached her car as her phone buzzed again against her thigh. The transition from intimate to ordinary still knocked her off balance. A third hard vibration. The screen's cold glow cut through the dark and displayed a message from Chief Hayes.

>*Zhang TBA*

>*Zhang arrested 1:30am.*

She checked the time. 1:23am. Seven minutes from now. He was going to be arrested in seven minutes.

New evidence?<

No response. Blackburn hit the call button. No answer. Hayes knew better.

She inhaled and steadied herself, slid into the driver's seat. Leather creaked and cooled beneath her. She took the wheel and noticed how hard she was gripping it. Her pulse settled. Her thoughts did not.

She exhaled and reopened the file in her mind. The case against James Zhang lacked substance. She had security footage showing he never left home, and gaming logs proving he was online when Jenna died. Multiple witnesses saw an empty car. The EDR was irreparable. They had found only a weak connection between their respective companies. Blackburn knew it was a bad arrest.

She backed out of the alley. Tires screamed nearby. A sleek autonomous car sliced past her bumper and clipped a pocket of air. The silver body caught a fragment of light and vanished. Her heart beat faster, then stabilized.

The engine's low hum filled the cabin and her fingers began a quiet rhythm on the wheel. She would try again. Blackburn tapped the screen and dialed again. Two rings, then Hayes's voice answered. Rough. Curt. A line hiss in the background.

"Hayes."

"Why is Zhang being arrested?" Blackburn kept her tone even. The edge remained just beneath it.

"Involuntary manslaughter," Hayes said. Each word clipped. "The Langston case."

"I asked why he was arrested, not the charge." She turned onto a side street and checked her mirrors, glass holding pale smears of daylight. "Owning a car that kills someone isn't the same as driving it. This doesn't add up. We need more evidence."

"You're not the one dealing with the mayor or Stan Raider breathing down your neck," Hayes snapped. His composure slipped. "The political pressure, public outrage, reporters are fanning the flames. Everyone wants action."

"So do I," Blackburn said. Her grip tightened until her knuckles whitened. "But not at the cost of due process. What if Zhang is innocent?" The hasty arrests were the ones that fell apart later.

Hayes breathed into the line. "I had enough for a warrant. The charges will hold." Resolute on the surface. She heard the strain underneath.

"That doesn't make it right," she said.

"Follow orders," Hayes said, voice firm. "Be at headquarters by seven-thirty for the press conference."

The call ended. Cold and final. She lowered the phone and stared through the windshield for a moment. Then she turned the wheel in a clean U and let the tires grip. She needed a couple of hours of rest and a shower to be anywhere near her best.

If the city charged manslaughter in a driverless hit, they needed impairment or negligence by the owner. Disabled safety features. Ignored recalls. Falsified update logs. Otherwise, it belonged in civil court or with the manufacturer.

Raider Straight Line cars maintained a reputation for flawless automation. Safety in glossy marketing and staged demonstrations. If Zhang's car had killed someone because of a system fault, criminal liability for him seemed tenuous. It pointed higher. If Hayes was moving to shield Raider, it wouldn't be New Dresden's first capitulation to a donor.

* * *

Blackburn pulled into the precinct lot and parked precisely. Out, lock, move. Her heels created a steady rhythm on concrete. She smoothed her grey suit, ran a hand lightly through her hair. She took the stairs two at a time and arrived at the chief's office at seven twenty-eight. Two minutes early.

"Good morning, Physica," Blackburn said to the chief's assistant.

"Good morning, Detective. The chief is expecting you," she said, gesturing for Blackburn to head to the office.

"Chief," Blackburn said as she walked into his office without knocking, "How did you get the warrant? What's your new evidence?"

Hayes sat and stared at her, his shoulders tense. "Detective," he said. "Sit."

Blackburn stopped before him. Composed exterior. Unyielding.

"Chief, when's the press conference?" Her voice was precise, each syllable distinct.

"Seven forty-five."

"You're giving me fifteen minutes?" Her tone left no room for negotiation.

"Yes. If anyone can handle it, you can." Hayes's words rang hollow, a compliment wrapped in manipulation.

Blackburn held his gaze. "Chief," she said, steady, "I want to see the evidence you used for the warrant."

Hayes stiffened. "Why?"

"It's my case," she said, her voice controlled but sharp. "And you pulled it out from under me."

He exhaled and passed her his tablet. The glass was warm from his hand. "It's all there. Zhang's car was identified as the one in the crash. GPS data puts it at the scene at the exact time of impact."

Blackburn scrolled. Blue light washed over her skin. Her eyes flashed, her attention sharper than his hurry. "We know that, sir. We have proof it was his car," she said flatly. "It doesn't prove he was driving."

"He's the registered owner," Hayes said, impatience creeping into his voice. "He had recent contact with the victim. That gave him time and opportunity to plan, and a potential motive. The car was conveniently incinerated, eliminating crucial evidence. His gaming logs and home security footage could easily have been manipulated by someone with his technical expertise. The lack of a driver actually supports premeditation. This was a remotely executed murder designed to create the perfect alibi."

"That's not how this works." Her words remained even. "If we're going after him, we need more than that. We need to know why that car malfunctioned."

Hayes rubbed his temples. "Look, I get it. But this isn't just about the investigation anymore. The mayor's office is on me, and Stan Raider wants action now before this blows up in their faces."

A thin smile was all she offered. Hayes had seen it before. "Then let's make sure it blows up in the right direction," she said. She handed the tablet back and moved to leave.

Blocked.

"Deputy Chief," she said as she stepped aside.

"Detective Blackburn," McLaughlin said as she stepped into the chief's office.

Blackburn wondered briefly if McLaughlin had been listening. Not her problem.

Her problem was she had just minutes to prepare.

Blackburn stood, precise in her movements, and crossed the hall. The hum of LEDs pressed at the edge of hearing. In the women's washroom, she met her reflection and opened the tap. Cool water over her hands. A faint citrus scent from the soap. She bent and let a clean splash take the heat out of her face.

The cold steadied her. The evening's indulgence receded to its right size. She blotted dry. Kendria flickered through her mind. Kendria's eyes when Blackburn covered them. A tight spark traced her fingers, a pleasant residue of control. She rubbed thumb against forefinger, then let it go.

She straightened. Jacket smooth. Collar aligned. The woman in the mirror was composed. She ran her fingers through her hair until it fell the way she liked, then squared her shoulders and headed to the press conference.

Blackburn surveyed the briefing room before her shoes met the floor. Reporters clustered in tight rows, voices kept low. Tripods stood like spare legs between chairs. Cameras waited with red lights dark. Chief Hayes away at the podium with one hand on his notes, face composed, eyes tracking each line. He nodded at Blackburn and the podium.

Her turn.

The media relations officer held the printed release tight against her clipboard. Brynn Cassidy sat in the front row. Notebook open. Pen poised. Phone recording. Her focus locked on Blackburn as soon as she appeared. They held one another's gaze for a beat. Brynn's shoulders squared. Blackburn noted the tell.

She crossed to the podium and let her fingers find the cold rim, grounding herself in metal and weight. One breath to set a rhythm. The air smelled of old paint and paper dust. Her badge pressed into her hip when she squared to the room, a familiar drag that marked where authority lived.

She gave the media officer a small nod. The woman nodded back and stepped away. Blackburn leaned into the microphone and cut through the remaining rustle.

"Good morning," she said, her words resonant and firm. "Thank you for coming on such short notice. My name is Detective Morgan Blackburn. B-L-A-C-K-B-U-R-N."

Silence settled hard and even. She held it until the last whisper died. Owning the start was half the work. She let the room come to her.

"New Dresden Police have made an arrest in connection with Jenna Langston's death."

The press leaned forward together. Fabric brushed. Chair legs creaked. Red lights blinked. Autofocus motors clicked. Pens scratched in quick lines. She waited a count, not for effect but to keep the pace in her hands.

"At this time, Mr. James Zhang is being charged with involuntary manslaughter," Blackburn announced.

Her grip tightened on the podium. Heat pulsed in her knuckles. Memory moved. Jenna's laugh at her shoulder. Breath warm against Blackburn's throat. Then the metal chill of the morgue. Blackburn set her feet and pressed the thoughts back until her breathing matched the room again. The work was here.

She cleared her throat and locked her focus just over the third row. The cameras would take her eyes, not her hands.

A voice cut clean. Brynn Cassidy, front row, pen stilled, phone raised and recording. She leaned forward until her knees touched the chair ahead.

"Detective Blackburn," Brynn began, tone clear and exact, "on what evidence was Mr. Zhang arrested?"

A small charge rose through Blackburn. She let it pass. She studied Brynn's line of approach instead. Hair controlled. Blazer precise. The question moved straight to the hinge. Amateur crossed her mind and left. Brynn had done enough to draw blood if Blackburn let her.

"I can't comment on ongoing investigations," Blackburn said smoothly, and watched frustration flare and then seal in Brynn's eyes.

Brynn's pen touched paper and paused. She didn't break pace.

"Was Mr. Zhang operating his vehicle manually at the time of Ms. Langston's death? Or did its autonomous system fail?"

Blackburn let one corner of her mouth lift. She kept still. The room tightened by inches. No one coughed. She pictured photos, the twisted metal. The twisted body. Subpoena to Raider already sent. Toxicology pending in a quiet lab. All of it moving. None of it for this room.

"As I said," Blackburn replied evenly, "Mr. Zhang has been charged with manslaughter. That's all I'm prepared to say at this time."

Hands rose across the rows. A few voices overlapped. Blackburn didn't move. Brynn wanted a signal. She wasn't going to get one.

Blackburn let the next rush of questions spend itself, then reached for the next control point.

"Sources indicate," Brynn said with a quick glance at her phone, "that the Raider Straight Line, Mr. Zhang's Raider Straight Line vehicle, was operating on its AI system at the time of impact." She leaned in, daring a correction. "If so, how does manslaughter apply?"

The shift ran through the room. Heads turned to Brynn, then back to Blackburn. Blackburn felt the move and matched it with a delay. One breath. No more. Her attention flicked to Hayes at her right. He didn't move. Good.

"Sources," Blackburn said coolly after a beat that stung just enough. A fake attribution for a wild guess. "The district attorney's office handles charges and classifications." Her gaze slid past Brynn with ice and returned to the faces ahead.

"You're leading this investigation, Detective. Are you saying you don't know the basis for the charges, or are you choosing not to share them?"

A brief stretch took hold as the room waited to see if she would snap. Blackburn let her shoulders ease half an inch and adjusted the mic with two fingers. The small movement reset the tempo. She marked the clock on the rear wall. Press windows were short by design. Control lived in seconds.

The corners of Blackburn's lips lifted. She let the expression stand for a breath, then let it go. Heat from the lights pressed against her skin. Attention pooled around her, steady and warm. She didn't have to like it to use it.

Her voice stayed level. "Chief Hayes obtained the warrant and made the arrest," she said, measured and resonant enough to fill the room. "Questions regarding the charges should be directed to either him or the District Attorney." The phrasing had not been cleared with counsel before she walked in.

Not her problem.

Blackburn watched it land. A ripple through the front rows. Reporters shifted their weight, recalibrating angles.

Brynn didn't deter. If anything, she pushed forward, hunger for an answer sharpening against the room's apprehension. "Are you distancing yourself from this arrest, Detective Blackburn?" Her chin lifted as she spoke, defiance glinting in her dark eyes.

"I'm stating facts," Blackburn said with calculated precision, her eyes locking onto Brynn's. "Chief Hayes obtained the warrant and made the arrest this morning." She let silence settle until the room took it in. A chair creaked. Someone's pen stopped tapping. The microphones hummed faintly.

Brynn's lips pursed before parting again. The motion was slow. Like she was taking a finger into her mouth. Like Kendria. "What about Stan Raider's statement that their AI systems have never failed a safety test? Was this indeed their first failure?"

A flicker crossed Blackburn's face and vanished. A single blink, the barest tilt of her head, as if weighing each word against the press of camera shutters.

"Good question," she said, and Brynn's mouth twitched with the smallest hint of satisfaction.

"No comment on any manufacturer statements," Blackburn continued, voice even and contained. She folded her hands as though closing a case file and set them on the podium's cool wood. "This press conference concerns James Zhang's arrest in connection with Jenna Langston's death."

If Brynn felt the pushback, she didn't show it. She leaned in, perfume cutting through the stale coffee in the air. Some submissive women were surprisingly bold. "But if the AI failed," Brynn countered, "isn't the Stan Raider Group ultimately responsible?"

For one fleeting moment, a fine crack ran through Blackburn's composure. Heat at the edges, then stillness. The light picked a hard line along her jaw. When she spoke, her tone was level.

"For someone so fixated on potential technology failings," Blackburn said, each word thoughtful, "you seem to have lost sight of what matters: a young woman is dead." The room went quiet. The soft whirr of a camera motor filled the gap.

She stepped back from the podium with unhurried poise. Cameras clicked in a staccato burst. She found Brynn Cassidy in the crowd and held her there, letting the distance between them feel intentional.

Blackburn's smile returned, small and controlled. It never reached her eyes. "Always a pleasure speaking with you, Ms. Cassidy," she said softly, each syllable precise. The overhead lights put a sheen on her skin; her breath stayed even.

She turned, mind already sorting the next steps. Hayes had signed the affidavit. The arrest stood on the record. She would keep it clean and move the case forward and let it explode toward Hayes. It belonged there. The plan slotted into place with the satisfaction of a file drawer closing.

She left the podium with a steady stride. Her heels sounded a quiet rhythm on the floor, tapping through the tangle of cables and tripods. At Brynn's row, she slowed, letting the pause do the work. Her voice stayed low. "Provocative questions, Ms. Cassidy," she said, tone clipped with interest. "I'm curious to see where they lead you."

The words stayed with her as she walked off, the press fading behind her into a muffled blur of voices and equipment hum. Hot lights and copier toner thinned in the hallway. Last night's interrogation of a different sort pressed at the edges of her control, and she tightened it without breaking stride, breath steady, shoulders level, every movement returned to order.

Chapter 18

The morning sun lifted over the city and laid light across the pavement. Kendria Chaplin adjusted her collar to cover the mark on her shoulder. The fabric brushed tender skin, a quiet reminder. Watching Blackburn's press conference on her phone while dressing had been surreal. The commanding detective at the podium wasn't that different from the woman who had picked her up and spun her hours ago.

She stepped out for breakfast and very hot coffee. The air had bite, clean and steadying, a chill that clarified everything it touched.

She had taken time to prepare herself. She showered, steam rising off tile and glass, then dressed with care and headed to her favorite coffee shop. News of an arrest in Jenna Langston's case lingered beneath her thoughts like a low current. She watched a brief clip of the conference again, drawn to Blackburn's control. Cool, dominant, and undeniably sexy.

Traffic needled the morning as she walked toward the shop. Horns snapped. Conversations blurred outside cafes. A single bark cut through it all. Sharp. Brief. Then it folded back into the street noise.

Kendria moved with ease. The vegan leather strap of her bag sat snug on her shoulder, the weight steady as its contents shifted with her pace. Receipts rasped, a tube of lipstick knocked softly, new scent samples clicked like small glass bones. The grounded routine calmed her. She ran through her list for the day. Pouring, wicking, blend tests.

She caught her reflection in a storefront. Hair neat. Shoulders square. Her skin held a clean glow in the light. Discipline suited her. The glass hardened her gaze to something exact.

A woman ahead drew her eye. She walked fast, gaze split between her phone and the sidewalk. Sun flared on the screen, flashing across her glasses. Her steps were precise, almost mechanical, shoes striking a metronome against concrete.

The woman's head snapped up. She slipped into a doorway and pressed against brick. Breath quickened. Her chest lifted in short pulls. She held herself where she was, as if hoping to disappear into mortar.

Kendria slowed and scanned. Her pulse climbed a notch, a thread tugged tight. She searched for the trigger of the stranger's alarm. Something, someone. Nothing stood out. Cars slid by, engines low. A few with the soft hum that marked autonomous models. Pedestrians stayed in their lanes, eyes forward, faces sealed.

The chill under Kendria's skin was small but real. The woman's fear had been sharp. Too sharp to ignore. Kendria considered approaching, offering a word to steady her. Before she decided, the woman stepped back into the flow. Brisk. Composed. She was gone by the next corner.

Kendria stopped and watched until the crowd swallowed the figure. A small crease formed between her brows as she sorted what she'd seen. The reaction had weight, like a scent note that lingered after the rest burned off.

Her coffee spot sat a block on, tucked in a narrow alcove. Glass doors, brick inked with graffiti. Layered tags and murals gave the wall a pulse. Color stacked on color, paint still faintly tacky in places.

The coffee smell drifted out warm and dense, cut by a faint sting of spray paint. Two notes that fit the street. She breathed in and pushed the door. Heat met her. Outside noise thinned, replaced by low conversation and the soft thrum of equipment. Steam hissed. Ceramic clicked against metal.

The barista nodded. Frankie. A young man with inked arms and a line of silver along his ear and brow. He didn't need to ask. His hand already reached for a large mug and filled it black. The stream hit the cup with a dark, steady sound.

She glanced at the glass case. Muffins leaned against each other, bagels speckled with seeds. And apples? A quiet laugh rose before she turned away. The sight tugged at last night. She felt the ghost of a bite on her tongue, a flash of heat under her collar, and then it passed, folded cleanly away.

The café's appeal lived in its wear. Tables of different heights stood on scuffed floors, their edges softened by years of elbows. Chairs bore thin scratches along their backs. Steam hissed at the espresso machine; a grinder whirred and fell quiet. In one corner, students bent over laptops, blue light on their faces as they murmured. By the window, an elderly man turned pages of a newspaper that sounded like dry leaves.

Kendria reached into her bag for her wallet, cloth worn smooth by time, and pulled a bill. She slid it to the barista as he passed her drink with an easy smile. Her fingers caught on loose coins in her pocket. The metal felt cool against her skin. She let them fall into the tip jar beside the register. The coins and wrinkled bills settled with a clean chime that cut through the low café hum.

"Thanks, Frankie. See you tomorrow," Kendria said with a quick wave.

Coffee in hand, she pushed through the glass door and stepped onto the sidewalk. Cool air met her, sharp after the café's heat. She paused. The cup warmed her fingers. The first sip tasted dark and clean and spread steady heat through her chest.

She turned to go. Something tugged at the edge of her vision.

An autonomous car. Sun flashed across its hood. The movement was wrong. The quiet motor blended with the street until it jumped the curb. It was on top of her.

Kendria stopped, cup lifted and forgotten. Everything narrowed to a few seconds. Her face stared back at her in the paint. Eyes wide.

The cup slipped from her hand. It hit with a dull knock. Coffee burst across the concrete and ran toward the gutter in a brown arc that steamed in the cool air.

Tires screamed. The stench of hot rubber cut through the morning. Kendria pressed into the doorway she had just left. Glass kissed her shoulder blades. She made herself small. Breath shallow. She tracked the angle of approach, the path that would either clip her or miss.

Metal scraped brick in a hard, narrow shriek. The car left a raw line across the wall and corrected. It surged forward and swung around the corner. One last squeal, then it was gone, sound unspooling down Oak.

She stayed where she was. Palm flat to the glass. Her pulse drummed hard, then steadied. Steam rose from the spilled coffee at her feet. The smell of burned rubber that would stay in her head. She analyzed what she had. Black sedan. No visible logo. No sound of warning. Southbound on Oak, then west on Tenth. Midmorning sun. Glare could have blinded forward sensors. Or someone told it to ignore the curb.

"Kenny? Kenny, are you okay?"

The voice cut cleanly through the noise. Kendria turned. Frankie stood close, eyes wide, breath fast. He pulled the door and guided her inside.

"Jesus, Kenny, that thing nearly mowed you down! Are you hurt?"

Kendria looked at her hands. They shook. "I don't think so," she said. "It came out of nowhere. Didn't even slow down."

"They're supposed to stop," Frankie said, voice rising. "Sensors. AI. Aren't they programmed for this stuff? What the hell happened?" He took her hands. His were warm. "This is like what happened with that woman just the other day."

"I don't know. For a second, I swear it sped up."

Frankie's grip tightened. "You need to call the cops," he said. "Do you want me to do it?"

"No," Kendria said quickly, shaking her head. "I'll call."

She drew a breath and looked past him to the street. People outside had stalled in mid-step. A few jogged to nowhere, then slowed and pretended it was fine. Inside, cups hovered near mouths. Conversation thinned, then found itself again, low and careful.

Kendria wiped her palms on her jeans and checked the time on her phone. She catalogued what she knew. Location. Direction of travel. Make and color. Any decals. Any plate. She had nothing on the plate. She had the path and the sound. She had damage on the wall that would show a paint transfer.

"Frankie, do you keep cameras on the door and the street?" Her voice came out even. Work talk. "If you do, pull the last ten minutes and save them. Don't overwrite anything."

He nodded fast. "Yeah. I can do that right now."

"Good. If you have a view of Tenth, grab that too." She glanced at the corner where the car had turned.

Frankie looked at her, surprised by the calm. "Okay. Okay, yeah."

Kendria picked up a napkin and dabbed coffee from the sleeve of her jacket. Her fingers steadied. The shakiness narrowed to a small tremor and stayed there. She watched the door as if the car might reappear, then forced herself to scan the room instead. The elderly man was still by the window, paper folded, eyes on her. The students had stopped pretending to work. The hiss of the steamer rose and fell, and someone set a cup down too hard, ceramic clicking on tile.

She stepped closer to the glass and looked at the scrape along the brick. Fresh. White dust from the mortar flecked the sidewalk. She followed the mark to the corner with her eyes. No skid marks on the approach. The tires had screamed on correction, not braking. That mattered.

Frankie came back from the register. "What should I tell them if they ask what you saw?"

"Tell them what you saw, honey. No horn. No attempt to stop." She kept her voice steady. "And say it looked deliberate. If they ask why, tell them it stayed on throttle after the curb."

Frankie swallowed. "That woman the other day. Same kind of car."

"Frankie, please." He skittered into the back room.

Kendria found her phone at the bottom of her bag. Her fingers wouldn't cooperate. She pressed her back to the cool glass and forced a steady breath. She dialed 911. One hand held the phone. The other kept moving, searching through receipts and keys as if motion might drain the adrenaline.

Inside the coffee shop, customers pulled close to their tables. Conversation thinned to a low hum. Eyes slid to her, then away, then back again.

"Did you see that?" a woman whispered urgently to her companion, clutching a paper cup too tightly. The lid creaked.

"She could've been killed," he said, shaking his head as if he could settle the image by force.

Frankie reappeared and stepped outside. The hinge rasped. He scanned the street, then found her face. A thin line creased his brow. It vanished as quickly as it had formed.

"Hello, I need to report an incident. Someone just tried to hit me with their car." Kendria kept her voice level.

"Ma'am, are you safe right now?"

"Yes," she said. The crowd cinched tighter around her. Screens rose. A man spoke without looking at her. "Hashtag KillerCar."

"Where are you located?"

"I'm at the 455 Coffee Shop on Oak Street," she said. She glanced at the window as if the building could brace her. When the door opened again, the scent of coffee and warm milk drifted out, normal life nudging against the edge of the moment.

"Can you still see the car?"

"No. It's gone."

"Can you tell me what happened?"

She inhaled slowly and steadied herself. "An autonomous car sped onto the sidewalk and aimed right at me. It scraped the building before speeding off. It wasn't an accident. It was deliberate."

The barista inside stopped where he stood and leaned toward the glass, listening.

"Did you see the car? Get a plate number?"

"No," she said, heat rising at the admission. "It all happened so fast." She folded her arms tight. "But I could tell it was one of those autonomous cars."

"Understood," the operator said. A faint hiss of city noise rode the line. "Officers are en route to your location now. Please stay where you are and remain on this call."

Kendria nodded, then remembered the operator couldn't see her. "Thank you," she said. "I'll wait here."

She let the phone anchor her and stayed with the basics. The glass was cool at her back. The murmur inside rose and fell with the steamer's hiss. Her breathing evened out gradually. She kept her attention on the sidewalk and the fresh scrape gouged into brick. She wouldn't let fear control her.

The image remained sharp in her mind. The car had come in too straight, too sure. The skin at the back of her neck stayed tight. She scanned the street. No engine. No wrong movement. A bus sighed at the far corner; a cyclist rolled past with a faint click of gears. None of it belonged to that car.

Sirens grew louder until they were upon her. A Straight Line patrol car pulled in and stopped square with the curb. Light bars washed the storefront in red and blue. Two stocky officers exited and examined the scuff on the wall, the crowd. Then her. She stepped through the door.

"Officers. It's me," Kendria called.

"Ma'am," the first officer said, approaching with his hands visible and calm, "are you alright? Do you need medical assistance?"

Kendria shook her head. Her hands still trembled. "No. No ambulance. I'm fine," she said, then pointed to the wall. "But someone just tried to run me over."

The second officer walked the edge of the building and traced the scrape with his eyes. He crouched, checked for debris, then looked back at her. "Can you walk us through what happened?" He glanced at the phone in her hand. "Were you recording the car?"

"No, I...I am on the phone with the 911 operator." She adjusted her grip and hit speaker without ending the call.

"You can end it now," the cop said. Kendria clicked the red button, ending the lifeline.

The first officer positioned himself to block foot traffic and waved a few onlookers back. Someone filmed. Someone else tucked their phone away when he met their eyes.

Kendria drew a breath that did nothing and gave her account. An autonomous vehicle had jumped the curb without warning and came straight at her. She pointed to what remained. Coffee puddled near the gutter in a thin brown sheen. Corner bricks wore a chalky scrape where metal had clipped stone.

Both officers kept it professional. Pens moved, pages rasping under their hands. No promises beyond what they could do. One stepped away to call in Traffic Services. His voice went low under the steady thrum of engines and the burr of street talk. A radio cracked and hissed against his shoulder. The other walked the line of the curb, eyes down, scanning for scuffs, paint, rubber. He crouched to photograph the brick and the coffee, the shutter clicking softly, then logged the time and location. He told a patrol aide to start pulling nearby camera feeds.

For a moment, they gave her space. The noise of the street pressed close, then eased like a tide. Her chest held a hard, shallow rhythm. Her hand went to her bag without thinking. Her fingers found Detective Blackburn's card, the cardstock thick and cool at the edges. She dialed with a shake she could not quite stop, the phone slick under her thumb.

The line clicked. Blackburn's voice came through, even and clear.

"Detective Blackburn," the voice said, clipped and composed. Professional.

"Morgan," she replied, her own tone strained but steadying as she spoke. "It's me. Someone just tried to run me over."

There was a brief silence. Blackburn's voice sharpened, concern evident. "Run you over? Are you hurt?"

"I'm fine," Kendria answered quickly, though her heart still raced. "But I need you to come here. It was terrifying."

"Are officers already there?"

"Yes, but—"

"The candle store?"

"No, the 455 Coffee Shop."

Blackburn cut in again, voice lower. "Listen to the officers. Stay where they can see you."

"They're not exactly—" she began, but Blackburn overrode her.

"I'll be there in a few minutes," Blackburn said firmly. A pause followed that made Kendria tense. "Stay inside."

The last words lingered with her. The tone and the instruction did not quite align. She almost asked why. Her mouth went dry. A soft click followed.

Blackburn had already ended the call. Kendria lowered the phone and watched the officer at the curb drag chalk along the scrape in the brick. The chalk squeaked and left dust on his knuckles. The other finished his transmission, the radio popping as it cleared, and glanced over to check her condition. Exhaust hung faint in the warm air. The coffee smell turned sour where it pooled. Glass in the corner glittered in the gutter. She stayed inside as instructed, far from the door and windows. Far from the outside. The warning remained clear in her mind. Stay inside.

Chapter 19

Car horns punched through the morning, brief and off-key bursts. Twenty minutes since Kendria's call. *Stay inside.*

Blackburn eased her black sedan through the fast traffic and parked half a block from the coffee shop. She stepped out. Heat rose off pavement. Sun on glass. Clean lines. She didn't belong here officially, but she walked like she did.

She approached the cluster of traffic officers, reading the set of shoulders and clipped chatter before she spoke. Radios hissed in small, bored bursts.

"Excuse me," she said to the nearest officer. Her voice carried natural authority, the kind that made people respond before they thought to question. "I'm here about Kendria Chaplin. She called me about what happened."

The young officer blinked. "Oh, uh, are you family?"

Blackburn's eyes went flat.

"Close friend," Blackburn replied smoothly, her eyes already scanning the scene with professional intensity. "She was pretty shaken up. What exactly happened here?"

The officer gestured to the brick. "A car clipped the side of that building. Almost hit someone. Ms. Chaplin, I guess. She was lucky."

Blackburn followed his hand. Silver paint transferred low on the wall. Fresh scuffs at bumper height. A shallow arc of rubber where someone corrected late, the mark still dark. No debris field to speak of. No glass. That suggested a glancing blow, not a full strike. She tracked the exit path to the lane where a driver could disappear in two turns.

"Did anyone get a plate number?"

"Just a little traffic incident. No one was hurt, no real property damage. Probably did more damage to the car than anything else."

"Security footage?"

"Ma'am," he said with a slight shrug. "Like I said, no injuries, minimal damage. It's not exactly a priority."

She let that sit. The city triaged what it could. People first. Paper later. Even small collisions told stories if someone bothered to listen.

"Was there anyone else around? Any other witnesses?"

"Ma'am, we don't need your help." The officer's tone shifted. "Move along."

"Bro," another officer warned, elbowing him. "Do you know who that is?"

"Some bossy bitch."

"Leave it, three seventy-nine," Blackburn said, holding up her hand. The cop blinked. Blackburn tapped her shoulder. He looked at his own. Badge number three seventy-nine. "Forty-two seventeen, thank you for your respect." Her gaze cooled on the first cop before she turned and walked away.

She logged what they had not. No canvass underway. No requests to the nearby stores for exterior camera pulls. No notice sent to the traffic network for a time slice on Oak. An autonomous car acting erratic, Kendria at the edge of it, and it lay in the hands of idiots.

She headed toward Coconut Glass Candles. New Dresden kept moving around her. Engines, the hiss of a bus brake, the low thrum of a city that didn't pause. Diesel hung faintly under the sweet bite of roasting beans. She scanned as she walked. Broken reflector chip winking near the curb. Nothing. A smear of metallic flake catching light. Maybe. She noted it and moved on.

Kendria surfaced in her mind, not as a case file but as weight in her palm and breath in her ear. Strong, disciplined, the body that held a pose until told to move. Trust as a chosen act, not a given. The image met the scrape on the wall and settled like a stone under her sternum. She named it quietly. Risk. Her investment required attention. She did not let the word fear get any traction.

She picked up speed. Comfort could sit beside extraction. She would get the sequence, the timing, the color of the car, the voice she'd heard if there was one. Official or not, she would reconstruct it. What was hers stayed intact.

At the door, she paused. Warm air carried layered scent from the shop. Wax and floral over heat off the street. Through the glass, color and flame. She slid a phone from her pocket. The case was smooth against her palm. She hit a saved number.

"Sgt. Beckett," she said as he answered, her tone clipped but edged with tension. "It's Morgan Blackburn. There was a car accident near that last case you gave me. On Oak Street."

"I heard about it. You're thinking this is tied to your anonymous car case?"

"Not sure yet," she replied, eyes narrowing as they swept over the shopfront. "Chief Hayes already made an arrest on that one, but something feels off about this accident scene." Her gaze lingered on shifting shadows inside as she spoke. The candle flames flickered, small and steady.

"Alright," Beckett replied after a beat. "I will keep you posted if we find anything worth sharing. You're very conscientious, Morgan. I like that." His tone softened toward the end, a low drop beneath street noise and footsteps that passed behind her.

She ended the call at the glass door of Coconut Glass Candles. Warm light spilled across the sidewalk. She tried the handle. Locked. She leaned in, breath fogging the pane, and peered inside.

Amber light washed the walls. Shadows moved, steady as breathing. The shop felt contained, a sealed pocket that refused the chaos that had bled into Kendria's hour. Inside, Kendria moved with economy. Blackburn knocked twice, her knuckles crisp against the glass.

Kendria looked up, eyes finding Blackburn's through the reflection. Relief surfaced and held, though tension still rode her shoulders. Their gazes held for a beat, charged with recognition. Kendria crossed the room in quick, even strides. She worked the lock and pulled the door open, gratitude showing under the unease.

"Morgan," Kendria breathed. "You came."

Blackburn stepped inside. Coconut and vanilla rose warm and dense. Kendria slid the bolt. Street noise thinned and fell away. The shop narrowed to light, heat, and the problem in front of them.

"I'm here," Blackburn said. Her voice remained even, softened at the edges. "I heard from traffic services what happened." She studied Kendria. "It must have been terrifying."

Kendria nodded, fingers lacing tight at her waist. Her gaze dropped as she spoke, voice low. "It was. I thought I was going to die."

Blackburn noticed the small tremor along Kendria's hands despite their grip. The shallow breaths. The effort it took to hold steady. Fear sat with her, and the shock of having survived. "You're okay," she said.

Candlelight flickered across glass. Heat from the flames couldn't touch the thin cold riding the room. Blackburn set her tone.

"I will take care of you," she said. The words landed as both a promise and an order.

Kendria's brow tensed. Gratitude and fear moved beneath it. "I'm so scared," she said, fingers twisting again. "The other woman, just a few blocks away. It made me think, maybe this isn't just a coincidence."

Blackburn gathered her in. She held Kendria against the warmth of her suit until their breathing evened. She did not think it was a coincidence.

"I'll look into every possibility," Blackburn said firmly. She pressed a brief kiss to the crown of Kendria's head, then stepped back. Her hands lingered before falling away. She straightened. Duty locked back into place. "Did you give your statement to the officers on scene?" she asked, tone professional.

Kendria nodded. Worry still marked her face, but some of the strain eased. "I did. I told them everything I could remember." She hesitated, teeth catching on her lower lip. "But I don't know if it was enough."

"If anything else comes to mind, call them immediately." The pull of the job cut through. Every detail mattered.

She turned to go.

"Wait," Kendria said. She stepped forward, voice sharp. "That's it? You can't just treat me like another case file. I'm not just a statistic or a witness in your investigation."

Blackburn stopped and turned back. Surprise flickered, then she leveled. "I…"

"You said you'd take care of me," Kendria said, voice trembling with hurt that gained strength as she spoke.

"I work homicides, Kendria," Blackburn said, keeping her cadence even. She straightened and met Kendria's eyes. "They see this as a traffic accident with no damage. I had to reach out to a desk jockey who's two years from retirement to get anything at all." The words slid cleanly, and she let them stand. Her tone eased as she added, "But I did it for you."

Kendria's expression shifted then, anger melting into something warmer as she looked up at Blackburn through wet lashes. A small smile touched her mouth. "You did it for me," she repeated softly.

The air eased. Blackburn drew her in again and held her. They stood like that, quiet, wax and lavender settling around them while the noise in Blackburn's head dropped to a manageable hum.

"I'll make it up to you," Kendria murmured, her fingers tracing the edge of a button on Blackburn's shirt. Fabric tugged under her touch. Kendria covered Blackburn's breast with her palm, pressure measured, intent clear, heat passing through cotton to skin.

"Not now. I need to get back to work," Blackburn said, her voice low but firm.

Kendria hesitated. "Right, of course. But can I walk you to your car?" She stepped back to the shelf. Her breath deepened. "I need to take back what's mine. My street."

Blackburn tapped a slow beat against the edge of her holster. "Take it back?" Her tone remained even. Curiosity thinned the set of her jaw.

Kendria paced. Morning light slid over glass and crystal, brief flares that cooled as she moved past. She stopped at the front window and pressed her palm flat against the cool pane. Outside, cars crept down the narrow block, paint clean, windows dark, exhaust a muted smear that the glass kept out.

Her fingers curled into a loose fist against the glass. "Bumpers and blind spots. That's all I see anymore."

Blackburn tilted her head. Her jaw tightened, then released. Overhead light caught the silver at her temples. She set her features into the shape she used with families and uniforms both, the working face that gave nothing away and kept the scene contained.

"We'll run more patrols." The words fell between them like stones; heavy, calculated, routine. "But this is still New Dresden. It isn't kind." She would flag the corridor for directed checks and pull camera coverage where she could. Say it was part of the Langston case.

A horn struck outside, blunt and close. Kendria flinched. She drew breath and tried again.

Her hand went to the door. Blackburn moved in, leather soles giving a small squeak on polished boards.

"Maybe it's better if you wait," Blackburn said quietly, the directive sitting just under the surface.

"No." Kendria snatched up a key ring from the counter; metal chimed as she straightened. "I refuse to let them cage my street." She turned, grabbed a small paper bag with handwritten designs. "I've got a delivery to later anyway," she said briskly. "The new yoga studio ordered a dozen sunners. Citrine for energy, pyrite for focus, carnelian for courage."

Blackburn watched her without comment. She logged the tremor in Kendria's fingers before the grip tightened, the lift of her chin, the way resolve arrived late but held. Details to note. Details she could use.

At last, Kendria reached the door and paused at the threshold where warm light from inside met gray shadow beyond. The street ahead looked both familiar and wrong. She fumbled the key at the lock; metal scraped on metal, a rough sound that dissolved into the low thrum building outside.

"Ready?"

"Ready." Kendria kept her voice low but clear. It carried new steadiness with thin seams where vulnerability showed beneath fresh resolve.

Blackburn lifted a finger for pause. A brief smile touched her mouth as she slid the phone away. She closed in at Kendria's shoulder, an arm light around her, and steered them to the sidewalk.

The morning was clean. The sun cut hard edges on the pavement and lifted heat from the concrete. A block behind them, the scene had been cleared. The traffic officers were gone. Only smears of silver on the brick marked where it had gone wrong. The faint tang of metal lingered. To anyone else, it looked routine. The city kept moving.

Kendria paused and took in the street. Kids laughed somewhere upwind, high and bright. Strangers traded small talk outside a convenience store. The air smelled of espresso and warm asphalt. Her chest rose and fell. The fear had settled. Something steadier had taken its place.

They walked. Black posts threw long shadows across cracked concrete. Heat mirrored up from the ground and warmed their legs. Blackburn scanned corners and alley mouths, checking reflective glass and parked bumpers. No idle autonomous vehicles sat with dark sensors. No engine whine. She logged plates by habit and marked escape routes without showing it. The day felt ordinary, not a warning.

"Isn't it beautiful?" Kendria asked softly, tilting her face toward the sky. Wisps of white drifted across the clean blue sky. The sun caught the curve of her cheekbone. "Days like this make everything feel lighter."

Blackburn nodded and squeezed her hand. Fingers laced. Skin warm against skin. "It is," she said, warmth threading through her controlled voice. "Weather like this, you could do almost anything with it." A thin smile.

Kendria turned to her, brown eyes bright with mischief and something weightier held back. "You know," she began, voice low but brimming with playful energy. "I'd love to see you again, but not tonight." She hesitated briefly before adding with a soft laugh, "I need to spend tonight with my daughter."

Blackburn raised an eyebrow. The corner of her mouth tipped, as if she had already made mental space for this information. She leaned closer, unhurriedly, reducing the space between them until breath warmed the air. "Wednesday night work for you?"

Kendria lit up. The answer rose fast and clean. "Wednesday is perfect!" Joy carried in her voice, easy against the street noise.

They moved at the same time. Then they were kissing. No rush. No flutter. Heat met heat. The taste of life and protection. It was clear, a neat exchange that held for a few quiet beats while traffic rolled and footsteps passed by.

Blackburn stepped back first, reluctance flickering through her gaze. "As much as I'd rather stay here, there's work waiting for me," she said. The softness stayed in the words. Her eyes dropped to the silver pendant at Kendria's throat where it rose and fell. Sun struck it and sent a thin flare across her collarbone.

"Me too," Kendria said. Her mouth curved in a small, unconvincing pout. Amusement edged her eyes.

Blackburn set a shoulder to the brick and used the cool to reset her pulse. Grit pressed through the fabric into her skin. She drew Kendria in again and kissed her. Slower. Measured. She took her time.

One hand threaded into Kendria's fingers, the other found her gun. Safety wrapped in a leather holster.

Kendria eased away. Trouble lived in her smile now, small and contained. Their fingers stayed linked, a simple hold that held more than it showed. She gave Blackburn's hand a light pull, a half step backward that invited pursuit. "Come on, Morgan," she breathed playfully. "Aren't you going to catch me?"

Blackburn leaned, watching the play spark across Kendria's features, tracking the shift in her stance and the street beyond her shoulder. A delivery truck hissed to a stop at the corner. "I'm not so easily led astray," she said, smooth as a caution. Her posture said she didn't mind the test.

Neither of them noticed the autonomous car gliding toward them along the narrow street. Its metal skin was filmed with grime, the panels dull and scored with old scars. The same hush that had made the moment feel safe now muffled the approaching threat as the electric motor propelled the vehicle forward with almost no sound.

Chapter 20

A thin mechanical whine cut through the street. Not an engine. Something programmed. Blackburn looked up. A silver autonomous sedan came fast, tires screaming across sun-heated asphalt. Kendria's hand slipped from hers. Their unspoken promise went with it. Blackburn's mouth opened to warn her. No time. No chance of protecting her this time.

The car hit Kendria mid-stride. The impact lifted and turned her. The bag in her hand spun free. Shards scattered across the lane, bright and hard, flashing in the light.

Blackburn stilled. Kendria hung for a breath against the white glare of the sky. The silver pendant Blackburn had noticed earlier flashed once and disappeared.

Kendria hit the pavement with a hard crack. She rolled and stopped. Still. Blood spread in a dark fan that edged outward. Her phone skidded and came to rest, the screen crazed with fractures.

Blackburn's knees gave and caught. She went down because her legs did, not because she chose to. Grit pressed into her palms. Lavender clung to the air and turned her stomach. Heat pushed up from the road against her shins. Ahead, the sedan rolled to a slow stop a few feet from Kendria. The bumper was dented and smeared dark. The car went quiet, status lights pulsing. Indifferent.

Blackburn moved on hands and knees. Deliberate. She reached for Kendria and set two fingers at the carotid. No pulse. No chest rise. She kept her hands off the neck. She would not move her. A Straight Line. She saw the sensor array and the forward camera. She pulled her phone and dialed, sweat slicking the back of her grip.

"This is Detective Blackburn, badge 259," she barked into the receiver even as she crawled closer to Kendria's lifeless shape sprawled on the pavement. "Requesting immediate medical response at 483 Oak Street. A pedestrian has been struck by a vehicle, critical condition."

Some bastard did this on her watch.

The angle of Kendria's head, the quiet of her body, the light gone from eyes that were laughing moments ago. Blackburn knew death. This one was wrong for other reasons.

People gathered. Phones went up. A ring of glass and faces. The soft clatter of someone stepping on a shard. Blackburn stayed on her knees beside Kendria. Not from grief. From control held in place while noise built around her. This was not just a loss. It was a feed. And she was in frame.

She planted one palm on the asphalt to steady herself, fingers spread, avoiding the pool of blood. A tight band cinched under her ribs. Not sorrow. Something colder. The air went metallic with heat and rubber. Sirens drifted in, thin and far. She marked exits, cameras on nearby storefronts, the traffic light with its lens pointed down the block. She noted the two nearest witnesses by clothing and position.

Then the voices cut through.

"Look at that. I bet she was just in the way. The dumb nigger didn't even see it coming!" The man in a red baseball hat sneered, phone held high to frame it all.

The man beside him, wearing a black baseball hat, chuckled, voice low and eager. "Yeah, she's not coming now, but I'd still hit that. Dead or not, she's got a body." His grin widened, bright with rot.

The red-hatted man snorted. "Only way I'd fuck a nigger is if she's dead. No other way."

Blackburn's vision narrowed. Her jaw set. A bead of sweat cut along her temple and dried. The noise, and cameras, and faces settled into a ledger. She logged red hat. Black hat. Ages, late twenties to mid-thirties. Heights, close. Location, three cars back. Curbside. She noted the angle of their phones for later subpoenas.

She rose with care. Nothing rushed. Her badge hung clearly. She scanned the sedan again. No driver. No one behind the wheel. The LIDAR dome on the roof ticked. A diagnostic LED blinked at a steady rate. Blackburn filed it. She spoke to dispatch with clipped detail and asked for traffic control, CSU, and a supervisor. She requested a tech from the AV unit.

The crowd pressed in half a step. Blackburn lifted a hand. Not a plea. A stop. Heat shimmered between her and the nearest faces. Her gaze moved over them and settled back on Kendria. The searing edge in her chest held steady. It wanted release. She caged it.

She listened to the car. No cooling fan. No fuel smell. She looked for external damage beyond the bumper, for fibers, for a caught thread. Nothing obvious. The shards from the bag were strewn in a broad arc. She would have to map it. She would have to hold the scene together until uniform got here.

Her attention cut back to the men with the hats. The red one had shifted for a better angle. The black one leaned in to whisper more poison and laugh. She marked the time on her phone and took two photos from the hip. Not art. Evidence.

Kendria lay quiet at her feet. The pendant was gone from view. The street heat rose in slow waves, warping the edges of shadow. Blackburn's pulse steadied to something usable. Sirens thickened, closer now, a layered wail. She squared herself toward the car, then toward the crowd, then back to the body. Kept breathing. Kept score. Kept the line between what she felt and what she would do next.

The crowd retreated when she turned toward the two men. Phones rose, screens held high. Faces tightened, eyes alert. The man in the red hat barely flinched before Blackburn's hand connected hard. The slap cracked across the plaza, a flat report bouncing off glass and stone. His head snapped aside. Blood spilled from his nose and striped his cheek. He stumbled, hat crooked, eyes wide. The metallic tang cut through the warm air.

"You disgusting bastard," Blackburn growled, her tone low and charged with venom. Her gaze held while he covered his face. Blood threaded between his fingers and dripped onto the hot concrete.

The man in black edged back, his phone trembling in both hands. "I got it! I got every second!" he shrieked. "You're finished! This is going online right now!" Spit brightened his lip. The recording light blinked red.

She turned to him sharply. Her shoulders remained square. Her hands settled by her sides. "Do it," she commanded coldly. "Let everyone see exactly what kind of filth you are."

The crowd murmured and created more space, sneaker soles rasping over grit. Blackburn ignored them. Kendria lay on the pavement, blood threading into the cracks in the asphalt. The color had already dulled toward brown. Blackburn fixed the position of the body, the spatter, the smear where a tire had crossed.

She crouched again. Knees to hot ground. Two fingers to Kendria's wrist. No pulse. She opened the airway, watched the chest, and checked again. She noted the time. Burned rubber and hot metal slicked the air. The weight in her chest settled cold and useful. She let it guide her. She had long ago learned what she could live with.

"Boss!" Sinclair's voice cut in. He pushed through the ring of onlookers, tie askew, shirt creased, collar damp. "I got here as fast as I could."

Blackburn glanced up and read his face. "You're quick," she said. Her fingers twitched once.

"Hampton's is just around the block." His eyes took in the scene. They stopped on Kendria. "Jesus."

Sirens swelled, the pitch rising and falling as they closed. Stopped. Two paramedics moved in with their kits and dropped beside

Kendria. One started compressions, arms locked and efficient, while the other cleared space and ripped open the pads. Alcohol and adhesive stung the heat.

An engine hummed to life. Headlights snapped on. Blackburn's head turned. The autonomous car rolled forward, smooth, confident, the electric whine distinct beneath the noise.

"Stop that car!" Blackburn's command cracked like a shot.

Sinclair ran. His shoes slid on grit. The vehicle kept its line through the gap in the crowd and accelerated. It slipped around the corner before he got close, tires whispering against the curb.

The paramedics kept their count. "One, two, three, four."

Blackburn scanned the curb and the lane the car had taken. Silver body. Raider Straight Line. A long scar along the side. Fresh damage. A dark smear low on the bumper. No plate visible from this angle. She raised her phone and took a quick frame of the lane and the corner for bearings. She fixed on two bystanders toward the edge of the plaza where the car had idled and fixed their faces in memory. Someone would have seen more.

Sinclair came back slowly, bent for breath, sweat bright at his hairline. Blackburn faced him. Her eyes were steady, the look flat and cold.

"What kind of detective lets critical evidence drive away?" Her words were clipped. "Did you misplace your legs? Or did you think asking politely might convince a machine to stop?"

Sinclair flushed and stumbled over himself. "I, I didn't think."

"Clearly," she said. "You didn't think. That's becoming a pattern, isn't it?" Blackburn took out her phone and keyed the screen.

Reeves answered on the second ring. "Detective Reeves."

"Oak Street," Blackburn snapped. "Now. Bring Cooper." Her voice stayed clipped, each word weighted. "Another autonomous car death. The vehicle fled the scene, a silver Raider Straight Line. Side damage. Front end damage. Blood on the bumper." She watched the paramedics working through their cycle, their pace steady and quiet. She added, "And Reeves? Issue a BOLO. I want that car found."

"Understood," Reeves replied without hesitation. "We'll be there in ten."

The paramedics traded a look, then stopped. One glanced up at Blackburn and shook his head. She nodded once, voice low. "Thank you for trying," she murmured. "Cover her."

They drew a white sheet over Kendria's body. The fabric whispered as it fell. Blackburn already had her phone to her ear. "Sergeant Beckett," she said briskly when the line connected. "It's Detective Blackburn. Another autonomous hit and run, same as Langston." Her gaze tracked the scene: cruisers strobing red and blue against dark glass, yellow tape snaking out and snapping in the air, units holding the line and logging statements while cameras blinked from the curb.

"Sweet Jesus. First a near miss and now"

Blackburn cut him off. "It's the same person."

"What? What do you mean?" Sgt. Beckett asked.

"The woman who was almost hit just half an hour ago? She's dead now. Hit and run."

"Oh, shit."

"Mmm. Oh, shit," Blackburn agreed.

She let the failure register and then set it aside.

Onlookers pressed near the barriers, voices rising and falling in a restless swell. She tightened her grip on the phone and dialed again. Chief Hayes this time. Her fingertips left blood on the screen.

Cooper and Reeves came in together, faces set, moving toward Sinclair for the first pass.

"What now?" Hayes barked through the speaker. He'd answered on the first ring.

Blackburn kept her tone flat. "Another woman dead," she stated. "Hit by an autonomous vehicle just over a block from Langston's scene."

Static cracked through. Hayes came back hot.

"Goddamn it!" he roared. "You're telling me we have Zhang locked up for Langston's murder, and now there's another killing just like it? How the hell do you explain that?"

Her patience slipped. "I told you not to arrest Zhang," she snapped. "I told you we weren't ready. This isn't my goddamn fault." She ended the call before he could answer.

Cooper stepped to her side, professional concern tipping toward something more personal. His gaze dropped to her clothes. She followed it. Blood on her black pants. Streaks on her white shirt. The fabric had started to stick. Enough.

Movement pulled her eye to a patrol car. The man in the red hat jabbed a finger toward her, face blotched, dried blood from nose to chin. He talked fast to an officer who kept pace with his words. The officer took notes, then steered him toward a waiting ambulance, the gurney wheels rattling over cracked asphalt.

Blackburn's jaw set. She held her ground and let the anger pass. Brynn Cassidy broke from the crowd, head down and moving, brown hair brushing her shoulders. Joseph followed close, camera gear thumping against his side, the strap creaking with each step.

Fuck this.

Blackburn stepped deeper into the scene, placing herself between Kendria's covered body and the crowd tight to the tape. She fixed on the numbered markers on the asphalt, the positions of debris, the camera angles already in play. She pulled herself into the work. Detective first, human second. Logic over emotion. Facts over fury.

Willow Adler slipped under the tape a moment later, glasses askew from the push through bodies. Her composure faltered when she saw Blackburn standing there, clothes stained, posture steady.

A breath caught in Willow's throat and came out as a thin whisper. "Oh no." The words barely rose over sirens and the churn of voices. The smell here was metal and coolant and blood on hot pavement.

Blackburn stayed still. Blood on her clothes registered as a fact, nothing more. Her eyes worked the scene, laying out the sequence. First responders moved, radio traffic snapped, then cleared. The light strobed across wet patches and the edges of glass. She let the noise wash past and kept to her lane.

Reeves approached carefully, suspicion running across his face when he noticed Willow. "How did you get here so fast?" he demanded, his voice edged with mistrust. The question hung heavy in the damp air.

Blackburn assumed the question was for her.

Chapter 21

Blackburn angled toward Reeves without committing. Blood had dried on her shirt in narrow dark seams, stiff against the fabric. It registered as proximity, not performance. The iron scent rose in the cold.

"I was standing next to Kendria Chaplin when the car hit her," she said, voice remaining even. No theatrics. "I was re-interviewing her about Jenna Langston's death. With Hayes having arrested Zhang, we needed more evidence."

Sinclair moved closer, eyes completing a swift assessment. His shirt clung, damp from the run. A fine line of sweat remained at his hairline despite the cold, his breath a pale cloud that dissipated quickly. "Are you hurt?" he asked quietly but directly.

"No." She dismissed it and shifted away from him, maintaining her focus on the scene. Phones clicked. Voices talked. Tape snapped in the wind.

Her phone vibrated against her hip. She answered. "Sir?"

"Don't you ever hang up on me again, Blackburn," Chief Hayes said, words low and clipped, breath close to the speaker.

"The victim was a witness in the Langston case." She kept her tone neutral.

Heads turned. Reeves, Sinclair, Cooper, Willow. No one spoke. Chaplin had been a direct connection to Langston; with Zhang in custody, the timing now carried significant weight.

"Get to my office now," Hayes said. "We need to address this."

"Understood. I'm on my way." She ended the call and faced her team. Blue strobes washed the sidewalk and slicked across faces. "Stay here. I want eyes on Forensics every second they're working this scene." She let the instructions settle. "Bag it all. Every damn thing."

Willow stepped in from the edge. Worry showed but remained contained. Her hands stayed steady on her tablet. "I should go with you," she offered softly, carefully.

Blackburn raised a hand. Final. "No." She kept her eyes on the scene. "Help with security footage. Same places as last time."

Willow held her gaze momentarily, then nodded and moved off to coordinate with the nearest patrol. The others returned to marking evidence, setting down numbered tents, logging witness statements. Traffic cones thumped into place while a tow truck idled a block away.

Blackburn slid into her car and turned the key. The engine caught cleanly and settled into a low hum. She adjusted the seat once, the leather cold against her back, and gripped the wheel. The shake in her palm had vanished, but the nerves there still remembered.

Through the glass she spotted Brynn Cassidy on the sidewalk with a camera crew. Cassidy's hair remained perfect despite the wind. The high beam of a light panel flattened her features to something glossy.

She spoke to the red cap man, the one who liked to provoke. He gave her that same slack smile.

Blackburn's palm pulsed at the memory of hitting him. Not the act. The decision. She noted it, then set it aside.

She pulled into traffic. The cabin filled with the mild scent of leather and warm air. The A/C ticked as it cooled. No music. No radio. One red light, then green. She checked the mirrors habitually. A delivery van settled behind her for half a block, its grille prominent in the rearview, then turned off with a slow blink of signal.

The precinct wasn't far. Good. She had calls to make and reports to secure before rumor became record. Jenna's files would need a fresh lock and stricter access controls. The traffic cam list needed expansion beyond the identified intersections. The tow report on the striking vehicle, if there was one, had to be pulled immediately.

If the driver ditched the car, he knew what she represented. If the driver kept the car, he, she or it would be found soon enough. Forensics would determine whether this was a genuine accident or something staged. Tire marks. Impact angle. Headlight glass. Paint transfer. The usual answers, if people allowed them time to speak.

She considered Hayes saying "address this" and heard the unspoken message. Zhang's arrest had started a countdown. Eliminating a suspect this quickly meant someone was paying attention. Or wanted them to think that.

She turned into the lot and took a space at the end facing the fence. She shut off the engine and sat briefly, hands loose on the wheel. It wasn't anger. It was the loss of someone who was hers.

She exited and locked the car with a chirp. The air smelled of exhaust and wet concrete. Her phone buzzed again. She ignored it until she passed the front desk with a nod at the sergeant's questioning look.

The text came from Willow. First clips coming in. East corner, northbound lane, twelve minutes before impact. A second message followed with a still of Kendria on the sidewalk. The image appeared grainy, a thumbnail ghost under the sun's glare.

Blackburn pocketed the phone. She felt Reeves's earlier question lingering between them, beneath the routine. It would remain there. There were better uses for breath.

At the elevator, she watched the floor numbers rise without focusing. Going nowhere. No time for the elevator. Brynn would publish a headline before noon. The red capped man would continue providing color. Neither mattered if they mapped Kendria's final route and arranged every camera along it. If lucky, the car's paint would indicate its model. If not, there would be nothing but speed and a clean exit.

The hum of LEDs and copier noise blended into the familiar sounds of a busy day. Coffee and paper scents filled the air. Blackburn moved through the hallway in a straight line. Conversations thinned. Heads turned. She let the looks pass off her like weather and kept going.

At the stairwell she took two steps at a time, her palm grazing the rail, metal cool against her skin. It wasn't urgency. It was defiance. She wouldn't slow down or signal compliance. The chief's door waited at the end of the hall, the frosted glass shut and certain. She pushed it open.

Chief Hayes didn't flinch. His eyes stayed on the monitor in front of him, its ghostly glow hollowing his eyes. The soft click of the door behind her marked her arrival. The clock on the wall ticked through the pause.

"Sit," Hayes said without looking up.

She stayed on her feet.

With a sigh that carried equal parts weariness and frustration, Hayes pinched the bridge of his nose. "What were you thinking?"

"About what?"

"The video." His voice hardened as he straightened in his chair. "'New Dresden Cop Attacks Bystander.' It's everywhere. Viral. The mayor already called. The press is hounding us. Do you make a habit of hitting people?"

As a matter of fact, yes.

She crossed her arms and met his stare. She could lay it out clearly. Kendria dead woman on the ground. The red capped man laughing. The palm of Blackburn's hand to the bridge of his nose when he turned. Blood on the sidewalk, the road, her clothes. Shock wiping the grin off his face. Sirens in the distance. In here, it would get stripped to codes and complaints. Excessive force. Insubordination. Another tick on her jacket.

She kept her mouth shut. The silence held.

Hayes closed the folder with a flat smack. "You're suspended," he said, voice flat but resolute. "Indefinitely."

Her fingers tightened on the badge, a small hesitation before she unclipped it. The leather warmed her palm; the metal felt heavier than it should have. She set it on the desk, then the service weapon beside it. Policy lived in the space those items left. She turned and walked out.

In the hallway, Physica, his administrative assistant, looked up. The air smelled like lemon cleaner. Their eyes met for a beat. "Thank you." Almost too soft to notice. She went back to sorting a stack of forms, paper whispering under her fingers.

Blackburn gave a slight nod and continued toward the stairs.

As she walked, heads lifted at her approach. Screens threw blue light across faces. Eyes flicked from the monitors to her and back again. Browsers closed. Conversations cut off mid-word. Across the atrium, Detective Cooper watched her. His expression revealed nothing.

Her heels marked a steady rhythm on the linoleum. Whispers gathered behind her and spread. She didn't react.

The stairwell cooled the air and muffled the noise. Poured concrete, a steel handrail, the brief echo of her steps spiraling down. The respite ended on the ground floor. She pushed the heavy door into the lobby. The smell of floor polish met her. They came into view. Brynn Cassidy and Joseph Miller, stationed by the entrance like guards barring an escape.

Brynn approached, microphone held steady. "Detective Blackburn, do you have any comment on the viral video showing you slapping a young man?"

Blackburn's gaze sharpened. Her voice remained clipped and controlled. "Have you seen the video yourself?"

"I have," Brynn said evenly. "You looked him dead in the eye, called him a bastard, and then punched him."

Blackburn's mouth tightened. "No," she said, cool and precise. "I called him a disgusting bastard, and it was an open-handed slap. The version you've seen has been doctored. Find another copy."

Brynn lifted her chin. "I've already run a segment on this story," she said.

"Then it seems accuracy isn't your strong suit," Blackburn said, her disdain unhidden. "Good thing you're not in law enforcement." She stepped past them and pushed through the glass doors. Air conditioning released her in a breath as the heat of the lot enveloped her, dry and immediate.

Sunlight flared across her windshield, highlighting old wiper scars. The metal door gave a hot click as it shut. Her hands set on the wheel, steady but firm. The engine turned over with a rough hum, and the vents pushed warm air before cooling. The city passed in familiar grids, high-rises catching glare, cracked pavement radiating heat, a patrol car cutting through a side street with lights throwing pale color against brick. Off the job pending review, everything felt exposed.

No shield.

No cover from the press unit.

IA would already have the file.

Traffic murmured in layered sound, tires on asphalt, a distant siren rising and falling. Her heart tapped too fast. She ran through the sequence again. The questions. The answers she should have given. The lines she crossed.

The memory came clean and fast. Kendria on the asphalt, eyes open to nothing. Blood pooling on warm pavement, the smell of iron lifted by heat. Skin still holding warmth in those first seconds. And then him, leaning in close, smiling through it. Breath sour. Words meant to strip the dead of dignity.

Kendria was hers. Had been hers.

Possession didn't help. It never did. Protection had been Blackburn's work. That border was broken. The rest was a flat field of loss and an anger she kept in a narrow channel so she could use it.

She pressed the accelerator, then made herself ease back. His name didn't matter. He didn't matter. Her hand had moved before she thought. A flat slap, contained. Enough to shut him up. Not enough to satisfy anything.

If only the other one hadn't backed away. If he'd stepped in when she told him to hold the scene. This mess wouldn't exist.

Now she was the story. Reckless cop on every loop. Screenshots, lower thirds, opinion panels. The video would keep circulating. So would he.

She rapped the wheel once. The sound cracked against the plastic and hung in the cabin. Kendria had slipped from her twice. First to that car. Then to the man who turned her memory into a stunt. Both times, control went out from under her.

Her phone buzzed in her pocket. She took a breath, braked at a red, and pulled it free. The name "Reeves" lit the screen above a message:

>*Boss. Shit hit the fan.*

Below it, a link in blue. "BREAKING: Investigation into hit-and-run death unveils shocking connections to New Dresden PD."

Cold settled under her ribs. She tapped. Grainy footage filled the screen. A still from a street cam. Her and Kendria outside a candle shop, hand-in-hand, the window crowded with wax pillars and soft light.

She closed the video and tossed her phone on the passenger seat.

In the distance, an autonomous car sliced through traffic like a blade through flesh, its silent hunger reminding her that the answers she demanded still pulsed just beyond her reach. Blackburn was not just a detective or a protector. She was an apex predator. New Dresden was her hunting ground. In that relentless stalking, she found communion with the dark.

9 781998 648337